Classic Celtic Fairy Tales

Classic Celtic Fairy Tales

Selected and edited by

JOHN MATTHEWS

Foreword by R.J. Stewart

Illustrated by Ian Daniels

BLANDFORD

To all storytellers everywhere,
and most especially to Robin and Bob for the
way in which they continue to bring life to
the ageless traditions

A BLANDFORD BOOK

First published in the UK 1997 by Blandford
A Cassell Imprint
Cassell Plc, Wellington House,
125 Strand, London WC2R 0BB

First published in paperback 1999

Distributed in the United States by Sterling Publishing Co., Inc.,
387 Park Avenue South, New York, NY 10016-8810

A Cataloguing-in-Publication Data entry for this title
is available from the British Library

ISBN 0-7137-2783-7

Typeset by Falcon Oast Graphic Art

Printed and bound by Kyodo Printing Co., Singapore

Frontispiece: *The King of the Red Shield, from the Leeching of*
Kayn's Leg

Contents

*Beira, Queen
of Winter*

Foreword

WE ARE COMING to the end of the century, to the end of an era of primarily materialistic consciousness in our world (which is to say most but not all of the planet, due to the predominantly western influence of the last 150 or more years). How intriguing, therefore, that we find a resurgence of interest in the humble fairy tradition. For at the close of the nineteenth century there was a similar resurgence, coming at the time of the collapse of Christianity as a dominant political force. Then it was science that ousted restrictive dogma; now it is science that ousts itself, as physics meets mysticism in the realms of energy and consciousness, and each finds that it has been there together before.

In this collection of tales, John Matthews has selected some of the gems from the vast hoard of Celtic tradition. Much of that hoard still lies untranslated in archives in Ireland and Wales, and we owe a debt today to the vigour of those nineteenth-century editors and translators who first brought much of this material into publication in English. Yet how different the general awareness is now from that of our grandparents and great-grandparents. Today Celtic tradition is widely published, even commercialized in terms of books, music, dance, art and patterns, clothing and tourism. In the last century, most people had never heard of the ancient Celts (including many Celts who were unaware of deep ancestry), and the folklore of the Irish, Scottish, Welsh and Breton peoples was seen as quaint peasant entertainment. It took the work of titans such as Lady Gregory, W.B. Yeats, Oscar Wilde, Lady Charlotte Guest, AE (George William Russell), Fiona Macleod (William Sharp) and, a little later, the American scholar W.Y. Evans Wentz to show the public that the Celtic tradition was vast, profound, complex and rich in multi-layered strata of poetry, vision, myth and mysticism. Many other writers, scholars, poets and researchers could be added to the list from this period of the late nineteenth to early twentieth centuries, when there was a profound sense of discovery, of inspiration, of revealing vast, hitherto ignored wealth for the first time in generations.

This was not strictly the case, of course, for the fairy tales, music, song, epic sagas and customs were still very active among the country people, and among their emigrant cousins and descendants in America; but the sense of revelation and restoration was certainly strong among the artistic, literary and academic minds of that period.

Today the oral traditions are very much attenuated, and the strength of family and tribal streams of consciousness and lore greatly weakened. Indeed, we are finding a type of false oral tradition generating itself from the wide audience for Celtic tradition that exists now. It may be difficult, even impossible, in the next century, to decide what is the true lineage of Celtic tradition and what has come out of the revival. Academic historical and source texts, of course, are datable, but the living awareness of people is more elusive.

There are many different attitudes to fairy tales: the Victorian revivalists were concerned with inspirational source material for their art, especially outside the restrictions imposed by dogmatic moribund state religion. The scholars were concerned with revealing a vast archive replete with historical, anthropological and cultural implications that had previously been denied, ignored and suppressed. Soon came the psychologists, who decided that fairy tales were the collective expression of the unconscious, and so sought to reduce them by systematizing them to fit preconceived theories. Not to forget, of course, the romantic, ethereal and theosophical strand of working with fairy lore, which is repeated today in the New Age approach to fairies and fairy tales as nursery escapism, nature palest blue-green in leaf and branch rather than red in tooth and claw. There is something for everyone in fairy tales, something to satisfy every stance, attitude, opinion, theory or escapism that ever was or ever will be. Yet there is more, much more, if we care to dig deep enough for it.

Fairy tales are found worldwide, and this Celtic selection could be paralleled with tales from any culture anywhere on the planet. This is because fairy tales embody truths about humanity, the land, the other orders or types of planetary life, and the planet itself. This embodying of truths is in a poetic visionary form, so while the tales may, and often do, mirror the unconscious mind, that is only the first stratum of awareness. Most important of all, and often forgotten, is that fairy tales are about fairies – not the pretty little gauzy winged sprites but the tremendous, gigantic, powerful, dreadful, beautiful beings described in this collection. Fiona Macleod gave the perfect description of fairy beings in one of the poems within *The Immortal Hour*: 'they laugh, and are glad, and are terrible'.

In our current revival of interest in fairy lore, there are many people who seek to work with this deeper level, communing with other orders of life (just as our ancestors did), but in a way apt and proper for the twenty-first century. It is one of the ways in which we can restore our relationship to the land, the environment, the planet, and bring that relationship back into health. The tales in this book give us some idea of how the Celtic ancestors understood the fairy races, and their mixed relationship to humanity. We can take this understanding and find insights within it that can inspire and inform us for the future.

R.J. Stewart, 1997

INTRODUCTION
Tales of Wonder, Tales of Life

THE CELTIC FAERY TALE tradition is one of the richest in the world, with hundreds of folk-tales, faery tales and tales of wonder to choose from (Joseph Jacobs estimated there were some 2,000 extant, of which 200 were in print, in 1892). Yet, surprisingly, there has been no new selection of these wonderful stories since the classic collections of Jacobs himself, and of the young W.B. Yeats in 1892, and those of the American Jeremiah Curtin in 1894, all of them appearing within a few years of each other. It therefore seemed timely to bring together a new selection for present-day readers to enjoy.

In assembling this collection I have been mindful of two things: that there is a vast field of virtually unknown tales from which to select, and that reprints of the above-mentioned authors' works are generally available. I have therefore sought out the rarer as well as the most representative of the genre, including only a handful from Curtin and one only from Jacobs. In doing so I am aware that there could have been at least another five volumes which would have contained a very different but no less exciting selection. If, therefore, you find that a particular favourite is missing, I can only say, by way of excuse, that I had to leave out at least 20 of my own favourites for every one that went in.

The volume you now hold in your hands contains some of the finest versions of these stories ever made. Many were collected from oral recital by some of the last surviving storytellers of Irish, Scottish, Welsh, Manx and Breton folk and faery tales. Many remain to this day almost forgotten in old and out-of-the-way books or obscure nineteenth-century journals. I have searched far and wide to find 17 of the best, many of which have not seen the light of day since the beginning of the century. It will be noticed that there is a preponderance of Irish and Scottish tales. This is simply because more stories were collected within these lands than in Cornwall or the Isle of Man. Jacobs noted the same situation when he came to compile his own great collections of *Celtic Fairy Tales* and *More Celtic Fairy Tales* (David Nutt, 1892 and 1894), pointing out that the Irish and the Scots were among the first people in Europe to collect their folk-tales. This is not to say that there are no Cornish or Manx tales, or indeed that the folk traditions of these two countries are any less valuable than those more widely represented here. Much of the literature published from the 1890s onwards tends to be more in the nature of overviews, with folklore traditions of wells, hills and lakes gathered together in one place, rather than the extended storytelling of, for example, the Irish *Seanachies*. In the case of the Breton story tradition, there is indeed a vast resource, but little has been published in English, and the scope of the present book did not permit the commissioning of new translations. This said, I am continuing to research and collect these out-of-the-way tales, with a view to publishing further volumes, and I am always interested in hearing from readers who possess volumes of their own which they might be willing to lend or have photocopied.

Despite the fact that these stories are classed as 'faery tales', a more proper description, and one which is more in keeping with Celtic tradition, would be 'wonder tales'. Tales of wonder they most certainly are, set in a world where literally anything can happen – and frequently does – where black is frequently white, and white any colour you care to name, and where heroes can grow overnight to such a size that their feet stick out of the window (see 'Coldfeet and the Queen of Lonesome Island', pages 14–23); where animals talk and know significantly more than humans; where to enter the place between the worlds is to find oneself in a perilous realm ruled by glamour and grammary, and where beauty is often synonymous with danger.

In her recent fascinating and exhaustive study of the fairy-tale tradition, *From the Beast to the Blonde* (Chatto & Windus, 1994), Marina Warner remarks:

> The verb 'to wonder' communicates the receptive state of marvelling as well as the active desire to know, to enquire, and as such it defines very well at least two characteristics of the traditional fairy tale: pleasure in the fantastic, curiosity about the real.

This is, in fact, a very important aspect of all these stories – they are rooted in what we would term the 'fantastic' (what earlier writers called 'superstition'); yet they are all essentially down-to-earth and matter-of-fact. The extraordinary happenings which take place within them are dealt with as everyday events. They emerge, in fact, from a recognition of the inherent reality of the fairy realm.

This is borne out by the statement of Curtin himself, who remarks in the introduction to *Tales of the Fairies and of the Ghost World* (Talbot Press, 1895) on the number of people in Ireland at that time who still believed in fairies. He quotes the words of a farmer, Maurice Fitzgerald, with whom he stayed while gathering stories from the area of the Dingle Peninsula:

When I was a boy . . . nine men in ten believed in fairies, and said so; now only one man in ten will *say* that he believes in them. If one of the nine believes, he will not tell you; he will keep his mind to himself. [My italics.]

He goes on to say:

It is very interesting indeed to find a society with even ten per cent of the population professed believers in fairies. Of the remaining ninety per cent, a majority are believers without profession, timid believers, men without the courage of their convictions. The minority of ninety per cent falls into two parts, one composed of people of various degrees of belief in the fairy creed and philosophy, the other unbelievers.

In our own time, it is safe to say that most people, if asked, would deny any such belief. However, there has been a recent upsurge of interest in the fairy traditions, which has seen the publication of several books on the subject, ranging from the lunatic to the inspired. Whatever one may think of these individually, they show a recognition, at a deep level, of the reality which these stories represent. Beyond this, the question of belief is immaterial. As R.J. Stewart notes in his *The Living World of Faery* (Gothic Image Publications, 1995): 'the faery tradition is not a faith, for faery beings exist whether we believe in them or not.'

The use of the spelling 'faery', as it applies both to the realm and to those who dwell there, is deliberate, and intended to differentiate between the kind of beings to be met with in these stories, and the images of the faery race as they appear in the best-known Victorian collections with which most of us grew up. 'Faery' is in line with the first recorded usage, in John Gower's *Confessio Amantis* (c.1450) in which the hero is described as being 'as if he were of Faerie' (v7065ff). 'Fairy' is a later spelling which is part and parcel of the Victorian image of these beings.

It could be argued, indeed, that the majority of misconceptions about the appearance and behaviour of the faery race are due to the diminishing of *all* the faery races to minute beings by popular Victorian writers: witness the number of winged and vapid sprites peering coyly from the pages of children's books published in the 1800s – at the same time, in many cases, as the great collectors were putting together their own very different findings, gleaned from the people of these islands.

Here, as writers such as W.Y. Evans Wentz in his monumental *The Fairy Faith in Celtic Countries* (Oxford University Press, 1911) and Thomas Keightley in his *The Fairy Mythology* (Wildwood House, reprinted 1981) so ably showed, the faery were perceived as the aboriginal race of these lands, who remembered and represented the old way of communion with the natural world. They did not seek to control or manipulate it by the use of iron, which is traditionally a metal which is inimical to them. If people see fewer of the faery today, it is the prevalence of concrete, iron and electricity that keeps us cushioned against their appearance. The Age of Reason and the Age of Industry have both contributed to the diminishment of faery, which has almost faded from the consciousness of our race. Yet, though we have scorned the enrichments of faery, we still have to pay the tithe of our imagination. Without the communion and otherworldly exchange between faery and our own world, we grow sick in soul.

The reason for this is not hard to discover, for there is another important aspect to the faery tradition which points the way to a deeper understanding of the age-old truths to be found there. I refer to what I will term the Celtic shamanic tradition. Shamanism (the word comes from the Tungusc region of Siberia) concerns those who are able to travel between the worlds, returning with prophecy, wisdom and healing lore. It was once a worldwide phenomenon, and although little now remains of its original form within these lands, vestiges have survived within the literature, traditions and folklore of the Celts. Thus you will find that in many of the notes for the tales in this book I have indicated, from my own researches and personal experience as a teacher of shamanism, where elements which are recognizably 'shamanistic' in quality are to be found.

Having worked at length on the early literature and mythology of the Celts (my findings are to be found in *Taliesin: Shamanism and the Bardic Mysteries in Britain and Ireland* (Aquarian Press, 1991) and subsequent books – see 'Further Reading') I am now convinced that a further dimension exists within the folklore and faery-tale traditions as well. This is beyond the scope of this introduction, although I hope to publish more on this in the near future. Meanwhile it is worth noting that a sensitive reading of these tales offers a world of information on what I believe were actual journeys to the otherworld, which, though never recorded, were remembered and passed down through generations of storytellers and wisdom-keepers until they reappeared as the faery traditions of these islands.

On the face of it, the majority of faery tales do not concern the faery race at all, but more often the actions of kings, queens, princes and princesses, stepmothers, witches, animal helpers and, above all, ordinary (and extraordinary) people. The term 'faery tale' is a catch-all for a vast treasury of lore, belief and mystery teaching, and it is for this reason that the faery tradition has recently become the stamping ground of psychologists, mystics and anthropologists, who have found there 'a reverence for, and a deep understanding of, life in all its myriad forms'. Faery tales can teach us a great deal about the world in which we live and the wonders that are hidden just beneath the surface of 'reality'. J.C. Cooper sums up the essential themes of faery in her book *Fairy Tales: Allegories of the Inner Life* (Aquarian Press, 1983):

> The most constantly recurring themes are those dealing with the descent of the soul into the world, its experience in life, initiation and the quest for unity and the trials and tribulations that beset its journey through the world. Possibly the best known and most frequent of motifs is that of Paradise Lost and Regained, of which the story of Cinderella is the classic example, though the theme runs through most fairy tales in the form of initial misfortune leading eventually to a happy ending.

This is indeed true of nearly all the stories gathered here. No matter what ordeals the heroes and heroines must pass through, there is always a satisfactory resolution, often delivered with a sly nod and wink to the lovers of 'reality'. Those who told these tales in the 1800s, and earlier, took the world of faery seriously and they took it as they found it – not attempting to put in meanings which are not there or extract significance where there is none. They did not seek to preach or to make fun of the faery race. In this they align themselves with a great tradition which has been stronger in this country than almost anywhere else in the world. (It should, however, be noted that as recently as the 1990s in Cape Breton, Nova Scotia, a Gaelic storyteller, Joe MacNeil, was giving his vast repertoire of stories to be recorded – a living proof of the power and vitality of the Celtic tradition.)

At the end of the day, these stories speak for themselves, and it is far more important to read them for the simple pleasure they offer than to speculate about their origins of meaning. Indeed, it should be said that they 'mean what they mean, and are what they are', and if we go no further than this we have already gone a good distance towards experiencing the innate truth contained within them.

To return to the great Jeremiah Curtin, in *Tales of the Fairies and of the Ghost World* (Talbot Press, 1895):

> The people of Ireland [for which we may read the Celtic peoples as a whole] have clung to their ancient beliefs with a vividness of faith which in our time is really phenomenal. Other nations have preserved large and (for science) precious heritages . . . but generally have preserved them in a kind of mechanical way. The residuum of beliefs which they give us lacks that connection with the present which is so striking in [this] case.

It is precisely this 'connection with the present' which shines out of the tales collected here. These are no dead and dusty documents but living elements of a continuing tradition which is every bit as real and powerful today as it ever was. It is to this belief that the book is dedicated, and to the faery people themselves, who must be vastly amused by our clumsy, earthbound inability to see creation as it really is, but who are also, I hope, cheered by our slightly less clumsy ability to preserve their history through the telling of these tales.

John Matthews
Oxford, 1997

COLDFEET AND THE QUEEN OF LONESOME ISLAND

NCE UPON A TIME, and a long time ago it was, there lived an old woman in Erin. This old woman's house was at the northeast corner of Mount Brandon. Of all the friends and relatives that ever she had in the world there was but one left, her only son, Sean, nicknamed Fuarcosa (Coldfeet).

The reason that people called the boy Coldfeet was this: When a child he was growing always; what of him did not grow one hour grew another; what did not grow in the day grew in the night; what did not grow in the night grew in the day; and he grew that fast that when seven years old he could not find room enough in his mother's house. When night came and he was sleeping, whatever corner of the house his head was in, it was out of doors that his feet were, and, of course, they were cold, especially in winter.

It was not long till his legs as well as his feet were out of the house, first to the knees, and then to the body. When fifteen years old it was all that he could do to put his head in, and he lived outdoors entirely. What the mother could gather in a year would not support the son for a day, he was that large and had such an appetite.

Coldfeet had to find his own food, and he had no means of living but to bring home sheep and bullocks from whatever place he met them.

He was going on in this way, faring rather ill than well, when one day above another he said, 'I think I must go into the great world, mother. I am half starving in this place. I can do little good for myself as I am, and no good at all for you.'

He rose early next morning, washed his face and hands, asked assistance and protection of God, and if he did not, may we. He left good health with his mother at parting, and away he went, crossing high hills, passing low dales, and kept on his way without halt or rest, the clear day going and the dark night coming, taking lodgings each evening wherever he found them, till at last he came to a high roomy castle.

He entered the castle without delaying outside, and when he went in, the owner asked was he a servant in search of a master.

'I am in search of a master,' said Coldfeet.

He engaged to herd cows for small hire and his keeping, and the time of his service was a day and a year.

Next morning, when Coldfeet was driving the cattle to pasture, his master was outside in the field before him, and said, 'You must take good care of yourself, for of all the herders who took service with me never a man but was killed by one or another of four giants who live next to my pastures. One of these giants has four, the next six, the third eight, and the fourth twelve heads on him.'

'By my hand!' said Coldfeet, 'I did not come here to be killed by the like of them. They will not hurt me, never fear.'

Coldfeet went on with the cattle, and when he came to the boundary he put them on the land of the giants. The cows were not long grazing when one of the giants at his castle caught the odor of the strange herder and rushed out. When coming at a distance he shouted, 'I smell the blood of a man from Erin; his liver and lights for my supper to-night, his blood for my morning dram, his jawbones for stepping-stones, his shins for hurleys!'

When the giant came up he cried, 'Ah, that is you, Coldfeet, and wasn't it the impudence in you to come here from the butt of Brandon Mountain and put cattle on my land to annoy me?'

'It isn't to give satisfaction to you that I am here, but to knock satisfaction out of your bones,' said Coldfeet.

With that the giant faced the herder, and the two went at each other and fought till near evening. They broke old trees and bent young ones; they made hard places soft and soft places hard; they made high places low and low places high; they made spring wells dry, and brought water through hard, gray rocks till near sunset, when Coldfeet took the heads off the giant and put the four skulls in muddy gaps to make a dry, solid road for the cows.

Coldfeet drove out his master's cattle on a second, third, and fourth morning; each day he killed a giant, each day the battle was fiercer, but on the fourth evening the fourth giant was dead.

On the fifth day Coldfeet was not long on the land of the dead giants when a dreadful enchanted old hag came out against him, and she raging with anger. She had nails of steel on her fingers and toes, each nail of them weighing seven pounds.

'Oh, you insolent, bloodthirsty villain,' screamed she, 'to come all the way from Brandon Mountain to kill my young sons, and, poor boys, only that timber is dear in this country it's in their cradles they'd be to-day instead of being murdered by you.'

'It isn't to give satisfaction to you that I'm here, you old witch, but to knock it out of your wicked old bones,' said Coldfeet.

'Glad would I be to tear you to pieces,' said the hag; 'but 'tis better to get some good of you first. I put you under spells of heavy enchantment that you cannot escape, not to eat two meals off the one table nor to sleep two nights in the one house till you go to the Queen of Lonesome Island, and bring the sword of light that never fails, the loaf of bread that is never eaten, and the bottle of water that is never drained.'

'Where is Lonesome Island?' asked Coldfeet.

'Follow your nose, and make out the place with your own wit,' said the hag.

Coldfeet drove the cows home in the evening, and said to his master, 'The giants will never harm you again; all their heads are in the muddy gaps from this to the end of the pasture, and there are good roads now for your cattle. I have been with you only five days, but another would not do my work in a day and a year; pay me my wages. You'll never have trouble again in finding men to mind cattle.'

The man paid Coldfeet his wages, gave him a good suit of clothes for the journey, and his blessing.

Away went Coldfeet now on the long road, and by my word it was a strange road to him. He went across high hills and low dales, passing each night where he found it, till the evening of the third day, when he came to a house where a little old man was living. The old man had lived in that house without leaving it for seven hundred years, and had not seen a living soul in that time.

Coldfeet gave good health to the old man, and received a hundred thousand welcomes in return.

'Will you give me a night's lodging?' asked Coldfeet.

'I will indeed,' said the old man, 'and is it any harm to ask, where are you going?'

'What harm in a plain question? I am going to Lonesome Island if I can find it.'

'You will travel to-morrow, and if you are loose and lively on the road you'll come at night to a house, and inside in it an old man like myself, only older. He will give you lodgings, and tell where to go the day after.'

Coldfeet rose very early next morning, ate his breakfast, asked aid of God, and if he didn't he let it alone. He left good health with the old man, and received his blessing. Away with him then over high hills and low dales, and if any one wished to see a great walker Coldfeet was the man to look at. He overtook the hare in the wind that was before him, and the hare in the wind behind could not overtake him; he went at that gait without halt or rest till he came in the heel of the evening to a small house, and went in. Inside in the house was a little old man sitting by the fire.

Coldfeet gave good health to the old man, and got a hundred thousand welcomes with a night's lodging.

'Why did you come, and where are you going?' asked the old man. 'Fourteen hundred years am I in this house alone, and not a living soul came in to see me till yourself came this evening.'

'I am going to Lonesome Island, if I can find it.'

'I have no knowledge of that place, but if you are a swift walker you will come to-morrow evening to an old man like myself, only older; he will tell you all that you need, and show you the way to the island.'

Next morning early Coldfeet went away after breakfast, leaving good health behind him and taking good wishes for the road. He travelled this day as on the other two days, only more swiftly, and at nightfall gave a greeting to the third old man.

*All the giants'
heads in the
muddy gaps of
Cattle Road*

'A hundred thousand welcomes,' said the old man. 'I am living alone in this house twenty-one hundred years, and not a living soul walked the way in that time. You are the first man I see in this house. Is it to stay with me that you are here?'

'It is not,' said Coldfeet, 'for I must be moving. I cannot spend two nights in the one house till I go to Lonesome Island, and I have no knowledge of where that place is.'

'Oh, then, it's the long road between this and Lonesome Island, but I'll tell where the place is, and how you are to go, if you go there. The road lies straight from my door to the sea. From the shore to the island no man has gone unless the queen brought him, but you may go if the strength and the courage are in you. I will give you this staff; it may help you. When you reach the sea throw the staff in the water, and you'll have a boat that will take you without sail or oar straight to the island. When you touch shore pull up the boat on the strand; it will turn into a staff and be again what it now is. The queen's castle goes whirling around always. It has only one door, and that on the roof of it. If you lean on the staff you can rise with one spring to the roof, go in at the door, and to the queen's chamber.

'The queen sleeps but one day in each year, and she will be sleeping to-morrow. The sword of light will be hanging at the head of her bed, the loaf and the bottle of water on the table near by. Seize the sword with the loaf and the bottle, and away with you, for the journey must be made in a day, and you must be on this side of those hills before nightfall. Do you think you can do that?'

'I will do it, or die in the trial,' said Coldfeet.

'If you make that journey you will do what no man has done yet,' said the old man. 'Before I came to live in this house champions and hundreds of king's sons tried to go to Lonesome Island, but not a man of them had the strength and the swiftness to go as far as the seashore, and that is but one part of the journey. All perished, and if their skulls are not crumbled, you'll see them to-morrow. The country is open and safe in the daytime, but when night falls the Queen of Lonesome Island sends her wild beasts to destroy every man they can find until daybreak. You must be in Lonesome Island to-morrow before noon, leave the place very soon after mid-day, and be on this side of those hills before nightfall, or perish.'

Next morning Coldfeet rose early, ate his breakfast, and started at day-break. Away he went swiftly over hills, dales, and level places, through a land where the wind never blows and the cock never crows, and though he went quickly the day before, he went five times more quickly that day, for the staff added speed to whatever man had it.

Coldfeet came to the sea, threw the staff into the water, and a boat was before him. Away he went in the boat, and before noon was in the chamber of the Queen of Lonesome Island. He found everything there as the old man had told him. Seizing the sword of light quickly and taking the bottle and loaf, he went toward the door; but there he halted, turned back, stopped a while with the queen. It was very near he was then to forgetting himself; but he sprang up, took one of the queen's golden garters, and away with him.

If Coldfeet strove to move swiftly when coming, he strove more in going back. On he raced over hills, dales, and flat places where the wind never blows and the cock never crows; he never stopped nor halted. When the sun was near setting he saw the last line of hills, and remembering that death was behind and not far from him, he used his last strength and was over the hill-tops at nightfall.

The whole country behind him was filled with wild beasts.

'Oh,' said the old man, 'but you are the hero, and I was in dread that you'd lose your life on the journey, and by my hand you had no time to spare.'

'I had not, indeed,' answered Coldfeet. 'Here is your staff, and many thanks for it.'

The two spent a pleasant evening together. Next morning Coldfeet left his blessing with the old man and went on, spent a night with each of the other old men, and never stopped after that till he reached the hag's castle. She was outside before him with the steel nails on her toes and fingers.

'Have you the sword, the bottle, and the loaf?' asked she.

'I have,' said Coldfeet; 'here they are.'

'Give them to me,' said the hag.

'If I was bound to bring the three things,' said Coldfeet, 'I was not bound to give them to you; I will keep them.'

'Give them here!' screamed the hag, raising her nails to rush at him.

With that Coldfeet drew the sword of light, and sent her head spinning through the sky in the way that 'tis not known in what part of the world it fell or did it fall in any place. He burned her body then, scattered the ashes, and went his way farther.

'I will go to my mother first of all,' thought he, and he travelled till evening. When his feet struck small stones on the road, the stones never stopped till they knocked wool off the spinning-wheels of old hags in the Eastern World. In the evening he came to a house and asked lodgings.

'I will give you lodgings, and welcome,' said the man of the house; 'but I have no food for you.'

'I have enough for us both,' said Coldfeet, 'and for twenty more if they were in it;' and he put the loaf on the table.

The man called his whole family. All had their fill, and left the loaf as large as it was before supper. The woman of the house made a loaf in the night like the one they had eaten from, and while Coldfeet was sleeping took his bread and left her own in the place of it. Away went Coldfeet next morning with the wrong loaf, and if he travelled differently from the day before it was because he travelled faster. In the evening he came to a house, and asked would they give him a night's lodging.

'We will, indeed,' said the woman, 'but we have no water to cook supper for you; the water is far away entirely, and no one to go for it.'

'I have water here in plenty,' said Coldfeet, putting his bottle on the table.

The woman took the bottle, poured water from it, filled one pot and then another, filled every vessel in the kitchen, and not a drop less in the bottle. What wonder, when no man or woman ever born could drain the bottle in a lifetime.

Said the woman to her husband that night, 'If we had the bottle, we needn't be killing ourselves running for water.'

'We need not,' said the man.

What did the woman do in the night, when Coldfeet was asleep, but take a bottle, fill it with water from one of the pots, and put that false bottle in place of the true one. Away went Coldfeet next morning, without knowledge of the harm done, and that day he travelled in the way that when he fell in running he had not time to rise, but rolled on till the speed that was under him brought him to his feet again. At sunset he was in sight of a house, and at dusk he was in it.

Coldfeet found welcome in the house, with food and lodgings.

'It is great darkness we are in,' said the man to Coldfeet; 'we have neither oil nor rushes.'

'I can give you light,' said Coldfeet, and he unsheathed the sword from Lonesome Island; it was clear inside the house as on a hilltop in sunlight.

When the people had gone to bed Coldfeet put the sword into its sheath, and all was dark again.

'Oh,' said the woman to her husband that night, 'if we had the sword we'd have light in the house always. You have an old sword above in the loft. Rise out of the bed now and put it in the place of that bright one.'

The man rose, took the two swords out doors, put the old blade in Coldfeet's sheath, and hid away Coldfeet's sword in the loft. Next morning Coldfeet went away, and never stopped till he came to his mother's cabin at the foot of Mount Brandon. The poor old woman was crying and lamenting every day. She felt sure that it was killed her son was, for she had never got tale or tidings of him. Many is the welcome she had for him, but if she had welcomes she had little to eat.

'Oh, then, mother, you needn't be complaining,' said Coldfeet, 'we have as much bread now as will do us a lifetime;' with that he put the loaf on the table, cut a slice for the mother, and began to eat himself. He was hungry, and the next thing he knew the loaf was gone.

'There is a little meal in the house,' said the mother. 'I'll go for water and make stirabout.'

'I have water here in plenty,' said Coldfeet. 'Bring a pot.'

The bottle was empty in a breath, and they hadn't what water would make stirabout nor half of it.

'Oh, then,' said Coldfeet, 'the old hag enchanted the three things before I killed her and knocked the strength out of every one of them.' With that he drew the sword, and it had no more light than any rusty old blade.

The mother and son had to live in the old way again; but as Coldfeet was far stronger than the first time, he didn't go hungry himself, and the mother had plenty. There were cattle in the country, and all the men in it couldn't keep them from Coldfeet or stop him. The old woman and the son had beef and mutton, and lived on for themselves at the foot of Brandon Mountain.

In three-quarters of a year the Queen of Lonesome Island had a son, the finest child that sun or moon could shine on, and he grew in the way that what of him didn't grow in the day grew in the night following, and what didn't grow that night grew the next day, and when he was two years old he was very large entirely.

The queen was grieving always for the loaf and the bottle, and there was no light in her chamber from the day the sword was gone. All at once she thought, 'The father of the boy took the three things. I will never sleep two nights in the one house till I find him.'

Away she went then with the boy, – went over the sea, went through the land where wind never blows and where cock never crows, came to the house of the oldest old man, stopped one night there, then stopped with the middle and the youngest old man. Where should she go next night but to the woman who stole the loaf from Coldfeet. When the queen sat down to supper the woman brought the loaf, cut slice after slice; the loaf was no smaller.

'Where did you get that loaf?' asked the queen.

'I baked it myself.'

'That is my loaf,' thought the queen.

The following evening she came to a house and found lodgings. At supper the woman poured water from a bottle, but the bottle was full always.

'Where did you get that bottle?'

'It was left to us,' said the woman; 'my grandfather had it.'

'That is my bottle,' thought the queen.

The next night she stopped at a house where a sword filled the whole place with light.

'Where did you find that beautiful sword?' asked the queen.

'My grandfather left it to me,' said the man. 'We have it hanging here always.'

'That is my sword,' said the queen to herself.

Next day the queen set out early, travelled quickly, and never stopped till she came near Brandon Mountain. At a distance she saw a man coming down hill with a fat bullock under each arm. He was carrying the beasts as easily as another would carry two geese. The man put the bullocks in a pen near a house at the foot of the mountain, came out toward the queen, and never stopped till he saluted her. When the man stopped, the boy broke away from the mother and ran to the stranger.

'How is this?' asked the queen; 'the child knows you.' She tried to take the boy, but he would not go to her.

'Have you lived always in this place?' asked the queen.

'I was born in that house beyond, and reared at the foot of that mountain before you. I went away from home once and killed four giants, the first with four, the second with six, the third with eight, and the fourth with twelve heads on him. When I had the giants killed, their mother came out against me, and she raging with vengeance. She wanted to kill me at first, but she did not. She put me under bonds of enchantment to go to the castle of the Queen of Lonesome Island, and bring the sword of light that can never fail to cut or give light, the loaf of bread that can never be eaten, and the bottle of water that can never be drained.'

'Did you go?' asked the queen.

'I did.'

'How could you go to Lonesome Island?'

21

'I journeyed and travelled, inquiring for the island, stopping one night at one place, and the next night at another, till I came to the house of a little man seven hundred years old. He sent me to a second man twice as old as himself, and the second to a third three times as old as the first man.

'The third old man showed me the road to Lonesome Island, and gave me a staff to assist me. When I reached the sea I made a boat of the staff, and it took me to the island. On the island the boat was a staff again.

'I sprang to the top of the queen's turning castle, went down and entered the chamber where she was sleeping, took the sword of light, with the loaf and the bottle, and was coming away again. I looked at the queen. The heart softened within me at sight of her beauty. I turned back and came near forgetting my life with her. I brought her gold garter with me, took the three things, sprang down from the castle, ran to the water, made a boat of the staff again, came quickly to mainland, and from that hour till darkness I ran with what strength I could draw from each bit of my body. Hardly had I crossed the hilltop and was before the door of the oldest old man when the country behind me was covered with wild beasts. I escaped death by one moment. I brought the three things to the hag who had sent me, but I did not give them. I struck the head from her, but before dying she destroyed them, for when I came home they were useless.'

'Have you the golden garter?'

'Here it is,' said the young man.

'What is your name?' asked the queen.

'Coldfeet,' said the stranger.

'You are the man,' said the queen. 'Long ago it was prophesied that a hero named Coldfeet would come to Lonesome Island without my request or assistance, and that our son would cover the whole world with his power. Come with me now to Lonesome Island.'

The queen gave Coldfeet's old mother good clothing, and said, 'You will live in my castle.'

They all left Brandon Mountain and journeyed on toward Lonesome Island till they reached the house where the sword of light was. It was night when they came and dark outside, but bright as day in the house from the sword, which was hanging on the wall.

'Where did you find this blade?' asked Coldfeet, catching the hilt of the sword.

'My grandfather had it,' said the woman.

'He had not,' said Coldfeet, 'and I ought to take the head off your husband for stealing it when I was here last.'

Coldfeet put the sword in his scabbard and kept it. Next day they reached the house where the bottle was, and Coldfeet took that. The following night he found the loaf and recovered it. All the old men were glad to see Coldfeet, especially the oldest, who loved him.

The queen with her son and Coldfeet with his mother arrived safely in Lonesome Island. They lived on in happiness; there is no account of their death, and they may be in it yet for aught we know.

NOTES

Source of tale: Jeremiah Curtin, *Hero Tales of Ireland*, London: Macmillan & Co., 1894.

Collected from John Malone, of Rahonian, west of Dingle in Ireland, by Jeremiah Curtin, this is a classic Celtic wonder tale in every sense, made up of many characteristic themes and motifs. There is the hero who grows quickly to more-than-normal size and is able to combat giants with ease; the triplicity of helpers; the classic triple quest – for the sword of light and the inexhaustible bottle and loaf. All of these themes are found repeatedly and with countless variations in the repertoire of Celtic storytellers.

The wise helpers, each one successively older than the last, are of particular interest. Here they are old men, but in a separate story they are animals. Indeed, in what may be part of a cycle of animal tales, the hawk of Achill, the salmon of Asseroe, and the stag of Slieve Fuaid are asked for information, and in each case send the hero on to ask 'my older cousin'. In the Welsh tale of 'Culhwch and Olwen', this is fleshed out considerably when the hero is sent in search of the lost child god Mabon. Again it is a combination of animals that gives aid to the search, and one can see something like a cosmogony in these tales, with each animal representing a more ancient period of time. This is reflected in a medieval verse which has survived from more ancient times, which reads:

Three years is the duration of the
    alder pole,
Three times the duration of the alder
    pole

Is the life of a dog in the green
    woodland;
And three times the age of the dog
Is the age of a good and active
    horse.
Thrice the age of the horse
Is that of a man – a short existence!
Thrice the age of man
Is that of the bounding hart;
Thrice the age of the stag
Is that of the melodious blackbird;
Thrice the age of the beautiful
    blackbird
Is that of the earth-grown oak;
Thrice the age of the oak
Is judged to be that of the earth
    itself . . .

Here we can catch a glimpse of a cosmological myth of great antiquity, no longer extant, but hinted at, tantalizingly, in these scraps of lore.

The Queen of Lonesome Island is very clearly an otherworldly figure, who sleeps on only one day a year. The fact that she gives birth nine months after the visit of Coldfeet is glossed over in the rather coy description of the theft of her garter, but the recognition of the ensuing child as the product of that visit makes it clear enough that the hero dallied long enough to father the next wonder child on the Queen – presumably without waking her! The mating of human beings and faery folk is a theme which occurs in countless of these stories, and gave rise to the belief that faery men were incapable of breeding without the help of human seed. The whole notion seems to stem from a deep-rooted desire among human beings for something 'other' to enter into their lives.

THE PRINCESS OF LAND-UNDER-WAVES

HEN NO WIND BLOWS and the surface of the sea is clear as crystal, the beauties of Land-under-Waves are revealed to human eyes. It is a fair country with green vales through which flow silvern streams, and the pebbles in the beds of the streams are flashing gems of varied hues. There are deep forests that glitter in eternal sunshine, and bright flowers that never fade. Rocks are of gold, and the sand is dust of silver.

On a calm morning in May, the Feans, who were great warriors in ancient Scotland, being the offspring of gods and goddesses, were sitting beside the Red Cataract, below which salmon moved slowly, resting themselves ere they began to leap towards the higher waters of the stream. The sun was shining bright, and the sea was without a ripple. With eyes of wonder the Feans gazed on the beauties of Land-under-Waves. None spoke, so deeply were they absorbed. They saw the silver sands, the rocks of gold, the gleaming forests, the beautiful flowers, and the bright streams that flow over beds covered with flashing gems.

As they gazed a boat was seen on the sea, and for a time the Feans were not sure whether it moved above the surface or below it. In time, however, as it drew near they saw that it was on the surface. The boat came towards the place where they sat, and they saw that a woman pulled the oars.

All the Feans rose to their feet. Finn, the King of the Feans, and Goll, his chief warrior, had keen sight, and when the boat was still afar off they saw that the woman had great beauty. She pulled two oars, which parted the sea, and the ripples seemed to set in motion all the trees and flowers of Land-under-Waves.

The boat came quickly, and when it grounded on the beach, the loveliest woman that ever eyes gazed upon rose out of it. Her face was mild and touched with a soft sadness. She was a stranger to the Feans, who knew well that she had come from afar, and they wondered whence she came and what were the tidings she brought.

The young woman walked towards Finn and saluted him, and for a time Finn and all the Feans were made silent by her exceeding great beauty. At length Finn spoke to her. 'You are welcome, fair young stranger,' he said. 'Tell us what tribe you are from, and what is the purpose of your journey to the land of the Feans.'

Softly spoke the young woman, saying: 'I am the daughter of King Under-Waves, and I shall tell you why I have come here. There is not a land beneath the sun which I have not searched for Finn and his brave warriors.'

'Beautiful maiden,' Finn said, 'will you not tell us why you have searched through the lands that are far and near, seeking to find us?'

'Then you are Finn and no other,' spoke the maiden.

'I am indeed Finn, and these who stand near me are my warriors.' It was thus that Finn made answer, speaking modestly, and yet not without pride.

'I have come to ask for your help,' said the maiden, 'and I shall have need of it very soon. Mine enemy pursues me even now.'

'I promise to help you, fair princess,' Finn assured her. 'Tell me who it is that pursues you.'

Said the maiden: 'He who pursues me over the ocean is a mighty and fearless warrior. His name is Dark Prince-of-Storm, and he is the son of the White King of Red-Shields. He means to seize the kingdom of my father and make me his bride. I have defied him, saying: "Finn shall take me to my home; he shall be my saviour. Great as is your prowess, you cannot fight and beat Finn and his heroic band."'

Oscar, the young hero and the grandson of Finn, spoke forth and said: 'Even if Finn were not here, the Dark Prince would not dare to seize you.'

As he spoke a shadow fell athwart the sea, blotting out the vision of Land-under-Waves. The Feans looked up, and they saw on the skyline a mighty warrior mounted on a blue-grey steed of ocean; white was its mane and white its tail, and white the foam that was driven from its nostrils and its mouth.

The warrior came swiftly towards the shore, and as his steed rode forward with great fury, waves rose and broke around it. The breath from its panting nostrils came over the sea like gusts of tempest.

On the warrior's head was a flashing helmet, and on his left arm a ridged shield. In his right hand he grasped a large heavy sword, and when he waved it on high it flashed bright like lightning.

Faster than a mountain torrent galloped his horse. The Feans admired the Dark Prince. He was a great and mighty warrior who bore himself like a king.

The steed came to land, and when it did so, the Dark Prince leapt from its back and strode up the beach.

Finn spoke to the fair daughter of the King Under-Waves and said: 'Is this the prince of whom you have spoken?'

Said the princess: 'It is he and no other. Oh, protect me now, for great is his power!'

Goll, the old warrior, and Oscar, the youthful hero, sprang forward and placed themselves between the Dark Prince and the fair princess. But the Dark Prince scorned to combat with him. He went towards Finn, who was

unarmed. Goll was made angry at once. He seized a spear and flung it at the stranger. It did not touch his body, but it split the ridged shield right through the middle. Then Oscar raised his spear and flung it from his left hand. It struck the warrior's steed and slew it. This was accounted a mighty deed, and Ossian, the bard of the Feans, and father of Oscar, celebrated it in song which is still sung in Scotland.

When the steed perished, Dark Prince turned round with rage and fury, and called for fifty heroes to combat against him. Then he said that he would overcome all the Feans and take away the fair princess.

A great battle was waged on the beach. The Dark Prince sprang upon the Feans, and fought with fierceness and great strength.

At length Goll went against him. Both fought with their swords alone, and never was seen before such a furious combat. Strong was the arm of Goll, and cunning the thrusts he gave. As he fought on, his battle power increased, and at length he struck down and slew the Dark Prince. Nor was ever such a hero overcome since the day when the Ocean Giant was slain.

When the Dark Prince was slain, the wind fell and the sea was hushed, and the sun at evening shone over the waters. Once again Land-under-Waves was revealed in all its beauty.

The princess bade farewell to all the Feans, and Finn went into a boat and went with her across the sea until they reached the gates of Land-under-Waves. The entrance to this wonderful land is a sea-cave on the Far Blue Isle of Ocean. When Finn took leave of the princess, she made him promise that if ever she had need of his help again, he would give it to her freely and quickly.

A year and a day went past, and then came a calm and beautiful morning. Once again the Feans sat on the shore below the Red Cataract, gazing on the beauties of Land-under-Waves. As they gazed, a boat came over the sea, and there was but one person in it.

Said Oscar: 'Who comes hither? Is it the princess of Land-under-Waves once more?'

Finn looked seaward and said: 'No, it is not the princess who comes hither, but a young man.'

The boat drew swiftly towards the shore, and when the man was within call he hailed Finn with words of greeting and praise.

'Who are you, and whence come you?' Finn asked.

Said the man: 'I am the messenger of the princess of Land-under-Waves. She is ill, and seems ready to die.'

There was great sorrow among the Feans when they heard the sad tidings.

'What is your message from the fair princess?' Finn asked.

Said the man: 'She bids you to remember your promise to help her in time of need.'

'I have never forgotten my promise,' Finn told him, 'and am ready now to fulfil it.'

Said the man: 'Then ask Jeermit, the healer, to come with me so that he may give healing to the Princess Under-Waves.'

Finn made a sign to Jeermit, and he rose up and went down the beach and entered the boat. Then the boat went out over the sea towards the Far Blue

The Feans watch Princess Under-Waves approach in a boat

27

Isle, and it went swiftly until it reached the sea-cave through which one must pass to enter Land-under-Waves.

Now Jeermit was the fairest of all the members of the Fean band. His father was Angus-the-Ever-Young, who conferred upon him the power to give healing for wounds and sickness. Jeermit had knowledge of curative herbs and life-giving waters, and he had the power, by touching a sufferer, to prolong life until he found the means to cure.

Jeermit was taken through the sea-cave of the Far Blue Isle, and for a time he saw naught, so thick was the darkness; but he heard the splashing of waves against the rocks. At length light broke forth, and the boat grounded. Jeermit stepped out, and found himself on a broad level plain. The boatman walked in front, and Jeermit followed him. They went on and on, and it seemed that their journey would never end. Jeermit saw a clump of red sphagnum moss, and plucked some and went on. Ere long he saw another clump, and plucked some more. A third time he came to a red moss clump, and from it too he plucked a portion. The boatman still led on and on, yet Jeermit never felt weary.

At length Jeermit saw before him a golden castle. He spoke to the boatman, saying: 'Whose castle is that?'

Said the boatman: 'It is the castle of King Under-Waves, and the princess lies within.'

Jeermit entered the castle. He saw many courtiers with pale faces. None spoke: all were hushed to silence with grief. The queen came towards him, and she seized his right hand and led him towards the chamber in which the dying princess lay.

Jeermit knelt beside her, and when he touched her the power of his healing entered her veins, and she opened her eyes. As soon as she beheld Jeermit of the Feans she smiled a sweet smile, and all who were in the chamber smiled too.

'I feel stronger already,' the princess told Jeermit. 'Great is the joy I feel to behold you. But the sickness has not yet left me, and I fear I shall die.'

'I have three portions of red moss,' said Jeermit. 'If you will take them in a drink they will heal you, because they are the three life drops of your heart.'

'Alas!' the princess exclaimed, 'I cannot drink of any water now except from the cup of the King of the Plain of Wonder.'

Now, great as was Jeermit's knowledge, he had never heard before of this magic cup.

'A wise woman has told that if I get three draughts from this cup I shall be cured,' said the princess. 'She said also that when I drink I must swallow the three portions of red moss from the Wide-Bare-Plain. The moss of healing you have already found, O Jeermit. But no man shall ever gain possession of the magic cup of the King of the Plain-of-Wonder, and I shall not therefore get it, and must die.'

Said Jeermit: 'There is not in the world above the sea, or the world below the sea, a single man who will keep the cup from me. Tell me where dwells the King of the Plain-of-Wonder. Is his palace far distant from here?'

'No, it is not far distant,' the princess told him. 'Plain-of-Wonder is the next kingdom to that of my father. The two kingdoms are divided by a river. You may reach that river, O Jeermit, but you may never be able to cross it.'

28

Said Jeermit: 'I now lay healing spells upon you, and you shall live until I return with the magic cup.'

When he had spoken thus, he rose up and walked out of the castle. The courtiers who had been sad when he entered were merry as he went away, and those who had been silent spoke one to another words of comfort and hope, because Jeermit had laid healing spells upon the princess.

The King and the Queen of Land-under-Waves bade the healer of the Feans farewell, and wished him a safe and speedy journey.

Jeermit went on alone in the direction of the Plain-of-Wonder. He went on and on until he reached the river of which the princess had spoken. Then he walked up and down the river bank searching for a ford, but he could not find one.

'I cannot cross over,' he said aloud. 'The princess has spoken truly.'

As he spoke a little brown man rose up out of the river. 'Jeermit,' he said, 'you are now in sore straits.'

Said Jeermit: 'Indeed I am. You have spoken wisely.'

'What would you give to one who would help you in your trouble?'

'Whatever he may ask of me.'

'All I ask for,' said the brown man, 'is your goodwill.'

'That you get freely,' said Jeermit to him.

'I shall carry you across the river,' said the little man.

'You cannot do that.'

'Yes, indeed I can.'

He stretched forth his hands and took Jeermit on his back, and walked across the river with him, treading the surface as if it were hard ground. As they crossed the river they passed an island over which hovered a dark mist.

'What island is that?' asked Jeermit.

'Its name,' the brown man told him, 'is Cold Isle-of-the-Dead. There is a well on the island, and the water of it is healing water.'

They reached the opposite bank, and the brown man said: 'You are going to the palace of King Ian of Wonder-Plain.'

'I am.'

'You desire to obtain the Cup of Healing.'

'That is true.'

'May you get it,' said the brown man, who thereupon entered the river.

Ere he disappeared he spoke again and said: 'Know you where you now are?'

'In the Kingdom of Plain-of-Wonder,' Jeermit said.

'That is true,' said the little brown man. 'It is also Land-under-Mountains. This river divides Land-under-Mountains from Land-under-Waves.'

Jeermit was about to ask a question, but ere he could speak the little brown man vanished from before his eyes.

Jeermit went on and on. There was no sun above him and yet all the land was bright. No darkness ever comes to Land-under-Mountains, and there is no morning there and no evening, but always endless day.

Jeermit went on and on until he saw a silver castle with a roof of gleaming crystal. The doors were shut, and guarded by armed warriors.

Jeermit blew a blast on his horn, and called out, 'Open and let me in.'

A warrior went towards him with drawn sword. Jeermit flung his spear and slew the warrior.

Then the doors of the castle were opened and King Ian came forth.

'Who are you, and whence come you?' he asked sternly.

'I am Jeermit,' was the answer he received.

'Son of Angus-the-Ever-Young, you are welcome,' exclaimed the king. 'Why did you not send a message that you were coming? It is sorrowful to think you have slain my greatest warrior.'

Said Jeermit: 'Give him to drink of the water in the Cup of Healing.'

'Bring forth the cup!' the king called.

The cup was brought forth, and the king gave it to Jeermit, saying: 'There is no virtue in the cup unless it is placed in hands of either Angus or his son.'

Jeermit touched the slain warrior's lips with the cup. He poured drops of the water into the man's mouth, and he sat up. Then he drank all the water in the cup, and rose to his feet strong and well again, for his wound had been healed.

Said Jeermit to the king: 'I have come hither to obtain this cup, and will now take it with me and go away.'

'So be it,' answered the king. 'I give you the cup freely. But remember that there is no longer any healing in it, for my mighty warrior has drunk the magic water.'

Jeermit was not too well pleased when the King of Wonder-Plain spoke thus. 'No matter,' said he; 'I shall take the cup with me.'

'I will send a boat to take you across the river and past the Cold-Isle-of-the-Dead,' the king said.

Said Jeermit: 'I thank you, but I have no need of a boat.'

'May you return soon,' the King said with a smile, for he believed that Jeermit would never be able to cross the river or pass the Cold-Isle-of-the-Dead.

Jeermit bade the king farewell and went away, as he had come, all alone. He went on and on until he reached the river. Then he sat down, and gloomy thoughts entered his mind. He had obtained the cup, but it was empty: he had returned to the river and could not cross it.

'Alas!' he exclaimed aloud, 'my errand is fruitless. The cup is of no use to me, and I cannot cross the river, and must needs return in shame to the King of Wonder-Plain.'

As he spoke the little brown man rose out of the river.

'You are again in sore straits, Jeermit,' he said.

'Indeed, I am,' answered the son of Angus. 'I got what I went for, but it is useless, and I cannot cross the river.'

'I shall carry you,' said the little brown man.

'So be it,' Jeermit answered.

The little brown man walked over the river with Jeermit on his shoulders, and went towards the Cold-Isle-of-the-Dead.

'Whither are you carrying me now?' asked Jeermit with fear in his heart.

Said the little brown man: 'You desire to heal the daughter of King Under-Waves.'

'That is true.'

*Princess Under-Waves
drinks from the
Cup of Healing*

'Your cup is empty, and you must fill it at the Well of Healing, on the
Cold-Isle-of-the-Dead. That is why I am carrying you towards the isle. You
must not get off my back or set foot on the shore, else you will never be able
to leave it. But have no fear. I shall kneel down beside the well, and you can
dip the cup in it, and carry off enough water to heal the princess.'

Jeermit was well pleased to hear these words, for he knew that the little
brown man was indeed his friend. He obtained the healing water in the manner
that was promised. Then the little brown man carried him to the opposite bank
of the river, and set him down on the border of Land-under-Waves.

31

'Now you are happy-hearted,' said the little brown man.

'Happy-hearted indeed,' Jeermit answered.

'Ere I bid you farewell I shall give you good advice,' said the little brown man.

'Why have you helped me as you have done?' Jeermit asked.

'Because your heart is warm, and you desire to do good to others,' said the little brown man. 'Men who do good to others will ever find friends in the Land of the Living, in the Land of the Dead, in Land-under-Waves, and in Land-under-Mountains.'

'I thank you,' Jeermit said. 'Now I am ready for your good advice, knowing that your friendship is true and lasting.'

Said the little brown man: 'You may give the princess water from the Cup-of-Healing, but she will not be cured unless you drop into the water three portions of sphagnum moss.'

'I have already found these portions on the broad level plain.'

'That is well,' said the other. 'Now I have more advice to offer you. When the princess is healed the king will offer you choice of reward. Take no thing he offers, but ask for a boat to convey you home again.'

'I will follow your advice,' Jeermit promised.

Then the two parted, and Jeermit went on and on until he came to the golden palace of King Under-Waves. The princess welcomed him when he was brought into her room, and said: 'No man ever before was given the cup you now carry.'

Said Jeermit: 'For your sake I should have got it, even if I had to fight an army.'

'I feared greatly that you would never return,' sighed the princess.

Jeermit put into the Cup-of-Healing the three portions of blood-red moss which he had found, and bade the princess to drink.

Thrice she drank, and each time she swallowed a portion of red moss. When she drank the last drop, having swallowed the third portion of red moss, she said: 'Now I am healed. Let a feast be made ready, and I shall sit at the board with you.'

There was great joy and merriment in the castle when the feast was held. Sorrow was put away, and music was sounded. When the feast was over, the king spoke to Jeermit and said: 'I would fain reward you for healing my daughter, the princess. I shall give you as much silver and gold as you desire, and you shall marry my daughter and become the heir to my throne.'

Said Jeermit: 'If I marry your daughter I cannot again return to my own land.'

'No, you cannot again return, except on rare and short visits. But here you will spend happy days, and everyone shall honour you.'

Said Jeermit: 'The only reward I ask for, O king, is a small one indeed.'

'I promise to give you whatever you ask for.'

Said Jeermit: 'Give me a boat, so that I may return again to my own land, which is very dear to me, and to my friends and kinsmen, the Feans, whom I love, and to Finn mac Cool, the great chief of men.'

'Your wish is granted,' the king said.

Then Jeermit bade farewell to all who were in the castle, and when he parted with the princess she said: 'I shall never forget you, Jeermit. You found me in suffering and gave me relief; you found me dying and gave me back my life again. When you return to your own land remember me, for I shall never pass an hour of life without thinking of you with joy and thankfulness.'

Jeermit crossed the level plain once again, and reached the place where the boat in which he had come lay safely moored. The boatman went into it and seized the oars, and Jeermit went in after him. Then the boat sped through the deep dark tunnel, where the waves splash unseen against the rocks, and passed out of the cave on the shore of Far-Blue-Isle. The boat then went speedily over the sea, and while it was yet afar off, Finn saw it coming. All the Feans gathered on the shore to bid Jeermit welcome.

'Long have we waited for you, son of Angus,' Finn said.

'What time has passed since I went away?' asked Jeermit, for it seemed to him that he had been absent for no more than a day and a night.

'Seven long years have passed since we bade you farewell,' Finn told him, 'and we feared greatly that you would never again come back to us.'

Said Jeermit: 'In the lands I visited there is no night, and no change in the year. Glad am I to return home once again.'

Then they all went to Finn's house, and a great feast was held in honour of Jeermit, who brought back with him the Cup-of-Healing which he had received from the King of Wonder-Plain.

NOTES

Source of tale: Donald A. Mackenzie, *Wonder Tales from Scottish Myth and Legend*, Glasgow: Blackie and Sons, 1917.

This fascinating and rather beautiful story is really a detailed description of the otherworld. Nominally it concerns Finn (Fionn mac Cumhaill) and the Feans (*fiana*) and their adventures with the Princess of Land-under-Waves. In the second part of the story, however, when Jeermit the Healer journeys to the land of the Princess to cure her mysterious and inexplicable illness, this becomes an excuse to describe the otherworld in its many forms and guises. The Plain of Wonder (Mag Mell), the Land-under-Mountains, the Cold-Isle-of-the-Dead and the Land of the Living are all widely disseminated names for the otherworld in Celtic tradition. Jeermit travels through each of them in search of the Cup of Healing (one of many such vessels which we shall encounter in this collection) and in the process we learn a little about each one.

Jeermit himself is better known in Irish mythology as Diarmaid ua Duibhne, the foster-son of the Irish love god Oenghus Mac in Og. In this guise he is best known as a poet and warrior who is irresistible to women because of a 'love-spot' given to him by a faery woman. In the most famous story of the Fionn cycle he elopes with Fionn's wife Gráinne and the pair are pursued and eventually hunted to their deaths.

The little brown man who comes out of the river appears elsewhere in both Welsh and Irish tradition, and in the story of 'Baranoir' from Curtin's collection of *Irish Folk Tales* (Talbot Press, 1944). He is always associated with water and is both wise and helpful to mortal heroes.

The version of the story which appears here was written by Donald Mackenzie, and is based on a much earlier story from the cycle of tales concerning Fionn and his warriors, several of whom are mentioned in the text. As always in tales where mortals visit the otherworld, time is different . What seems to Jeermit only a few days is in fact seven years. He is perhaps lucky that only this much time had passed, since in many other instances several hundred years go by in but a day.

THE LAD OF THE SKIN COVERINGS

O N A CERTAIN DAY OF OLD, Finn thought that he would go to hunt to the White Glen. He took with him as many of his men as were at hand at the time, and they went to the Glen.

The hunt began, and when it was over no man who was present ever saw such a sight of dead deer.

It was a custom with the Fein (Féinn), after they had gathered together the deer they killed, to sit down and take a rest. They would then divide the deer among them, each man taking with him a small or large burden as he was able. But on this day they killed many more than all that were at the hunt could take with them.

While Finn was considering what he should do with the remainder, he gave a look, and saw a Big Lad coming over the side of the mountain, and making straight for the place in which they were assembled with so great speed that never before did they see a man so fast as he. 'Some one is coming towards us here,' said Finn, 'and 'tis before him his business is, or else I am deceived.' They all stood looking at the Big Lad who was coming, but he took not a long time till he was in their very midst.

He saluted Finn frankly, energetically, fluently; and Finn saluted him with the equivalent of the same words. Then Finn asked of him whence did he come, or whither was he going, or what was he wanting. He sad that he was the Son of the Lady of Green Insh (*Innis Uaine*), and that he came from that as far as this seeking a Master. Finn answered, 'I have need of a servant, and I do not care although I engage thee if we agree about the reward.' 'That would not be my advice to thee,' said Conan. 'Conan, thou hadst better keep quiet, and mind thine own business; and I will do my business,' said the Big Lad. Every one present was wondering at the Big Lad's dress, for it consisted of skin coverings. Not less did they wonder at the appearance of his great strength of body. And they were somewhat afraid that he would disgrace them before he would part with them. Finn then asked of him what reward would he be asking to the end of a day and year? The Big Lad said that he asked nothing but that there should be no apartness of meat or of drink between them at the table within, or on the plain without, or in any place in which they should take food to the end of the day and year. 'Thou shalt get that,' said Finn; and they agreed.

Then they began to lift the deer with them. One would take with him one, and another would take with him two, till all had their burdens except the Big Lad. But they left many more deer than they took with them. Finn then told the Big Lad to take with him a burden. The Big Lad began to pull the longest and the finest part of the heather that he could see, till he had a great heap beside him. Then he began to make a rope of the heather, and to place a deer on every deer's length that he would twine till he had every deer that was left in one burden.

When the burden was ready he told the rest to lift it on his back. They came, and as many went about the burden as could surround it; but though as many and as many more of the Fein would have been assembled as were present on that day they could not put wind between it and (the) earth. When the Big Lad saw this he told them to stand out of his way. He then took hold of the rope and put a turn of its end about his fist, he bent his back, put a balk on his foot, and threw the burden over his shoulder. Every one of the Fein looked at his neighbour, but spake not a word.

When the Big Lad got the burden steady on his back he said, 'I am but a stranger in this place; let one of you therefore go before to direct me in the way.' Every one looked at his neighbour to see who would go. At last Conan answered that he would go if the rest would carry his deer home. Finn said that his deer would be carried home if he would take the lead. Conan threw the deer off him, sprang before the Big Lad, and told him to follow him.

Conan went away as fast as he could, and the Big Lad went away after him. There were two big nails on the two big toes of the Big Lad, and they went but a short distance when he left not a hair's-breadth of skin on the back of Conan between the top of his two shoulders and the back of his two feet with the two big nails which were on his feet. At last Conan began to lose his distance, for he was growing weak with loss of blood; and in a short time he was under the necessity of stopping and of sitting down where he was. When the Big Lad saw that Conan yielded he went past him, and stop he made not till he let his burden go at the dwelling of Finn.

Then he sprang in, and put on a fire. He cooked food for every man who was at the hunt, and set the food of each man apart, except his own food and that of Finn. The Fein came home at last; and when they went in they wondered greatly to see the food ready before them, but they made no remark.

After the supper (was over) the Fein sent for Finn, and Conan spoke and said: 'Did I not tell thee that we should get disgraced by the Lad whom thou didst engage? His match in strength is not in the Fein. Thou must put him out of our way until his time shall be out.' 'Well,' said Finn, 'I do not know what I can do with him unless I send him away to Lochlan to seek the four-sided cup, and he has there a day and a year's journey however well he may walk.'

They were all quite pleased with this, and told Finn to send him off as soon

as he could. Finn answered and said: 'Before a sun shall rise on a dwelling he
will get his leave to travel on the journey.'

Without delay he sent for the Lad of the Skin Coverings, and said to him
that he was sorry to ask him to go on this long journey, but that he hoped he
would not refuse. The Big Lad asked him on what business was he sending
him, or whither had he to go? Finn said that he got word from Lochlan that
he would get the four-sided cup if he would send a man for it. 'I sent them
word to come and meet us with it, and that we would go and meet them. I
am desirous that thou wilt go to seek it to-morrow, and I know that they will
meet thee coming with it.' 'Well, Finn,' said the Big Lad, 'thou knowest and
art assured that they shall not meet me with it, for numerous are the heroes
who have shed their blood on the field beneath the spears of Lochlan for the
sake of the four-sided cup which they have had since four-and-twenty years,
and which thou hast not yet got. How now dost thou think, Finn, that I can
take it out (of their hands) unassisted? But since I promised to do what thou
wouldst ask me, I will go seek it for thee.'

On the next morning, before a sun shone, the Big Lad was ready for the
journey. Then he lifted his own skin-coverings on him, and strode away; and
the swift March wind which was before him he would overtake, and the swift
March wind which was behind him would not keep (pace) with him. At that
rate of travelling onwards he did not slacken the speed of his chace till he
struck his palm against a (door) bar at the palace of the King of Lochlan that
night.

The palace of the King of Lochlan was kept by seven guards. The Big Lad
knocked (at the gate of) the first guard, and the first guard asked him whence
was he, or whither was he going? He replied that he was a servant who had
come from Finn, King of the Fein, on a message to the King of Lochlan. Word
went to the King that such a man was at the door. The King asked if any man
was with him. The Lad-in-waiting said that there was not. The King then
gave orders to let him in. The (gate of the) first guard was opened for him,
and he got in, and in like manner every (gate with a) guard until he got
through the seven guards. He was taken into the place where the King was,
and the King told him to sit down. The Big Lad sat, for he was tired after the
journey which he had made. He gave a look through the room, and noticed
as beautiful a cup as he ever saw standing on a table. He said to the King of
Lochlan, 'That is a beautiful vessel which thou hast there.' The King said that
it was that, and also a cup of virtues. The Big Lad asked what virtues did it
possess? The King answered that there was no fill that he would order to be
in it which would not be in it immediately. The Big Lad, being thirsty after
the journey which he had made, thought that its full of water on the table
would be a good thing. Then he rose up, took hold of the cup, and drank all
that was in it. He next turned his face to the door; and if he asked for an
opening in, he asked not for an opening out, for he leaped over the seven
guards, having the cup with him.

Then he lifted his own skin-coverings on him, and strode away on the
path on which he came; and the swift March wind which was before him he
would overtake, but the swift March wind which was behind him would not
keep (pace) with him. At that rate of travelling onwards he did not slacken

the speed of his chace till he struck his palm against a (door) bar at Finn's dwelling on that night.

He went in, and handed the cup to Finn. 'Thou wert not long away,' said Finn. 'Did I not tell thee before thou didst leave that they would meet thee coming with it?' The Big Lad answered: 'Thou knowest and art assured that they did not meet me coming with it. But I reached Lochlan, and I got the cup in the King's palace, and I made the journey forward and back again.'

'Silence, babbler!' said Conan. 'There are some in the Fein who can run on ben-side or on glen-strath as well as thou canst, and they could not do the journey in double the time in which thou sayest thou didst it. But come to cut a leap with me as far as the Green Lakelet at the foot of Ben Aidan, and I will know if thou hast made the journey.' 'O, Conan! I am more needful of food and a little wink of sleep than of going to cut leaps with thee.' 'If thou wilt not go, we will not believe that thou hast made the journey,' said Conan.

The Big Lad rose and went with him; and they reached the Green Lakelet. Conan asked the Big Lad to cut a leap across the Lakelet. 'It is thou that brought me here, and I am tired,' said the Big Lad; 'therefore cut the first leap thyself.' Conan took a race and cut a leap, but sank to the balls of his two hips in the leafy marsh on the other side of the Lakelet. The Big Lad cut his leap without any race, and went over Conan's head on the hard ground on the other side of the Lakelet. He then leaped it back back-foremost, and forward front-foremost, before Conan got his haunches out of the bog.

When Conan got his feet on the hard ground he said that the roots gave way under his feet, and that he sank! 'But come and race with me to the top of Ben Aidan, and I will know if thou hast made the journey.' 'Conan, I am more needful of a little wink of sleep than of going to race with thee to the top of Ben Aidan.' However, he went. At a stride or two the Big Lad went past Conan, and gave not another look after him till he was on the top of the Ben. He then stretched himself on a green hillock and slept.

He knew not how long he slept, but it was the panting of Conan climbing the Ben which wakened him. He sprang quickly to his feet, and said, 'Did I make the journey now, Conan?' 'Come, wrestle with me, and I will know if thou hast made the journey,' said Conan. They embraced each other. Conan told the Big Lad to put his turn. 'Put thou thy turn first, Conan, for it is thou who wanted to begin.' Conan tried to put his turn, but he did not move the Big Lad.

The Big Lad then bent over Conan, and with his weight threw him, and bound his three smalls with his leather garter.

The Big Lad now took it as an insult that the most contemptible man in the Fein was despising and bullying him; and he gave a vow that he would not return to Finn any more. He went away, and left Conan bound on the top of the Ben.

The night was coming, and Finn was wondering that the two men who went away were not returning. At last fear struck him that the Big Lad had killed Conan, and therefore he told his men that they must go seek them. Before the sun rose on the next morning he divided his men in companies, and sent a company to each corner of the Ben, and told them to travel on till they should all meet on the top of the Ben. About the evening of the day they met, and found Conan bound by his three smalls in one thong.

Finn told one of his men to go over, and unbind Conan. Oscar went, and took a long time trying to do that, but for every knot which he would untie seven other knots would go on the thong. At last he said to Finn, 'I cannot loose this thong!' Then Goll sprang over, thinking that he could do better. He began to untie the thong; but, as happened to Oscar, it beat him. If it was not tighter when he ceased, it was not a bit looser. At last he lifted up his head in wrath, and said, 'There is not a man in the Fein who can unbind Conan!'

Finn now got afraid that Conan would be dead before they could get him released. But he remembered his knowledge set of teeth; and having put his finger under it he discovered that there was not a man in the world who could unbind him but the Smith of the White Glen, or else the man who bound him.

He then sent away Goll and Oscar to tell the Smith what befell Conan. They reached the Smith, and told him the business on which they were. The Smith told them to gather together every four-footed beast which was between the back of Ben Aidan and the top of the White Glen, and send them past the door of his smithy. 'And,' said he, 'if I then come out in peace good is my peace, but if I come out in wrath evil is my wrath.'

Oscar and Goll then returned to Finn, and told him what the Smith said to them. Finn said that the hunt must be started. The hunt was started, and that was the Great Hunt of the White Glen. Since the first hunt was started never was there so great a number of four-footed beasts assembled as were (together) on that day. Then they sent them past the door of the smithy. The Smith came out and asked what was yonder? They answered, 'All the four-footed beasts between the top of Ben Aidan and the head of the White Glen, as he wanted.' The Smith said, 'You have done well enough, but turn back every one of those creatures to the place from which you have taken them, and I will then go to unbind Conan.' They did that, and the Smith went to the top of Ben Aidan, and released Conan.

When Conan got released he was so ashamed on account of what befell him that he drew away down the Ben as fast as he could, and that he cast not a look behind him till he went out to the neck in the sea. Out of that, he would not come for Finn or for a man in the Fein. But the tide was rising at the time, and when the water began to enter his mouth he thought that it was better for him to go ashore, and return home after the rest.

On a certain evening after that, when Finn and his men were coming home from the Hunting-ben they beheld a Lad coming to meet them. He took his way where Finn was, and said to him that he was sent from the Queen of Roy (*Ruaidh*) to Finn, King of the Fein, and that he was laying on him as crosses, and as spells, and as seven fairy fetters of travelling and straying, that he would neither stop nor take rest until he would reach the Queen of Roy's (*Ruaidh*) place. Having said this he turned towards them the back of his head, and departed; and they had not a second look of him.

The Fein looked at each other, for they thought that some evil was to happen to Finn, because no man was asked to go but himself. They said to him that they were sorry because he was going alone, and because they knew not when he would come, or where they would go to seek him. But Finn said to them that they were not to be anxious about his coming to the end of a day and year.

Out of that standing he departed with his arms on him. He travelled onward far long and full long over bens, and glens, and heights, and a stop went not on his foot till he came in sight of Green Insh (*Innis Uaine*). There he beheld a man going to lift a burden of rushes on his back. When he saw the man throwing the burden over his shoulder he thought that he was the Lad of the Skin Coverings. He began to approach him under cover (make earth-hiding on him) till he got near him. Then he showed himself, and when the man who was there looked at him in the face he knew that he was the Lad of the Skin Coverings. He sprang with a hasty step where he was, seized him in his two arms, and said, 'Darling of all men in the world! is it thou?' The Big Lad answered and said, 'If I were thy darling of all the men in the world, the most insignificant man whom thou hadst in the Fein would not have been bullying me, and making me the subject of mocking witticisms.' 'Well,' said Finn, 'I was sorry enough, but I could not help it. I was afraid that the men would rise up against me, and become unruly; I therefore left Conan in his opinion. But I knew thou didst make the journey, and we will be as good friends to each other as we ever were. Wilt thou go with me once more on this little journey?' 'Well,' said the Big Lad, 'I do not know. Look down in yonder hollow under us, and thou shalt see my mother on her knees cutting rushes, and a turn of her right breast over her left shoulder. If thou shalt get a hold of the end of the breast do not let it go till thou shalt get thy first request from her.'

Finn went away a while on his hands and feet, and another while dragging himself (along) on his belly, till he got within a distance to take a spring. Then he gave a spring, and got a hold of the end of the breast. The Lady of Green Insh cried who was there? He replied, that Finn, King of the Fein, was there, asking his first boon of her. She said what boon would he ask that he would not get? He said, 'Let thy son go with me once more on this little journey.' The Lady said, 'If I had known that it was that which thou wouldst ask, thou wouldst not have got it though thou shouldst take the breast from my chest, but since I promised it thou shalt get it. But I will have one promise from thee before thou goest, and that is that thou shalt take home to me

The Lad of the Skin Coverings brings back the four-sided cup

himself and all that shall fall with him.' 'I hope that the matter will not end in that way, and that he will return home whole.' 'If he will, good shall not befall thee, Finn. However, be off on your journey.'

Then Finn and the Big Lad went away on their journey, ascending hills and descending hollows, travelling over bens and glens and knolls till the gloaming of night was coming on them. They were growing weary, and were wishing to reach some place where they would get permission to take rest. They were but a short time travelling after that, when they beheld an exceedingly fine place before them, with fine large houses built on large green fields. Finn said to the Big Lad, 'Let us take courage, for we are not far from houses.' Shortly after that they reached the place.

Finn saw a man coming to meet them, and he knew that he was the very Lad who came with the message to him.

He asked of him what need had he of him now? The Lad answered and said that there were two big houses opposite him, one with door-posts of gold and doors of gold, and the other with door-posts of silver and doors of silver, that he was to take his choice of them to stay in, and that he would see when he would enter what he had to do there. The Lad having said this turned away from them, and left them where they were standing.

Finn looked in the face of the Big Lad, and said to him, 'Which one of these houses shall we take to stay in?' The Big Lad said, 'We will have the more honourable one; we will take the one with the doors of gold.'

They took their way over to the door. The Big Lad laid hold of the bar, and opened the door. Then they went in. When they looked there was a great sight before them, but the Big Lad thought nothing of it. There were eighteen score and eight Avasks (*Amhaisg*) standing on the floor. When they got Finn and the Big Lad inside the door they sprang towards it, and shut it; and put on it eighteen score and eight bars. The Big Lad went and put on it one great bar, and so firmly did he put the bar on that every bar they put on fell off. Then the Avasks made eighteen score and eight laughs; but the Big Lad made one great guffaw of a laugh and deafened all that they made. Then the Avasks said, 'What is the cause of thy laugh, little man?' The Big Lad said, 'What is the cause of your own laughter, big men all?' They said, 'The cause of our laughter is that it is a pretty, clustering, yellow head of hair which thou hast on thee to be used as a football out on yonder strand to-morrow.' 'Well,' said the Big Lad, 'the cause of my laugh is that I will seize the man of you with the biggest head and smallest legs, and that I will brain all the rest of you with him.' He then saw a man with a big head; and having laid hold of him by the smalls of his two feet he began braining them in one end of the band and stopped not till he went out at the other end. When he was done he had only as much of the feet as he held in his fists.

He and Finn put the dead bodies out, and made three heaps of them at the door. They shut the door then, and made food ready, for there was abundance of it in the house.

After they had taken the food the Big Lad asked of Finn, 'Whether wilt thou sleep or watch the door?' Finn answered, 'Sleep thou, and I will watch the door.' And so they did. But before the Big Lad slept Finn asked of him, 'With what shall I waken thee if distress shall come upon me at the door?'

'Strike the pillar (or block) of stone, which is behind the hearth, on me in the breast-bone, or else take with thy dirk the breadth of thy thumb from the top of my head.' 'Quite right,' said Finn, 'sleep on.'

Finn was watching the door, but for a long time he was feeling nothing coming. At break of dawn he noticed the conversation of ten hundred coming to the door. He lifted the block of stone, and struck the Big Lad with it in the chest. The Big Lad sprang quickly to his feet, and asked Finn what he felt? 'The conversation of ten hundred is at the door,' said Finn. 'That is right yet,' said the Big Lad, 'let me out.'

The Big Lad went out to meet them. He began in one end of them, attacked them violently below and above them, and left none of them alive to tell the evil tale, but one man with one eye, one ear, one hand, and one foot, and he let him go. Then he and Finn collected the dead bodies, and put them in the three heaps with the rest. They afterwards went in, and waited till the next night came.

After supper the Big Lad asked of Finn, 'Whether wilt thou sleep or watch to-night?' Finn said, 'Sleep thou, and I will watch.' The Big Lad went to sleep, and Finn was watching the door. A short time before sunrise, Finn heard the conversation of two thousand coming, or the Son of the King of Light alone. He sprang up, and with his dirk took the breadth of the face of his thumb from the top of the Big Lad's head. Instantly the Big Lad sprang to his feet, and asked of Finn what did he feel? Finn answered, 'The conversation of two thousand, or the Son of the King of Light alone is at the door.' 'Oh, then, I dare say that thou must be as good as thy promise to my mother,' said the Big Lad, 'but let thou me out.' Finn opened the door, the Big Lad went out, and it was the Son of the King of Light who was before him.

Then the two champions embraced each other, and wrestled from sunrise to sunset, but the one threw not the other, and the one spake not to the other during the whole time. They let each other go, and each one of them went his own way. Early next morning, before sunrise, the Big Lad went out, and his companion met him. They wrestled from sunrise to sunset, but the one threw not the other, and the one spake not to the other. They let each other go, and each one of them went his own way. The third day the heroes met, and embraced each other. They fought all day long till twilight, and the two fell side by side cold and dead on the ground.

Finn was dreadfully sorry for the Big Lad. But he remembered his promise to the Lad's mother, and said to himself that it must be fulfilled. He took out the silk covering which was over them where they slept, wrapped it about the two bodies, and took them with him on his back. He drew away with a hard step over bens and glens and hillocks, ascending hills and descending hollows, and stop or rest he made not till he reached the house of Green Insh (*Innis Uaine*).

The mother of the Big Lad met him at the door, and said to him, 'Hast thou come?' Finn answered that he had come, but not as he would wish. She said to him, 'Didst thou do as I told thee?' Finn said, 'Yes, but I am sorry indeed that I had to do it.' She said, 'Everything is right. Come in.' Finn went in, and laid the burden on the floor. He unloosed the covering, and the two lads were locked in each other's arms as they fell.

The Big Lad and the Son of the King of Light lie dead on the ground

43

When the Lady of Green Insh saw the two lads she smiled and said, 'Finn, my Darling, well is it for me that thou didst go on this journey.' She then went over into a closet, and having lifted a flag which was on the floor, took out a little vessel of balsam which she had there. She then placed the two lads mouth to mouth, face to face, knee to knee, thumb to thumb, and rubbed the balsam to the soles of their feet, to the crowns of their heads, and to all parts of their skins which touched each other. The two lads stood up on the floor kissing one another.

'Now, Finn,' said she, 'there thou hast my two sons. This one was stolen from me in his infancy, and I was without him till now. But since thou has done as I told thee, thou art welcome to stay here as long as thou desirest.'

They were so merry in the house of Green Insh that the time went past unknown to them. On a certain night the Lady of Green Insh said to Finn, 'To-morrow there will be a day and a year since thou didst leave the Fein, and they have given up hope of thee. The man of them who is not whetting his sword is pointing his spear to-night for the purpose of going away to seek thee. Make ready to depart to-morrow, and I will let my son go with thee. For if thou shalt arrive alone they will give thee such a tumultuous welcome that they will smother and kill thee. But when you will arrive my son will enter before thee, and say to them, if they will promise him that they will rise up one after another to give thee a quiet, sensible welcome, that he will bring their earthly king home whole and sound to them.'

Finn agreed to this with all his heart, and he and the Big Lad went away on their journey homewards on the morning of the next day. They had a long distance to go, but they took not long accomplishing it.

When they reached Finn's Hall (*Talla*) the Big Lad went in first, and what his mother said proved true. Every man was getting ready his sword and spear. The Big Lad asked of them what were they doing? They told him that. Then the Big Lad said to them what his mother told him to say. They willingly consented to do that. He then called on Finn to come in. Finn came, and one rose after another as they promised. They got their earthly king back once more. The Big Lad returned home, and if he has not died since he is alive still.

NOTES

Source of tale: J. MacDougal, *Folk and Hero Tales of Argyllshire*, London: David Nutt, 1891.

This story is a typical wonder tale from the vast cycle which constellated around the hero Finn (Fionn mac Cumhaill) and his band of warriors, this time called the Fein (*fiana*). These tales are found both in Ireland and Scotland, and are direct evidence of the amount of interaction between the two branches of Gaeldom. The story was collected by Alexander Cameron from his grandfather, an old soldier who died at Ardnamurchan in Scotland around the middle of the nineteenth century. The tale was widely known, and is found in variant forms all over Scotland and Ireland. (An Irish version, 'The Bent Grey Lad', was published by D. MacInnes in his *Folk and Hero Tales of Argyllshire*, Folklore Society, 1890).

The characters within the story are typical of this type of wonder tale. Thus Finn's heroes, who here feature only as background, were all possessed of extraordinary abilities, such as being able to outrun deer, breathe for long periods under water or observe events taking place hundreds of miles away. Their meeting with the Lad of the Skin Coverings, whose abilities outstrip their own, is an occasion for high comedy.

The casual brutality of the story, as in the episode where the Lad uses one of his adversaries (the Avasks, who were a kind of Highland berserker) to beat the rest to death, is also very much a part of these tales, where everything is exaggerated to the point where it becomes comic, at the same time expressing a view of the heroic past which is peopled with fantastic characters, magic and wonder.

The Lad and his mother are part of a huge gallery of such beings, who possess otherworldly characteristics and powers, but who are encountered in a perfectly normal, everyday situations. In fact, they are otherworldly beings, and their relationship with the human world is defined in their own terms. Thus Finn's taking hold of the Lady of the Green Insh by the breast places him in the relation of foster-son to her, so that, according to Celtic law, she must grant him a boon; while the presence of the Smith of the White Glen adds a further otherworldly dimension to the tale, since smiths are traditionally beings possessed of great magic (not only in Celtic tradition) and are known to possess the keys to the lands of faery.

Several details in the story suggest an underlying cosmographic meaning. MacDougal, the editor and translator of the tale, suggests that the Lad of the Skin Coverings and his brother, the Son of the King of Light, represent Dawn and Daylight; and that the Lady of the Green Insh is their mother, the Night. Finn himself is the Sun, and his journey to the Queen of Roy (red) is the passage of the sun across the heavens. The golden and silver doors may possibly represent the sun and moon together at the same time in the western sky as dusk falls.

The four-sided cup which the Lad of the Skin Coverings is sent after is here described in terms of a wishing cup, where one has only to think of a certain drink to have it full to the brim. Elsewhere Finn's cup is known as the Cup of Victory, and is frequently the object of theft by his enemies. An even more famous 'four-sided cup' is the Cup of Truth, owned by the otherworld god Manannán, which breaks when an untruth is spoken in its presence, but is restored when a truth is uttered.

In all this is a wonderful example of the wonder tale at its best, displaying all the verbal hyperbole in which Celtic storytellers love to indulge, as well as suggesting a possible source in the remembered journeys of ancient Celtic 'shamans'.

THE BARE-STRIPPING HANGMAN

EFORE NOW THERE WAS a King in Ireland who was twice married, and who had a son by each of his wives. The name of the first wife's son was Cormac, and the name of the second wife's son was Alastir (Alexander). His father was very proud of Cormac, and was always accustomed to take him with him to the Hunting-hill.

The King had a Hen-wife, who, with a sad and sorrowful countenance, went, on a certain day, in to the place where the Queen was. The Queen asked what was troubling her? 'Great is that and not little, Queen of misery!' said the Hen-wife. 'What does that mean?' 'That the King is so fond of Cormac, the son of the first wife, that he will leave the kingdom to him, and that your son will be penniless.' 'If that is the King's pleasure, it cannot be helped.' 'Oh! nevertheless, the case need not so happen. If thou wilt give me what I shall ask of thee I will make thy son King.' 'What then is the reward which thou wilt ask for doing that?' 'That is not much: as much meal as will thicken the little black jar and as much butter as will make it thin, the full of my two (outer) ear-holes of wool, and the breadth of one of my haunches of flesh.' 'How much meal will thicken the little black jar?' 'Fourteen chalders.' 'How much butter will make it thin?' 'As much as thy seven cow-houses will produce to the end of seven years.' 'What now is the full of thy two ear-holes of wool?' 'As much as thy seven sheep-houses will produce in seven years.' 'And what now is the breadth of one of thy haunches of flesh?' 'As much as thy seven ox-houses will produce to the end of seven years.' 'That is a great deal, woman.' 'Yes, but it is little in comparison with the third of Ireland.' 'It is,' said the Queen, 'and thou shalt get it. But what plan wilt thou take for making my son King?' 'Cormac was yesterday complaining that he was not well. When the hunters will come home thou shalt say to the King that Cormac must stay at home to-morrow, and that Alastir must go in his stead to the Hunting-hill. I will make a drink for Cormac, and thou shalt give it to him after the rest have gone away, and he shall never again trouble thy son from being King.' This pleased the Queen well, and she promised that she would do as the Hen-wife told her.

The women were thinking that no one was hearing them while they were devising mischief; but all the time Alastir was eavesdropping behind the door, and was very much displeased, because he and Cormac were as fond of each other as two brothers ever were. He considered what he should do, and resolved to tell the women's intention to Cormac as soon as he would come home.

Cormac came home about evening. He was pretty tired, and was not feeling better than he was in the morning. Alastir went where he was, and told him everything that happened between his mother and the Hen-wife. Poor Cormac got afraid, and said to Alastir what should he do? Alastir replied, 'Have courage, and I will devise a scheme by which we shall get out of their way, and we shall not trouble them any more. To-morrow I shall go with my father to the Hunting-hill, but I shall not proceed far on the way when I shall say that I will return home because I do not like going to the hill. Before I arrive my mother will go in with the drink to thee. Thou shalt take hold of the cup out of her hand, but for man or thing that thou hast ever seen, taste not out of it, and put it not near thy mouth. Thou shalt lift thy hand as if thou wert going to drink; and then thou shalt spring out, holding it in thy hand. I will have the two fleetest horses in the stable waiting for thee, and we will go away.' And so they did.

Next day he went but a short distance with his father, when he refused to go farther, and returned home. He knew the time when Cormac would get the drink, and resolved that the horses should be ready as he promised. But scarcely had he them saddled, when Cormac came out in haste, having the cup with him in his hand. Alastir cried to him, 'Leap into thy saddle quickly, and stick to what thou hast.'

He did that, and they both went off as fast as the horses' feet would carry them. They kept going forward without stop or rest until their horses were giving up. Then they dismounted and sat down in the place where they were.

Alastir said to Cormac, 'Show me the cup now.' He took hold of the cup from his brother's hand, and having got a little stick, said, 'We shall now see what stuff is in the cup.' He dipped the stick in the stuff, and put a drop of it in an ear of each one of the horses. 'What art thou doing in that manner?' said Cormac. 'Wait a little, and thou shalt see,' said Alastir. In a short time the horses began to go round in a state of dizziness, and before long they fell cold and dead on the earth. 'Think you, Cormac, what would have happened to you if you had drunk the potion?' 'What, but that I should have been dead now,' said Cormac.

While they were conversing four ravens came, and settled on the carcasses of the horses. They began to peck the eyes out of the horses, and when they ate the eyes they flew away in the air. But they went only a short distance, when they uttered piercing screams and fell dead on the earth. 'What now is thy opinion of the drink, Cormac?' 'What, but if I had drunk of it that I would not have been here at present,' said Cormac.

Alastir rose up, and having taken the four ravens with him in a napkin, he and his brother went away again on their journey. Alastir was keeping a step in advance, because he had virtues about him by which he knew what was to meet them. They kept going forward till they came to a small town.

Alastir went in to a Cooking-house in the town, and told the Cook to dress the ravens as well as he ever dressed birds, but not to put finger or hand near his mouth till he had them dressed, and till he had washed his hands well, and very well. 'What does that mean?' said the Cook. 'I never before dressed food which I might not taste.' 'Taste not and eat not a bit of these, otherwise thou shalt not get them at all.' The Cook promised to do as he was told.

After the Cook had dressed the ravens, and received payment for his labour, Alastir tied them in his napkin, and he and Cormac departed again on their journey. On the way, Alastir said, 'There is a large wood before us in which are staying four-and-twenty robbers who never allowed a man to pass them without killing him, and who will not let us pass if they can prevent us.' 'What shall we do?' said Cormac. 'Leave that to me,' replied Alastir.

When they were going through the wood they noticed a pretty little plain above the road on which they were walking, and the robbers lying on their backs basking themselves in the sun at the upper end of the plain. They kept going forward, but when they were just passing beneath the place in which the robbers were, two of them cried, 'Who are the two impertinent fellows who would dare pass by on this way without asking us?' They all took their way down where the two strangers were, and said to them that they were going to strike their heads off them. 'Oh, then,' said Alastir, 'there is no help for it. We are tired and hungry, and if you would allow us to eat a bite of food before you would put us to death, we would be obliged to you.' 'If you have food, take it quickly,' said the robbers. 'We have food,' said Alastir, 'and you too will get some of it if you like.'

Then he opened the napkin, and divided the ravens into twenty-six pieces, a piece for every man in the company. 'Now,' said he, 'you shall wait until you are all served, and you shall begin to eat together, for if some of you eat their own share first they will fight the rest for their share, and you will wound and kill each other.' Hereupon the robbers made a loud mocking laugh, but they said that they would do as they were told. When they were all served, Alastir lifted up his hand, and cried, 'Eat now.' They did so, and praised the food. But it was not long till one after another of them began to sit, and every one that sat fell asleep, and out of that sleep he was waking no more. At last they were all in the sleep of death.

'Now,' said Alastir, 'that is over, and the way is clear before us as far as the Castle of the King of Riddles. Thou shalt travel as the King of Ireland, and I will travel as thy Servant. If thou art told to do anything thou shalt say that it is the Servant who does that in the country out of which thou hast come. When thou shalt reach the Castle of the King of Riddles thou must put a Riddle or solve a Riddle, and if thou do not that thy head shall be placed on a stake in the wall, which is before the door. Many of our sort reached the Castle before us, and as they could not put a riddle or solve a riddle, their heads were placed on the stakes of the wall. There is one stake still empty, and thy head shall be placed on it if neither thou, nor I for thee, will put or solve a riddle to-night.'

They reached the Castle. The King of Riddles gave them a great welcome, for he thought that it was to ask his daughter they came, like those who preceded them. They were but a short time in when food was placed before them, but ere they began to take it the King of Riddles said, 'King of Ireland, put a riddle or solve a riddle.' The King of Ireland answered, and said, 'It is the Servant who does that in the country from which I came.' 'Get thy Servant down, then,' said the King of Riddles. The Servant came. 'Servant of the King of Ireland, put a riddle or solve a riddle,' said the Riddle King. The Servant answered, 'One killed two, two killed four, four killed twenty-four, and two escaped.' The King of Riddles thought, but he could not solve the riddle. At last he said to the Servant, 'Go away just now, and thou shalt get the solution of the riddle to-morrow.' After the dinner was over they spent the rest of the night telling interesting tales until bedtime came.

Then the King of Riddles sent word for his daughter and her twelve maidens in attendance. He said to the maidens that whoever of them would find the solution of the riddle from the beginning from the Servant of the King of Ireland would get his son in marriage and half the kingdom. They said that they would try. He then turned to his daughter, and promised her her choice of a sweetheart and half the kingdom, if she could find the solution of the riddle from the beginning.

The maidens were awhile considering in what manner they could find out the solution of the riddle. At last they agreed to put the Servant in the very coldest and worst room which was in the Castle, where there were holes on the walls, and the windows were broken, and wind and rain (were) coming in at them; that they would put his Master in the best room which was in the house; and that they would say to the Servant that he would get as good a bed and room as his Master had if he would tell the solution of the riddle from the beginning. And they did so.

The Servant was not very long in bed when he felt the door opening. He turned on his pillow, and beheld a young, comely maiden standing on the floor. He understood very well what was on her mind. The maiden said, 'Is it sleep to thee, Servant of the King of Ireland?' 'It is not sleep to me; for it is no sleeping quarters I have got, wind and cold under me, and wind and rain over me. Far will I carry the name of this house when I shall go away.' 'Thou shalt get as good a bed as thy Master has, if thou tell me the solution of the riddle from the beginning.' But he did not tell her that, and he allowed her to go back to the rest without it. They then came one after another, but it befell them as it befell her.

As soon as the last of them went out, the Servant went to his Master's room, and the Master went to the Servant's room. He was but a short time there when the King's daughter went in. She said, as the maidens before her said: 'Is it sleep to thee, Servant of the King of Ireland?' 'It is not sleep to me; for it is no sleeping quarters I have got, with wind and cold under me, and wind and rain above me. Far will I carry the name of this house when I shall go away.' 'Well, thou shalt get as good a bed as thy Master has if thou wilt tell me the solution of the riddle from the beginning.' But he did not tell her that, and she went away.

Next morning the King of Riddles asked the maidens if they had got the solution of the riddle? They said that they had not. He then asked of his daughter if she got it, and she said that she had not.

When they sat down at their breakfast the King of Riddles said: 'King of Ireland, put a riddle or solve a riddle.' 'As I told thee last night, it is my Servant who is accustomed to put a riddle or answer a riddle for me.' 'Get thy servant down, then.' The Servant came. 'Servant of the King of Ireland, put a riddle or solve a riddle,' said the King of Riddles. 'I did not get the solution of the first riddle yet,' said the Servant. 'Thou insolent fellow, is it keeping up chat with me thou art? Put a riddle or solve a riddle, otherwise thy head shall be struck off thee at breakfast time, and placed on a pale in the wall.' 'I will put a riddle, then,' said the Servant. 'Let me hear it,' said the King of Riddles.

[The Servant put a riddle which he composed on the things which befell himself and his Master on the night before. The King of Riddles solved that riddle, but the first one beat him. To shorten this part of the tale, the King of Riddles gave his daughter to the King of Ireland.]

Alastir remained many days with them, passing the time hunting and fishing. On a certain day, while he was fishing on a rock near the sea, and thinking what he should do – go away or stay with Cormac – he heard a loud splash in the sea at the foot of the rock. Before he got time to look one way or another, a large Dog-Otter sprang out of the water, seized him by the two ankles, and went out with him on the sea. He saw not again a blink of earth or of sky until he was left above the reach of the tide in the very prettiest bay he ever saw, with smooth, white sand from the margin of the wave to the green grass. He was now in Lochlan.

In a short time the Dog-Otter returned, having a fresh-water salmon with him in his mouth. He left the salmon at Alastir's feet, and said to him: 'When thou art going on any long journey, or when any hardship is coming upon thee, take a bite of this fish beforehand. Here thou shalt make a bothy, and shalt stay in it till thou shalt see more than me, and till thou shalt get more than my advice.'

He put up the bothy that same night. He then boiled a piece of the salmon, and after eating it he felt stronger than he ever was.

On the next morning he rose up, and went out before breakfast to the end of his bothy. He stood, and saw the Great White-buttocked Deer coming straight towards the place in which he was standing, and the White Red-eared Hound after him, chasing him keenly. When the Deer was nearing him, the Hound had hold after hold of the Deer; and in going past, the Hound gave forth a bark, and sprang at the neck of the Deer, and left him dead at Alastir's feet.

'Now,' said the Hound to Alastir, 'thou wert faithful to thy brother, and thou shalt receive thy reward. When thou art going on any long journey, or when any hardship is coming upon thee, thou shalt eat beforehand a bite of the fresh-water salmon, and a bite of this deer, and from anything which thou shalt (afterwards) see or hear no further injury shall befall thee. And before that will fail thee thou shalt be told what thou art to do.' Then the White Red-eared Hound wished him good success, and departed.

Alastir took the deer in to his bothy, and left it beside the salmon. He made ready his breakfast, and ate a piece of the salmon and a piece of the deer. He then went out, and having given a look away from him, he saw coming a large-sized man having the appearance of a King, and twelve Champions with him. They came straight to the place in which he was.

The King said to him: 'How hadst thou the courage or the boldness of coming to kill my large White-buttocked deer?' 'Thy deer came of its own accord my way, I had need of food, and I killed thy deer,' said Alastir. 'Well,' said the King, 'since thou didst kill my deer, thou must fight with my Champions until thou shalt fall or until they shall.' 'I am alone, King,' said Alastir, 'you are many, along with that I am without a sword.' 'Thou shalt not be without a sword,' said the King; 'thou shalt get my sword, and if thou take thy life out of peril with it, it shall be thine own.' 'I will try, at any rate,' said Alastir. 'But I ask of thee as a favour that thou wilt let me eat a bite of food before I shall begin.' 'Thou shalt get that,' said the King, while he was reaching him his sword.

He went into his bothy, and ate a bite of the fish and a bite of the deer. When he was done he thrust the King's sword into the carcass of the deer, and it went as easily through it as though it were water. 'The success of this thrust be with each stroke,' said Alastir. He felt that he himself was in great courage and in full strength, and turned out to the fight.

The King said that he would get the advantage of the Fein – man after man. One of the Champions was sent out opposite him. But they were not long at swordplay when the Champion of the King fell, heavily wounded, on the ground. Alastir shouted to the next man to come on. He came; but in a short time he fell wounded on the ground like the first man. A like thing befell the third man.

When the King saw his three Champions dropping blood and dying, he said to the Stranger, 'Whatever place is thy native country, thou art a Champion at any rate.' Alastir then called to the rest to come on quickly if he had to go through them all. But the King put a stop to the contest. He turned to Alastir, and said to him, 'Thou hast won thy sword with victory, and thou shalt get it. Go with me and I will make thee better off than thou art here.' Then Alastir asked of him as a kindness to leave the bothy standing as it was, since he did not know but that he must return to it yet. He got his request, and went away with the King.

On the way, the King was under a heavy stupor for the loss of his three Champions. But at last he said to himself, that the one he had found was as good as the three he had lost. They kept going forward through wood, over heath, and over moss, until they arrived at a fine large Castle the like of which Alastir never saw before. The King told him to go in along with him. The Champions took their own way, and Alastir entered with the King.

Food and drink were put before Alastir, and the King told him to eat and drink. He replied that he would not eat a bite of his food, and that he would not drink a drop of his drink until he would tell him the reason why he brought him yonder. The King understood that he had a Champion, and said that he would tell him that.

'I had four daughters. Three of them were taken from me by the Big Giant who is staying in the Black Corrie of *Ben Breck* (or the Speckled Mountain). He came at first at the time of the going down of the Sun, and took away the first of them in my own presence and in the presence of my Champions, and I saw her no more. I sent my Champions after him, and they followed him to his Castle. But when they reached it, as a sudden blast of east wind would strip bracken in winter, he swept the heads off them. Only one escaped to tell me the tale of distress. At the end of seven years he came again, and as it happened at first it happened that time. At the end of another seven years he came, and took the third one with him. My Champions resolved that they would have revenge on him, and that they would bring my daughter home to me. They went away under full armour to watch the Castle of the Black Corrie of the *Ben Breck*. After they had watched it during three rounds of the Sun they got no opportunity of the Giant. At last they were growing heavy for want of sleep and weak for want of food, and therefore resolved that they would go to the Castle and see what was within. They found the way to the Den of the Giant, and saw that he was in a heavy sleep. They said to each other that that was the time for them to have revenge for the King's daughter, and to take the head off the Giant. They sprang towards him, and struck off his head with their swords. No sooner had they done that than a large golden eagle sprang down, and struck the first Champion on the face, and knocked him down. The golden eagle did the same thing on the next man. When the rest saw that, they fled. But scarcely had they got outside through the gate of the Castle than they saw the Giant coming after them, and his head on him as it was before. When they saw him, they stretched away, and those of them who escaped made no stay until they arrived here. But those of them that fell into his hands, he bared to the skin, and hanged up on hooks against the turrets of the Castle. Now, the fourth one of my daughters is about a day and year of the age of the rest when they were stolen from me. But to any one who will bring home to me the Black Brood-mare which is on the Ben, and on which a halter never went, belong my daughter and as far as the half of my kingdom.'

'Good is thine offer, King,' said Alastir. 'He is a sorry fellow that would not make his utmost endeavour to earn it.' 'I knew that thou wert a Champion,' said the King, 'and if thou wilt do it thou shalt get thy promised reward, and much more. On the morning of next day thou shalt reach my Stable, and wilt get thy choice of a bridle.'

On the next morning, Alastir reached the Stable, and found many men and Champions before him who were going to try and catch the Black Brood-mare, as he himself was, for the sake of getting the King's daughter as a reward. The Stable was opened, and each one selected a bridle for himself.

They then went away to the mountain to catch the Black Brood-mare. They were travelling through glens, over bens, and through hollows until they got a sight of her. Alastir tried to get before her, but as soon as she saw him she ascended the face of the Ben, sending water out of the stones, and fire out of the streams, fleeing from him. They followed after her until the darkening of night came on them, and then they turned home without her.

When they reached the Castle they told the King how it befell them. He said to them that another day was coming, and that another sun was to go round, and that to the man who would bring home to him the Black Brood-mare at the end of a tether would belong his daughter, and as far as the half of his kingdom. When they heard this, every man and every Champion made ready to go to the Ben before sunrise on the following day.

When the next morning came each one of them turned away in the full belief that it was with himself the victory would be when returning. They reached the Ben. Some of them were going on their bellies through hollows, some creeping along the beds of streams, others were peeping over ridges, and taking advantage of every gap to see if they could get a sight of the Black Brood-mare. At last they saw her on the sunny side of the Glen-of-the-Sun (*Gleann-na-gréine*). Each man made ready as well as he could, to catch her. But no better befell them that day than on the day before, for she was sending water out of the stones and fire out of the streams fleeing before them. At the going down of the sun, they were further from her than they were in the morning. Then they returned home weariedly, sadly, hungrily.

When they reached the Castle the King sent out his Gillie-in-attendance, to ask with whom the victory was. The Gillie brought word back to him that they had seen her, but that they got not within catching distance of her, or even within a stone-cast of her. Then the King sent word to them that the morrow was the third day of their trial, and that he would be as good as his promise to any one of them who would bring home to him at end of rein, the Black Brood-mare. When they heard this, each running Champion and each fighting Champion was under heavy anxiety, for they could not do more than they had already done. But they resolved that they would once more try to catch her.

After the supper was over, Alastir, as he was going through the Castle, met the Sorceress (*Iorasglach-ùrlair*) of the King. 'Son of the King of Ireland,' said she, 'thou art wearied, sad, and under a heavy stupor.' Alastir answered that he was. 'Thou didst not take the advice of thy friends. To-night thou shalt go back to thine own bothy, and thou shalt take a bite of the fish and a bite of the deer. But before thou go away thou shalt turn back where the King is, and thou shalt say to him that to-morrow is the last day which you have for catching the Black Brood-mare, and that thou shalt not go after her unless thou shalt get thy choice of a bridle before thou wilt depart. He will then go with thee, and when you reach the Stable thou wilt see a door on thy right hand, and thou shalt tell him to open the door in order that thou shalt take thy choice of a bridle out of that place. He will open the door for thee, and thou shalt see hanging from the wall an old bridle which was not in the head of horse or mare for twenty-seven years, and thou shalt take it with thee. When thou wilt reach the mountain thou shalt give the rest the slip (or turn about a bush), and go before the Black Brood-mare. As soon as thou wilt come in sight of her thou shalt shake the bridle towards her; and she will come with a neigh and put her head in the bridle. Thou shalt then leap on her back, and ride her home to the King.'

Alastir went away from the Sorceress as well pleased as he was since the day the Dog Otter left him ashore in the land of Lochlan.

On the third day the Champions got ready, and went away to the Mountain to catch the Black Brood-mare. When they reached they took advantage of every cover till they thought that they were as near her as they could get. But Alastir gave them the slip, and left them. He did not stop until he got ahead of the Black Brood-mare. She was coming, bearing a terrible appearance, driving water out of the stones and fire out of the streams with the speed of her running. Then Alastir lifted up the bridle and shook it towards her. As soon as the Brood-mare heard the jingling of the bridle she stood, and made a hard neigh, which Mac-talla of the rocks (echo) answered four miles round. She laid down her two ears along the back of her head, she came at the gallop, and thrust her head into the bridle. Then Alastir leaped on her back, and rode her home to the King. When the other Champions saw the stranger riding away with the Black Brood-mare, all their *sud* and their *sad* (*cheerfulness* and *hope*) forsook them, and they returned home.

On this night the King came out to meet them. When he saw that it was the Stranger who had the victory he took his way over where he was, went on his two knees to do him honour, and said, 'I thought that thou wert a Champion indeed, and thou hast proved it at last. Now, ask any cattle or person, jewel or value, which is in my kingdom, and thou shalt get it along with the reward which I promised for this deed.'

The King made a great feast on that night. But before the feast was over word came to the King from the Big Giant of the Black Castle in the Ben Breck (Speckled Mountain) that he would come for the fourth daughter at the end of a day and year from that night. This message put the King in ill humour and in anxiety. He turned to the Champions, and said to them that he was sorry because he could not fulfil what he had promised unless they themselves would find out the place in which the soul of the Bare-Stripping Hangman was hid, and kill him. 'My Champions struck his head off already, but he put it on him again, and he was as alive as he ever was. He defied them, and said that in spite of them he would take all my daughters with him. Now, he is coming at the end of a day and year from this night, and to the man of you who will put him out of life shall belong my daughter and all my kingdom.'

All the Champions were under anxiety because they did not know how they could kill the Bare-Stripping Hangman. But when they separated, the Sorceress (*Iorasglach-ùrlair*) met Alastir, and said to him, 'Son of the King of Ireland, I hope that thou hast received thy reward to-night.' He told her everything that happened, and how the condition on which the King's daughter would be found was harder now than it was before. She was lying on the floor, and she rose up quickly in a sitting posture. She took hold of her hair in her hand, and made a loud laugh, and said, 'Son of the King of Ireland, success was always with thee and shall be with thee still if thou wilt take my advice.' 'If I can I will do anything that thou wilt ask of me, for I have found thee true thus far, and I have full confidence in thee now,' said Alastir. 'Well, said the Sorceress (*Iorasglach*), 'from the spot on which thou art standing thou shalt go away under full armour, and remember that thou shalt not part with the King's sword until thou get a better. Thou shalt go first to thy bothy and eat a bite of the deer and a bite of the fish. Thou shalt then come out to the door of thy bothy, and thou shalt set thy face towards the Rocky Path of the Yellow Mountain (Ben Buie), and thou shalt not look behind thee, and thou shalt not turn a step back for any difficulty or hardship which may meet thee until thou reach the Great Castle which is at the end of the Mountain Path. There thou shalt see a woman looking out at the high window of the Castle.' The Sorceress now took a writing out of her bosom, and said, 'When thou shalt see the woman thou shalt know her, and say to her that thou hast a writing for her. She will then come and open the door to thee, and tell thee what thou hast to do after that. Thou mayest now set off on thy journey. The blessing of the King is in thy company, the blessing of his daughter is with thee, and thou hast my blessing. Now, whatsoever thing the woman will ask thee to say or do, be sure that thou fulfil it.'

Alastir took courage, and went away straight to his bothy, and on the next morning, before sunrise, he departed on his journey through the Rocky Mountain Path of Ben Buie (Yellow Mountain). He kept going forward far long and full long until the Path grew so full of fissures and sharp-pointed rocks that he was under the necessity of hanging on his belly to go over them. At last even the jagged rocks failed, and there was nothing before him but a great chasm between lofty precipices which were as deep under him as they were high over his head. He gave a look on each side of him, and saw the Path running in to the side of one of the precipices in so narrow a ledge that there was not the breadth of a footsole in it. Then he got afraid that he was astray, and he was going to return. But a large buzzard came flying across over his head, and cried to him, 'Son of the King of Ireland, remember the advice of the Sorceress (*Iorasglach-ùrlair*).' At once he remembered his promise to the Sorceress, and said to himself that he would go forward as long as the breath would be in him. He was then hanging from cliff to cliff and leaping from ledge to ledge, until the path began to grow better. At last he got on the smooth way. He then went as fast as he could go over the rocks, for the evening was coming and a sight of the Castle was not to be seen. The ascent was so steep that he could make no great speed. But he won the top at last. He said to himself that he would not take long now, and he ran as fast as he could down the hill-side. He was thinking that when he got to the foot of the brae every hardship would be over, but when he reached it they were, to all appearance, only beginning. Instead of the Castle, he saw a large Red Lake before him. He gave a look on each side of him to see if he could behold a way in which he could get over the Lake, but he saw only rocky precipices, and it was enough for a bird on the wing to go over them. He was in a dilemma (house of conference) whether he should return or go forward, when he heard the buzzard crying over his head, 'Son of the King of Ireland, take neither fright nor apprehension in presence of any difficulty or hardship which will meet thee.' When he heard this he took courage, and kept going forward on the Path into the Lake. At first he wondered that he was not sinking in the Lake, but in a short time he saw that the road on which he was walking was scarcely covered with water. He kept straight on the path until he arrived at the other side of the Lake. As soon as he got his feet on dry land he lifted up his head, and saw a beautiful green field before him, and a large Castle at the end of the field. Twilight had come, and therefore he hastened forward to the Castle.

When he reached the Castle, he saw a woman looking out at one of the windows. He cried that he had a letter for her. She descended quickly, and opened the door to him. He handed her the letter. She caught it out of his hand, and told him to wait until she would see what was in it. As soon as she read the letter she bounded towards him and seized his hand in both her hands, and kissed it. She took him in, and asked of him what way did he come? He said that he came through the Rocky Path of Ben Buie (Yellow Mountain). 'If so,' said she, 'thou hast need of meat and of drink.' She set meat and drink before him, and told him to be quick, because he had a great deal to do.

As soon as he was done she took him in to the armoury, and told him to try whether he could lift the sword which was over against the wall. He tried that, but he could not put wind between it and the earth. She opened a press which was on a side of the house, and took out of it a little bottle of balsam. She drew a cup of gold, and put a little drop out of the little bottle into it, and said to him, 'Drink of it.' He did that. He again seized the sword, and he could lift it with both hands. She gave him another little drop, and then he could lift the sword with one hand. She gave him the third drop, and no sooner did he drink it than he felt stronger than he ever was. He seized the sword, and he could work with it as lightly and airily as he could work with the King's sword.

'Now,' she said to him, 'there is a big Giant having two heads on him, staying in this Castle, and he is coming home in a short time. Come with me, and I will set thee standing on the *ùdabac* (or porch), where thou shalt get an opportunity of striking him when he stoops to come in under the lintel. Be sure that thou strike him well, and send the two heads off him: for if thou send but one head off him, he will take hold of that one, and kill thee with it, as he did many others before thee.'

He went away without delay, and stood on the porch (*ùdabac*) as she told him. He was not long there when he saw the Giant coming with a fairy motion.

When he reached the door he bent his heads, and gave a grunt. Alastir took the advantage of him, and struck him with all his might. With the stroke he threw one of the heads off him, and half of the other head. Then the Giant gave dreadful leaps and screams, but before he found time to turn round, Alastir struck the other half of the second head off him, and he fell a dead carcass on the earth.

The woman came out, and said to him, 'Well done, Son of the King of Ireland. Success is with thee, for my father's blessing is with thee.' He then asked of her who she was. She replied that she was the oldest daughter the King of Ben Buie had. 'Thou art going away,' she said, 'to seek the soul of the Bare-Stripping Hangman, in order that thou mayest save my youngest sister from him. Come in and I will let thee away on thy journey before a sun will rise tomorrow.'

He went in, she washed his feet, and he went to bed.

Before the red-cock (heath-cock) crowed, and before a sun rose on dwelling or on mountain, she was on foot, and had breakfast waiting him. After he had risen and got his breakfast, she took a letter out of her bosom, and handed it to him, saying, 'Thou shalt keep this carefully until thou reach the Great Castle of the eight turrets, and thou shalt give it to the woman whom thou shalt see looking out at one of the roof windows of the Castle.' She gave a pull on her own little bottle of balsam, and on her cup of gold, and gave him a drink. She then put him on the head of the way, she wished a blessing to accompany him, and said that she would remain yonder until he would return. He left the King's sword in the Castle, and went away with the sword of the Giant. The path on which he was walking was smoother than the one on which he travelled the day before. He got on well, but the distance was so long that the night began to come upon him before he came in sight of the Castle. About the greying of the evening he saw the turrets of the Castle far from him. He took courage and hardened his step, and though it was a long distance from him, he took not long to reach it.

There were such high walls about the Castle that he was not seeing by what way he could get in. But he gave his head a lift, and saw a woman looking out at a window, and cried that he had a letter for her. She came down and opened a large iron door which was on the wall. After she had read the letter, she took hold of him by the hand and brought him in.

She then looked at the sword which he had, and asked him where did he find it? He told her that he got it from the woman who was in the Castle in which he was the night before. There was another large sword standing beside the wall, and she told him to try if he could lift it. With difficulty he put wind between it and the earth. 'None that came before thee did even that much,' said the woman. She gave him a drink out of her little bottle of balsam in a cup of gold, and then he could play the sword with both hands. She gave him the next drink, and he could play the Giant's sword as nimbly as he could play the sword of the King.

'Now,' said she, 'thou hast no time to lose. The Great Giant of the three heads, three humps, and three knobs is staying here, and he will come home in a moment. Come with me and I will put thee in a place where thou shalt get an opportunity of striking him.' He went with her, and she set him standing on a bank which was on the opening side of the great iron door on the wall. Then she said, 'When the Giant stoops to come under the lintel, be sure to strike him before he can get his heads lifted, and to send the three off him with the first stroke, for if he get time to rise he will take thee assunder in bits, as he did those that came before thee.'

The Giant came, and stooped beneath the lintel, but before he got through the door, Alastir struck him with all his might, and sent two of his heads off and half the third. The Giant gave a leap, and one of the humps struck the lintel and put it out (of its place). Then he fell, and before he got time to rise and give the next leap, Alastir struck him the second time, and sent the other half of the third head off him. With a great, melancholy groan the Giant fell a dead carcass on the ground.

The woman came out then and said, 'Well done, Son of the King of Ireland. The blessing of my father and of my sister is with thee, and thou shalt have my blessing now.' Then he asked of her who she was? She answered that she was the second daughter of the King of Ben Buie. 'Thou art going away to seek the soul of the Bare-Stripping Hangman, in order that thou mayest save my youngest sister from him, and if thou come alive out of the next Castle which thou shalt reach, thou needst not be afraid of either thing or person that may meet thee any more, for everything shall succeed with thee to the end of thy journey. But thou hast no time to lose.' She took him in, served him with meat and drink, and put him to bed.

After he had got his breakfast next morning she gave him a drink out of her little bottle of balsam in a cup of gold. She then put her hand in her bosom, and took out of it a letter, and said to him, 'Thou shalt give this to the woman whom thou shalt see standing in the door of the Castle to which thou shalt come.'

He now went away, having with him the great sword with which he struck the heads off the Giant. He got on smoothly until he arrived at the next Castle, a great shapeless mass of a place without window or turret on it. He saw the woman standing in the door, and cried to her that he had a letter for her. She seized the letter, and after she had read it, she laid hold of him by the hand, and took him in.

She washed his hands and feet with a mixture of water and milk. She then looked at his sword, and said to him, where did he find yon blade? He replied that he found it in the Castle in which he was last night. 'Since thou hast got thus far, thy sword will serve thee, and thou shalt not part with it as long as the breath is in thee till thou reach the end of thy journey. The Great Fiery Dragon of the Seven Serpent Heads and of the Venomous Sting is staying in this Castle. *She* will come at sunrise to-morrow, and thou must meet her outside, for if she get inside, neither thou nor I will be seen alive any more.' She then sent him to sleep in a warm, comfortable bed.

She herself remained awake, and when the time for him to rise came, she wakened him. She gave him his breakfast, and after his breakfast a drink out of her little bottle of balsam in her cup of gold. He then grasped his sword, and turned out.

Scarcely had he got over the threshold of the door when he felt the Dragon coming. He made ready for her, and as soon as she came a hard contest began between them. He was defending himself from the heads, while she was wounding him with a large sting which she had in the end of her tail. They carried on the fight to the time of the going down of the sun. Then she said to him, 'Thy bed is thine to-night yet, but meet me before sunrise to-morrow.' The Dragon went her own way, and he returned in to the Castle.

The woman washed his sores, put balsam to every wound which was on his body, and sent him to bed.

When he awoke next morning he felt that he was as whole and sound as he ever was. After he had risen, and had got his breakfast and a drink of the balsam, he took with him his sword and went to meet the Dragon. They fought from morning to evening, he defending himself from the heads, and she wounding him with the sting of her tail. At going down of sun they stopped. She went her own way, and he returned to the Castle.

The woman served him this night as she did on the night before. When he awoke on the third morning he was as whole of his sores as he ever was. After he had got his breakfast and a drink of the balsam, he grasped his sword, and went to meet the Dragon.

On this morning he heard her coming with horrible screaming. But he thought that since he stood the two days before, he would try her this day yet. The Monster came, and they went at each other. She was shooting stings out of each mouth at him, and he was defending himself from her with his sword.

About the greying of the evening he was growing weak, but if he was, he understood that she also was losing her strength. This gave him courage, and he closed boldly with her. At the going down of the sun she gave up, and stretched herself on the ground.

'Now,' said she, 'thou hast vanquished me, but the advantage was with thee. At night thou wert getting thy sores washed and healed, and thou wert warm and comfortable at the fireside in my Castle. But if I had got half an hour's time of the warmth of the fire, thou hadst returned no more than those who came before thee.' Alastir now drew his sword, and with seven strokes sent the seven heads off the Dragon. But at the seventh stroke she gave her tail a lift, and struck him in the side. He fell as if he were dead, and he neither saw nor felt anything further until he awoke about midnight.

The woman was then washing and healing his sores. When she was done of that she put him to bed. On the next morning she went where he was, and asked of him how he felt. He answered that he felt strong (and) sound. 'That is good,' said she; 'the greater part of thy trials are now past.'

When he arose and got his breakfast, she said to him, 'Thou hast killed the Great Giant of the Two Heads in the Castle at the end of the Rocky Path of Ben Buie, thou hast killed the Great Giant of the Three Heads, Three Humps, and Three Knobs in the Great Castle of the Seven Turrets, and thou hast killed the Fiery Dragon of the Seven Serpent Heads and of the Venomous Sting in this Gloomy Castle. Only one of those who came before thee on the journey on which thou art going got thus far. He came over the Rocky Path of the Yellow Mountain (Ben Buie), and over the Path of the Red Lake almost drowned. He got through broken ground past the first two Castles, but he could not go past this Castle without going through it. The Fiery Dragon met him at the door, and killed him. But thou hast come on the right path, and success was with thee thus far. I will not keep thee longer, for thou hast many things yet to do. Thou hast got but a day and year for killing the Bare-Stripping Hangman, and if thou hast not thy work finished before then, he will take away with him my fourth sister as he took us. I will go with thee, and put thee on the head of the way. Thou shalt neither stop nor rest until thou reach the Great Barn of the Seven Stoops (*Crùb*), of the Seven Bends (*Lùb*), and of the Seven Couples. Thou shalt see under the Barn on the Yellow Knoll of the Sun, a really old Man cutting divot with a turf-spade. Thou shalt tell him the business on which thou art, and he will tell thee what thou must say and do after that. Thou shalt take advice from every one that will give it to thee faithfully. The blessing of the King is with thee, the blessing of the Sorceress is with thee, the blessing of Sunbeam, my sister, is with thee, the blessing of Light-of-Shade is with thee, and thou hast also my blessing. Be going on thy journey, and everything will be right when thou returnest.'

Then he went away. He was travelling onwards far long and full long. When he began to grow wearied he remembered his achievements and his victory. This lightened his mind, and he got on his way well. In the very midst of his thoughts he came in at the head of the very prettiest Glen he ever beheld. He said to himself, 'It must be that I am not now far from the Great Barn of the Seven Couples.' Before he let the word out of his mouth, he beheld the Barn a little before him, and the very prettiest Knoll that he ever

saw, shining like gold in the sun, in the bottom of the Glen, and the very Man of the oldest appearance whom he ever beheld, cutting divot with a turf-spade on one side of the Knoll.

He took his way where the Man was, and gave him the salutation of the day. The man answered him briskly and vigorously, much younger in his talk than he was in his appearance, and asked him where was he from? 'I came from the Castle of the King of Lochlan, through the Rocky Path of the Ben Buie, through the Castle at the end of the Path where I killed the Great Giant of the Two Heads, through the Great Castle of the Eight Turrets where I killed the Great Giant of the Three Heads, Three Humps, and Three Knobs, through the Gloomy Castle of the Fiery Dragon of the Seven Serpent Heads and of the Venomous Sting, and from that as far as this, to see if thou wouldst tell me where I can find the Soul of the Bare-Stripping Hangman?' The Old Man gave him a look in the face, and said, 'Let me see thy sword, Hero.' Alastir drew his sword out of the scabbard, and handed it to him. The Old Man took hold of the sword between his two fingers, and put it between him and the light. He then handed it back and said, 'Let me see thee flourishing thy sword, Hero.' Alastir seized the sword, and gave a back sweep and a front sweep with it as lightly as though it were the deer-knife that would be in his fist. The Old Man bounded towards him and took him by the hand and said, 'Hero, thou hast come the way thou hast mentioned. I cannot tell thee where the Soul of the Bare-Stripping Hangman is now, for it fled out of the place where it was four days ago. But it may be that my father will tell thee.' 'Oh, is thy father alive, or can I see him?' 'He is alive. Yonder he is carrying the divot on his back. Go where he is and ask him.'

Alastir reached the Man carrying the divot, and asked of him if he knew where the Soul of the Bare-Stripping Hangman was hidden. The Old Man answered, 'No, it fled out of the place where it was three days ago. But it may be that my father will tell thee.' 'Oh, is thy father alive, or may I see him?' 'Oh, he is alive, and thou canst also see him. Yonder he is, over there casting the divot.' Alastir reached the man who was casting the divot, and said to him, could he tell where the Soul of the Bare-Stripping Hangman was hidden? He answered, 'I cannot, for it fled out of the place where it was two days since. But it may be that my father will tell thee.' 'Oov, Oov, sir, can I see thy father, or is he able to speak to me, for he must be very old?' 'Oh, thou canst see him, and he can speak to thee. Yonder he is laying the divot.' Alastir reached the man who was laying the divot, and asked of him, could he tell where the Soul of the Bare-Stripping Hangman was hidden? He answered, 'I cannot, for it fled out of the place where it was yesterday. But reach my father, and he will tell thee where thou canst find it.' 'What sort of man is thy father? Can I see him, or can he speak to me?' 'Thou shalt see him, and he will speak to thee, and tell thee what thou hast to do after this.' 'But where shall I see him?' 'He is in a little bunch (*sopan*) of moss behind the crooked stick (*maide-cròm*). But I myself must go with thee. When thou art speaking to him thou shalt take extreme care that thou go not within hands' length of him, for if he get a hold of a bit of thy body, he will bruise thee like a grain of barley under a quern-stone. Before you part he will ask a hold of thy hand, and if thou give it to him he will bruise it until it shall be as small as the pin of a

Alastir fights the Great Fiery Dragon of the Seven Serpent Heads

61

black pudding. But here is a wedge of oak,' handing him a stout piece off the head of a caber, 'and thou shalt give it to him when he asks thy hand.'

They went in to the house where the Old Man was. The divot-layer took down a large armful of moss from behind the crooked stick (*maide-cròm*), and laid it on the hearth-stone. 'The little bunch (*sopan*) is great, sir,' said the Son of the King of Ireland. 'Greater than that is my father within it,' said the divot-layer. He took his father out of the little bunch (bunchie), and placed him on the flag-stone. 'What is thy need of me now, son,' said the father. 'It is a long time since thou didst seek me.' The son answered, 'There is a Young Champion here who is seeking to know where the Soul of the Bare-Stripping Hangman is hidden.' 'Son of King Cormac in Ireland, which way hast thou come thus far?' inquired the Man of the Little-bunch of Moss. Alastir told him every step he took from the day he left his father's house, and everything that befell him up to that day. 'Truthfully thou hast told me everything, Son of the King of Ireland. Thy father has burnt the Hen-wife, and thy mother is under sorrow for thee. Her prayer and her blessing follow thee, the blessing of the Young King of Riddles follows thee, the blessing of the Young Queen of Riddles follows thee, the blessing of the King of Lochlan follows thee, the blessing and victory of the Sorceress follow thee, and my blessing will follow thee. Thou wert faithful to thy brother, and every man and beast that shall meet thee will be faithful to thee. And, brave Hero, give me a shake of thy hand, and I will tell thee where thou shalt find the Soul of the Bare-Stripping Hangman.' The Old Man stretched out his hand, and Alastir stretched out the wedge of oak to him. He seized the wedge, gave it a bruising and a shaking, and made pulp (*cothan*) of it. When he let it go he said, 'Son of the King of Ireland, hard is thy hand, and it would need be thus far. Thou art tired, thirsty and hungry, thou art worthy of meat and drink, and thou shalt get both. After thy supper thou shalt go to bed, and at sunrise to-morrow thou shalt be ready for thy journey. Thou shalt keep going forward without turning, without stopping, without looking behind thee till thou reach the Thick-foliaged Grove of the Trees (*Doire Dlùth-dhuilleach nan Craobh*). Thou shalt see there the Swift-footed Hind of the Cliffs, near which neither dog nor man ever got. Thou shalt catch her, open her, and find a Salmon in her stomach. Thou shalt open the Salmon, and in its belly thou shalt find the Green Duck of the Smooth Feathers. In the belly of the Duck thou shalt find an Egg, and thou shalt catch the Egg and break it before it touch the ground. For if it touch the ground thou shalt never after that see king, or man, or men. But though thy hand is hard it will not break the Egg without my help.' He felt beside him in the moss, and took out of it a little jar. He handed the jar to Alastir, and said, 'There is ointment for thee. As soon as thou shalt reach the Thick-foliaged Grove of the Trees thou shalt pour the ointment on thy hands, and rub with them every bit of thy skin which happens to be naked, or which thou mayest think that the blood of Hind, or scale of Salmon, or feather of Duck, or shell of Egg will touch. Thou shalt accept hospitality from every man or beast that gives it thee without asking. And thou thyself shalt know what thou hast to do after that. Catch this ointment now, and take it with thee, and be ready for thy journey as I told thee.' Alastir knew that it was not safe for him to stretch out his hand for the little jar. So he stretched out his sword, and said, 'Put the little jar on the point of my finger.' The Old Man did that, and grasped the sword in his hand, and bruised it till it was as round as a bit of stick. Then he said, 'Thou shalt accomplish thy task. Thou shalt then return on the way on which thou hast come. Thou shalt take the King of Lochlan's daughters out of the Castles in which they are, (and bring them) with thee. Thou shalt then take thy way to the Castle of the Speckled Mountain (Ben Breck), where thou shalt find the Great Giant stretched dead on the floor. Thou shalt cut off him the head and the feet as far as the knees, and shalt take them with thee to the Castle of the King of Lochlan. When thou shalt arrive at the Castle thou shalt put on a great fire, and when it is in the heat of its burning thou shalt throw them on the top of the fire. As soon as they shall get a singeing in the flame they shall become as handsome a young man as man ever saw. He is a brother of the King of Lochlan, who was stolen from his mother, when he was a child, by the Fiery Dragon. She was keeping him yonder under spells, doing every mischief he could on the King until thou didst come. Now, do as I told thee, and my blessing will accompany thee.'

On the next day Alastir went away on his journey. He kept going forward far long and full long. The evening was coming on him, the calm, still clouds of day were departing, and the dark, gloomy clouds of night were approaching, the little nestling, folding, yellow-tipped birds were taking to rest at the roots of the bushes, and in the tops of the tree tufts, and in the snuggest, pretty sheltered little holms they could choose for themselves. At last he was growing tired, and weak with hunger. He gave a look before him, and whom did he see but the Dog of the Great Headland? When they met each other, the kind Dog gave him a salutation and welcome heartily. He asked of him whither was he going? Alastir told him that he was going to seek the Soul of the Bare-Stripping Hangman. The Dog said to him, 'The night is coming, and thou art wearied; come with me, and I will give thee the best hospitality I can to-night.' He went with the Dog willingly. They reached the Lair of the Dog, and that was the dry, comfortable place, with abundance of fire, venison of deer, and of hinds and roes. He got enough to eat, and a warm, comfortable bed, with the skins of stags under him, and the skins of hinds and roes over him.

Next morning he got his breakfast of the same kind of food as he had at his supper. When he was going away the kind Dog said to him, 'Any time a strong tooth that will not yield its hold, or a fast strong foot that will travel on the rocky top (*creachann*) of mountain, or run on the floor of glen, will do thee service, think of me, and I will be at thy side.' He gave the kind Dog great thanks, and departed on his journey.

He kept going forward far long and full long, until he was growing tired and evening was coming on. He gave a look before him, and whom did he see coming to meet him but the Brown Otter of the Stream of Guidance. When they met, the Otter gave him a cheery salutation, and asked of him where was he going? Alastir told him that. 'The night is coming and thou art wearied; come with me to-night, and thou shalt get the best hospitality I can give.' He went with the Otter to his Cairn. That was the warm, comfortable place, with abundance of fire and enough of the fish of salmon and grilse. He got his supper well and very well, and as easy a bed as he ever slept on of the smooth bent of the fresh-water Lakes. Next morning he got his breakfast of the same sort as he had for his supper on the night before. When he was going away, the Otter said to him, 'Any time a strong tail to swim under water, or to stem each current and rapid, will be of service to thee, think of me, and I will be at thy side.' Alastir gave thanks to the kindly Otter, and departed.

He travelled on far long and full long, until he was growing tired and night was coming. He gave a look before him, and whom did he see squatting on a stone, but the Great Falcon of the Rock of Cliffs? When they met, the Falcon asked of him where was he going? and Alastir told him the journey on which he was. 'The night is coming, and thou art wearied and hungry,' said the Falcon; 'thou hadst better stay with me to-night, and I will give thee the best hospitality I can.' He went with the Falcon to his own sheltered cliff. That was the dry, comfortable place, where he got abundance of the flesh of every kind of birds, and a bed of feathers as easy as he ever lay on. Next morning, after he had got his breakfast, the Falcon said to him, 'Any time a strong, supple wing which can travel through air or over mountain will be of service to thee, think of me, and I will be at thy side.'

He did not go far forward, when he came in sight of the Thick-foliaged Grove of the Trees. He reached the Grove, and scarcely had he got in when the Swift-footed Hind of the Cliffs sprang out and ascended the mountain. He stretched away after her, but the faster he went the farther she would be from him. When he exhausted himself pursuing her, he thought of the Dog, and said, 'Would not the Dog of the Great Headland be useful here now?' No sooner did the word go out of his mouth than the Dog was at his side. He told the Dog that he was exhausted following the Hind, and that he was then farther from her than he was when he began to pursue her.

The Dog went after her, and he went after the Dog till they reached the side of the Green Lakelet. Then the Dog caught the Hind, and left her at Alastir's feet. It was then that Alastir remembered the ointment. He poured it quickly on his hands, and rubbed it to every bit of his skin that the Hind's blood might touch. He then tackled the Hind, and opened her. But if he did open her it was not without a fight, for her hoofs were so sharp and her feet so strong that if it were not for the ointment she would take him asunder in bits. When he opened the stomach the Salmon leaped out of it into the Green Lakelet.

He went after the Salmon round the Lakelet; but when he would be at one bank, the Salmon would be under another bank. At last he remembered the Brown Otter of the Stream of Guidance, and on the spot he was at his side. He told the Otter that the Salmon was in the Lakelet, and that he could not get a hold of it. The Otter sprang out quickly into the water, and in a short time came back with the Salmon, and laid it at Alastir's feet. Alastir seized the Salmon, but as soon as he made a hole on its belly, the Duck of the Smooth Feather and Green Back sprang out, and flew to the other side of the Lakelet, and lay down there. He went after her; but when he reached that side on which she was, she rose and went back to the side which he had left. When he saw that he could not catch her, he remembered the Great Falcon of the Rock of the Cliffs, and in an instant he was at his side. He told him how the Duck got away, and that he could not catch her. The Falcon sprang quickly after her, and in an instant came with her and left her at Alastir's feet.

Alastir remembered that if the egg should touch the ground everything was lost. He therefore opened the Duck cautiously, and as soon as the Egg came in sight he seized it quickly in his hand, but the Egg gave a bounce out of his fist, and sprang the three heights of a man in the air. But before it struck the earth, Alastir got a hold of it, and gave it a hard bruising between his two hands and two knees, and crushed it in fragments.

He had now finished everything which he had got to do. He therefore returned the way he came. He found the path as smooth and safe as it formerly was full of obstacles and dangers. In a short time he reached the Gloomy Castle of the Fiery Serpent. The woman met him at the door, and cried, 'Darling of the Men of the World! thou hast conquered, and thou shalt receive thy reward.' She went away with him, and in a short time they reached the Great Castle of the Eight Turrets. Light-of-Shade met them at the door, and went away with them. Then they reached the Great Castle at the end of the Rocky Path, and found Sunbeam waiting them. She went away with them, and they reached the Castle of the Great Giant of Ben Breck, and found him stretched dead on the floor. Alastir seized his own Great Sword, and took the head and feet as far as the knees off him. He tied them up and took them with him.

'Now,' said Sunbeam, 'to-night is the night in which the Great Giant was to come for my youngest sister, and my father is in heavy sorrow, because he is sure that thou hast been killed, since thou didst not return before now. He has all his men assembled to meet the Giant when he will arrive. But his sorrow will be turned to cheerfulness, and his sadness to laughter. When he comes to meet us, thou shalt tell him how it befell thee since the day in which thou didst depart to this night.'

When they were nearing the Castle, they saw a great host awaiting the coming of the Giant. The King and all in the Castle were sad and sorrowful for the maiden who was to be taken from them. But in the midst of their grief, the King gave a look out of the window, and saw Alastir coming with three women in his company, and the head and feet of the Giant over his shoulder. He sprang out to meet him, seized him between his two arms, and kissed him. 'Darling of the Men of the World! I knew that victory would be with thee, and I will be as good as my promise to thee. But since thou hast brought home all my daughters, thou shalt get thy choice of them, from the oldest one to the youngest.' 'Well,' said Alastir, 'she whom I went to save from the Bare-Stripping Hangman is my choice.' When each of the rest heard this she was sorry that he did not choose herself. But since he won the victory, and did so much for them, they all consented that he should get the one he chose.

The King then asked Alastir what was he going to do with the head and feet of the Giant. 'Before I eat food or take a drink thou shalt see that,' said Alastir. He then got fuel, and made a large fire, and when the fire was in the heat of its burning, he threw the head and feet in the midst of the flame. As soon as the hair of the head was singed and the skin of the feet burnt, the very handsomest young man they ever beheld sprang out of the fire. 'Oh, the son of my father and mother who was stolen in his childhood!' said the King, springing over and embracing him in his arms. When they saluted each other, they all went in to the Castle.

65

The King resolved that Alastir and his daughter should be married that very night. But when Alastir heard this, he said, 'King of Lochlan, thine offer is good enough. But I will not marry thy daughter, nor will I enter into possession of a bit of thy kingdom, until thou shalt send for the Young King of Riddles and the Young Queen of Riddles to the wedding.' The King now fell into great anxiety, because he did not know in what direction he should send for them. In the midst of his thoughts he remembered the Sorceress. He went where she was, and told her Alastir's request. 'Get thou everything else ready, and I will have them here before sunrise to-morrow,' said the Sorceress. And what she said proved true. The first look the King gave next morning in the direction of the sea, he saw two coracles (*curachs*) coming to the shore. Out of one of them came Cormac and his wife, and out of the other came the Sorceress.

Alastir sprang out to meet them, and that was the affectionate welcome they gave each other! The King came to meet them, and he gave them a cordial salutation. They went to the Castle, and the marriage was consummated. After the marriage was over, they made a great feast which lasted a day and year. At the end of that time Cormac and his wife returned to their own place, and Alastir and his wife went with them. Cormac remained in the Castle of the King of Riddles, but Alastir went back to his father's place. When his mother saw him she gave him a great welcome, and his father rejoiced greatly when he heard that Cormac was the Young King of Riddles. The King now made another great feast for Alastir and his wife and for all who were about him.

And I got nothing but butter on a live coal, porridge in a basket, (and) paper shoes. They sent me (for water) to the stream, and they (the paper shoes) came to an end.

Notes

Source of tale: J. MacDougal, *Folk and Hero Tales of Argyllshire*, London: David Nutt, 1891.

This tale was told to the great collector Alexander Cameron by a famous old storyteller named Donald McPhie in the 1800s. It is one of the longest and most complex stories (even though somewhat abridged) in this collection. It possesses all the characteristics of the classic wonder tale: a daring and resourceful hero, numerous twists and turns in the plot, a terrible adversary in the shape of the giant Bare-Stripping Hangman of the title, and a generous sprinkling of other-worldly helpers. Several tales exist which have similar themes and structure, including the Russian 'Koschei the Deathless', which became the subject of an opera by Rimsky-Korsakov, and 'The Giant Who Had No Heart in His Body', which is found in both Norse and English versions. The latter theme, in which the soul of the giant is hidden somewhere else, is one of the most widespread and fascinating aspects of folklore tradition. It suggests the idea that certain beings were able to separate themselves from their souls and hide these elsewhere – again a notion which is encountered in shamanic practice both here and in the rest of the world.

Lochlann, where much of the action takes place, is frequently used as a name for the otherworld, though it in fact refers to Scandinavia and was widely used as a term meaning 'foreigner'. As in all stories where the otherworld is invoked, the events which occur within its boundaries are not subject to the same laws of cause and effect as the outer world.

The hen-wife, as seems to be the case in nearly every story in which she appears, is a mischief-maker, skilled in the use of small magic, and in this case she becomes a mediator of the usual evil stepmother theme – though of course the queen must go along with the plot for it to work. The subsequent use of the opening elements of the story to form the riddle which Alastir sets the King of the Riddles is ingenious. We, as audience, know the answer of course, and can smile at the king's inability to work it out.

The second part of the story, in which Alastir seeks for the soul of the Great Giant, is a triumph of imaginative power and intricacy. Just as Alastir is himself seeking the place where the giant has hidden his soul, he has also to return again and again to his bothy to eat of the flesh of the white deer and drink of the brew – both need to return to the seat of their power from time to time, and in both cases the power is held elsewhere.

The sequence of animal helpers, each of which offers its special skills to the hero, and which is at his side as soon as he thinks of it, is reminiscent of the myth of Taliesin, where the wise child Gwion changes shape into the form of the animal which best suits his need. (See my book *Taliesin: Shamanism and the Bardic Mysteries in Britain and Ireland*, Aquarian Press, 1991, for more on this.) This is a very clear memory of earlier shamanic techniques, in which the shaman seeks the help of animal totems for his inspired flights into the other-

world. Of course, we have once again the familiar sequence of the 'oldest of the old', which is present in 'Coldfeet and the Queen of Lonesome Island' (see pages 14–23) and elsewhere. Here it is worked out in more detail, including the fascinating notion of the oldest old man being kept in a clump of moss and taken forth only when required to be consulted. This suggests a hidden soul-part which may be consulted at need and is the repository of an essential wisdom. A similar incident is found in another tale, 'The Man in the Tuft of Wool', in *A History of the Highlands* by D. McLauchlan, Vol. 2 (publisher unknown).

The description of the helpful sorceress also possesses some interesting details. She is lying down on the floor when Alastir asks for her help. She then sits up and grasps her hair, and is at once able to tell him what to do. Both these actions reflect a strong shamanistic element. Lying on the floor is a practical method of journeying, out of the body but in contact with the earth; hair, in Celtic tradition, is always associated with power. In another version of the story the sorceress strikes the earth three times before she utters a saying – an action which is also found in the accounts of ancient magical practice. Finally, as recently as this year I heard the account of a journey taken by one of my own shamanic students in which the cutting of hair was described as a ritual to gain power. These factors more than convince me of the continuing validity of the imagery to be found in these tales.

At the end of the story we suddenly discover the names of two of the three daughters of the King of Lochlann: Light-of-Shade and Sunbeam. Could it be that, as in the story of 'The Lad of the Skin Coverings' (see pages 35–45), we have a vestige here of a far more ancient, cosmological story? Given the extraordinary imagery of the tale, I think it more than likely that the otherworldly characters were once seen as patterns of 'inner-earth' stars, for it is said of the underworld that there are stars within it, just as there are stars in the heavens.

BEIRA, QUEEN OF WINTER

ARK BEIRA WAS THE MOTHER of all the gods and goddesses in Scotland. She was of great height and very old, and everyone feared her. When roused to anger she was as fierce as the biting north wind and harsh as the tempest-stricken sea. Each winter she reigned as Queen of the Four Red Divisions of the world, and none disputed her sway. But when the sweet spring season drew nigh, her subjects began to rebel against her and to long for the coming of the Summer King, Angus of the White Steed, and Bride, his beautiful queen, who were loved by all, for they were the bringers of plenty and of bright and happy days. It enraged Beira greatly to find her power passing away, and she tried her utmost to prolong the winter season by raising spring storms and sending blighting frost to kill early flowers and keep the grass from growing.

Beira lived for hundreds and hundreds of years. The reason she did not die of old age was because, at the beginning of every spring, she drank the magic waters of the Well of Youth which bubbles up in the Green Island of the West. This was a floating island where summer was the only season, and the trees were always bright with blossom and laden with fruit. It drifted about on the silver tides of the blue Atlantic, and sometimes appeared off the western coasts of Ireland and sometimes close to the Hebrides. Many bold mariners have steered their galleys up and down the ocean, searching for Green Island in vain. On a calm morning they might sail past its shores and yet never know it was near at hand, for oft-times it lay hidden in a twinkling mist. Men have caught glimpses of it from the shore, but while they gazed on its beauties with eyes of wonder, it vanished suddenly from sight by sinking beneath the waves like the setting sun. Beira, however, always knew where to find Green Island when the time came for her to visit it.

The waters of the Well of Youth are most potent when the days begin to grow longer, and most potent of all on the first of the lengthening days of spring. Beira always visited the island on the night before the first lengthening day – that is, on the last night of her reign as Queen of Winter. All alone in

68

the darkness she sat beside the Well of Youth, waiting for the dawn. When the first faint beam of light appeared in the eastern sky, she drank the water as it bubbled fresh from a crevice in the rock. It was necessary that she should drink of this magic water before any bird visited the well and before any dog barked. If a bird drank first, or a dog barked ere she began to drink, dark old Beira would crumble into dust.

As soon as Beira tasted the magic water, in silence and alone, she began to grow young again. She left the island and, returning to Scotland, fell into a magic sleep. When, at length, she awoke, in bright sunshine, she rose up as a beautiful girl with long hair yellow as buds of broom, cheeks red as rowan berries, and blue eyes that sparkled like the summer sea in sunshine. Then she went to and fro through Scotland, clad in a robe of green and crowned with a chaplet of bright flowers of many hues. No fairer goddess was to be found in all the land, save Bride, the peerless Queen of Summer.

As each month went past, however, Beira aged quickly. She reached full womanhood in mid-summer, and when autumn came on her brows wrinkled and her beauty began to fade. When the season of winter returned once again, she became an old and withered hag, and began to reign as the fierce Queen Beira. Often on stormy nights in early winter she wandered about, singing this sorrowful song–

> O life that ebbs like the sea!
>   I am weary and old, I am weary and old –
> Oh! how can I happy be
>   All alone in the dark and the cold.
>
> I'm the old Beira again,
>   My mantle no longer is green,
> I think of my beauty with pain
>   And the days when another was queen.
>
> My arms are withered and thin,
>   My hair once golden is grey;
> 'T is winter – my reign doth begin –
>   Youth's summer has faded away.
>
> Youth's summer and autumn have fled –
>   I am weary and old, I am weary and old.
> Every flower must fade and fall dead
>   When the winds blow cold, when the winds blow cold.

The aged Beira was fearsome to look upon. She had only one eye, but the sight of it was keen and sharp as ice and as swift as the mackerel of the ocean. Her complexion was a dull, dark blue, and this is how she sang about it:–

> Why is my face so dark, so dark?
>   So dark, oho! so dark, ohee!
> Out in all weathers I wander alone
>   In the mire, in the cold, ah me!

69

Her teeth were red as rust, and her locks, which lay heavily on her shoulders, were white as an aspen covered with hoar frost. On her head she wore a spotted mutch. All her clothing was grey, and she was never seen without her great dun-coloured shawl, which was drawn closely round her shoulders.

It is told that in the days when the world was young Beira saw land where there is now water and water where there is now land.

Once a wizard spoke to her and said: 'Tell me your age, O sharp old woman.'

Beira answered: 'I have long ceased to count the years. But I shall tell you what I have seen. Yonder is the seal-haunted rock of Skerryvore in the midst of the sea. I remember when it was a mountain surrounded by fields. I saw the fields ploughed, and the barley that grew upon them was sharp and juicy. Yonder is a loch. I remember when it was a small round well. In these days I was a fair young girl, and now I am very old and frail and dark and miserable.'

It is told also that Beira let loose many rivers and formed many lochs, sometimes willingly and sometimes against her will, and that she also shaped many bens and glens. All the hills in Ross-shire are said to have been made by Beira.

There was once a well on Ben Cruachan, in Argyll, from which Beira drew water daily. Each morning at sunrise she lifted off the slab that covered it, and each evening at sunset she laid it above the well again. It happened that one evening she forgot to cover the well. Then the proper order of things was disturbed. As soon as the sun went down the water rose in great volume and streamed down the mountain side, roaring like a tempest-swollen sea. When day dawned, Beira found that the valley beneath was filled with water. It was in this way that Loch Awe came to be.

Beira had another well in Inverness-shire which had to be kept covered in like manner from sunset till sunrise. One of her maids, whose name was Nessa, had charge of the well. It happened that one evening the maid was late in going to the well to cover it. When she drew near she beheld the water flowing so fast from it that she turned away and ran for her life. Beira watched her from the top of Ben Nevis, which was her mountain throne, and cried: 'You have neglected your duty. Now you will run for ever and never leave water.'

The maiden was at once changed into a river, and the loch and the river which runs from it towards the sea were named after her. That is why the loch is called Loch Ness and the river the river Ness.

Once a year, when the night on which she was transformed comes round, Ness (Nessa) arises out of the river in her girl form, and sings a sad sweet song in the pale moonlight. It is said that her voice is clearer and more beautiful than that of any bird, and her music more melodious than the golden harps and silvern pipes of fairyland.

In the days when rivers broke loose and lochs were made, Beira set herself to build the mountains of Scotland. When at work she carried on her back a great creel filled with rocks and earth. Sometimes as she leapt from hill to hill her creel tilted sideways, and rocks and earth fell from it into lochs and

*Beira, Queen
of Winter*

71

formed islands. Many islands are spoken of as 'spillings from the creel of the big old woman'.

Beira had eight hags who were her servants. They also carried creels, and one after the other they emptied out their creels until a mountain was piled up nigh to the clouds.

*Beira strikes her
magic hammer on the
mountain rocks*

One of the reasons why Beira made the mountains was to use them as stepping stones; another was to provide houses for her giant sons. Many of her sons were very quarrelsome; they fought continually one against another. To punish those of them who disobeyed her, Beira shut the offenders up in mountain houses, and from these they could not escape without her permission. But this did not keep them from fighting. Every morning they climbed to the tops of their mountain houses and threw great boulders at one another. That is why so many big grey boulders now lie on steep slopes and are scattered through the valleys. Other giant sons of Beira dwelt in deep caves. Some were horned like deer, and others had many heads. So strong were they that they could pick up cattle and, throwing them over their shoulders, carry them away to roast them for their meals. Each giant son of Beira was called a Fooar.

It was Beira who built Ben Wyvis. She found it a hard task, for she had to do all the work alone, her hag servants being busy elsewhere. One day, when she had grown very weary, she stumbled and upset her creel. All the rocks and earth it contained fell out in a heap, and formed the mountain which is called Little Wyvis.

The only tool that Beira used was a magic hammer. When she struck it lightly on the ground the soil became as hard as iron; when she struck it heavily on the ground a valley was formed. After she had built up a mountain, she gave it its special form by splintering the rocks with her hammer. If she had made all the hills of the same shape, she would not have been able to recognize one from another.

After the mountains were all formed, Beira took great delight in wandering between them and over them. She was always followed by wild animals. The foxes barked with delight when they beheld her, wolves howled to greet her, and eagles shrieked with joy in mid-air. Beira had great herds and flocks to which she gave her protection – nimble-footed deer, high-horned cattle, shaggy grey goats, black swine, and sheep that had snow-white fleeces. She charmed her deer against the huntsmen, and when she visited a deer forest she helped them to escape from the hunters. During early winter she milked the hinds on the tops of mountains, but when the winds rose so high that the froth was blown from the milking pails, she drove the hinds down to the valleys. The froth was frozen on the crests of high hills, and lay there snow-white and beautiful. When the winter torrents began to pour down the mountain sides, leaping from ledge to ledge, the people said: 'Beira is milking her shaggy goats, and streams of milk are pouring down over high rocks.'

Beira washed her great shawl in the sea, for there was no lake big enough for the purpose. The part she chose for her washing is the strait between the western islands of Jura and Scarba. Beira's 'washing-pot' is the whirlpool, there called Corry-vreckan. It was so named because the son of a Scottish king, named Breckan, was drowned in it, his boat having been upset by the waves raised by Beira.

Three days before the Queen of Winter began her work her hag servants made ready the water for her, and the Corry could then be heard snorting and fuming for twenty miles around. On the fourth day Beira threw her shawl into the whirlpool, and tramped it with her feet until the edge of the Corry overflowed with foam. When she had finished her washing she laid her shawl on the mountains to dry, and as soon as she lifted it up, all the mountains of Scotland were white with snow to signify that the great Queen had begun her reign. . . .

NOTES

Source of tale: Donald A. Mackenzie, *Wonder Tales from Scottish Myth and Legend*, Glasgow: Blackie and Sons, 1917.

This is almost not a story at all, but rather an account, based upon the most ancient level of folk-memory, of the creation of the earth. Beira is generally associated with the Beara Peninsula, in west Munster, Ireland, where she is called the Cailleach or Old Woman. She is also well known in Scotland and Wales, where she is simply known as the Old Woman or the Mountain Mother. In each case she was seen as carrying the stuff of the mountains in her apron or basket (creel) and letting these fall from time to time, thus accounting for the great blocks of granite scattered across the land. Her struggle with Bride, the Queen of Summer, is well known, but, with the coming of Christianity to Ireland, just as the Goddess Bride became Saint Bridget, so Beira came to be reduced from an ancient goddess to an old nun. The poem quoted in this story exists in a much longer form, dating from the ninth century. Here Beira speaks in her Christianized voice, though sometimes a gleam of earlier, pagan times shows through:

I'm the yellow one of Beare,
Smocks of silk I once would wear.
Now no shawl to cover me:
Ebb-tide is the blood in me.

Money's all you care about,
Wealth and power without a doubt:
We loved people in my youth –
That's the craft of simple truth . . .

Once their gifting was to me
Steeds and chariots like a sea,
Richly flowing from the grace
Of a king of blessed face.

Now my body's sharp to me,
Seeks a home beyond the sea.
My body's credit falls like sand:
Soon I'll be in God's Son's hand. . . .

(translated by Caítlin Matthews)

A note in the *Medieval Irish Book of Lecan* says that the Cailleach originated in the area known as Corco Duibne, of whose people it was said that 'they shall never be without some wonderful cailleach among them'. The same text says: 'This is why she was called the Old Woman of Beare: she had fifty foster-children in Beare. She passed into seven periods of youth, so that every husband used to pass from her to death of old age and so that her grandchildren were peoples and races.' This is both a foundation myth and a creation myth, and it is obvious that the stories about Beira (Beara) must have been handed down from a very early period. Her foster-sons, here called *Fooar* are, as noted by the story's original teller, probably the same as the Irish Fomorians, a race of monstrous people who were finally defeated by the incoming Milesians: the settlers from whom the present-day Irish draw their ancestral roots. Despite the statement that the Scottish Fooar are different from the Irish, I suspect they shared the same function as one of the primal races which Beira is said to have brought forth.

'Mutch' is the old Scottish name for a woman's cap. The story has been slightly edited.

THE STONES OF PLOUVINEC

N THE LITTLE VILLAGE OF PLOUVINEC there once lived a poor stone-cutter named Bernet. Bernet was an honest and industrious young man, and yet he never seemed to succeed in the world. Work as he might, he was always poor. This was a great grief to him, for he was in love with the beautiful Madeleine Pornec, and she was the daughter of the richest man in Plouvinec.

Madeleine had many suitors, but she cared for none of them except Bernet. She would gladly have married him in spite of his poverty, but her father was covetous as well as rich. He had no wish for a poor son in-law, and Madeleine was so beautiful he expected her to marry some rich merchant, or a well-to-do farmer at least. But if Madeleine could not have Bernet for a husband, she was determined that she would have no one.

There came a winter when Bernet found himself poorer than he had ever been before. Scarcely anyone seemed to have any need for a stonecutter, and even for such work as he did get he was poorly paid. He learned to know what it meant to go without a meal and to be cold as well as hungry.

As Christmas drew near, the landlord of the inn at Plouvinec decided to give a feast for all the good folk of the village, and Bernet was invited along with all the rest.

He was glad enough to go to the feast, for he knew that Madeleine was to be there, and even if he did not have a chance to talk to her, he could at least look at her, and that would be better than nothing.

The feast was a fine one. There was plenty to eat and drink, and all was of the best, and the more the guests feasted, the merrier they grew. If Bernet and Madeleine ate little and spoke less, no one noticed it. People were too busy filling their own stomachs and laughing at the jokes that were cracked. The fun was at its height when the door was pushed open, and a ragged, ill-looking beggar slipped into the room.

At the sight of him the laughter and merriment died away. This beggar was well known to all the people of the village, though none knew whence he came nor where he went when he was away on his wanderings. He was sly and crafty, and he was feared as well as disliked, for it was said that he had the evil eye. Whether he had or not, it was well known that no one had ever offended him without having some misfortune happen soon after.

'I heard there was a great feast here to-night,' said the beggar in a humble voice, 'and that all the village had been bidden to it. Perhaps, when all have eaten, there may be some scraps that I might pick up.'

'Scraps there are in plenty,' answered the landlord, 'but it is not scraps that I am offering to anyone to-night. Draw up a chair to the table, and eat and drink what you will. There is more than enough for all.' But the landlord looked none too well pleased as he spoke. It was a piece of ill-luck to have the beggar come to his house this night of all nights, to spoil the pleasure of the guests.

The beggar drew up to the table as the landlord bade him, but the fun and merriment were ended. Presently the guests began to leave the table, and after thanking their host, they went away to their own homes.

When the beggar had eaten and drunk to his heart's content, he pushed back his chair from the table.

'I have eaten well,' said he to the landlord. 'Is there not now some corner where I can spend the night?'

'There is the stable,' answered the landlord grudgingly. 'Every room in the house is full, but if you choose to sleep there among the clean hay, I am not the one to say you nay.'

Well, the beggar was well content with that. He went out to the stable, and there he snuggled down among the soft hay, and soon he was fast asleep. He had slept for some hours, and it was midnight, when he suddenly awoke with a startled feeling that he was not alone in the stable. In the darkness two strange voices were talking together.

'Well, brother, how goes it since last Christmas?' asked one voice.

'Poorly, brother, but poorly,' answered the other. 'Methinks the work has been heavier these last twelve months than ever before.'

The beggar, listening as he lay in the hay, wondered who could be talking there at this hour of the night. Then he discovered that the voices came from the stalls near by; the ox and the donkey were talking together.

The beggar was so surprised that he almost exclaimed aloud, but he restrained himself. He remembered a story he had often heard, but had never before believed, that on every Christmas night it is given to the dumb beasts in the stalls to talk in human tones for a short time. It was said that those who had been lucky enough to hear them at such times had sometimes learned strange secrets from their talk. Now the beggar lay listening with all his ears, and scarcely daring to breathe lest he should disturb them.

'It has been a hard year for me too,' said the ox, answering what the donkey had just said. 'I would our master had some of the treasure that lies hidden under the stones of Plouvinec. Then he could buy more oxen and more donkeys, and the work would be easier for us.'

'The treasure! What treasure is that?' asked the donkey.

The ox seemed very much surprised. 'Have you never heard? I thought every one knew of the hidden treasure under the stones.'

77

'Tell me about it,' said the donkey, 'for I dearly love a tale.'

The ox was not loath to do this. At once it began:

'You know the barren heath just outside of Plouvinec, and the great stones that lie there, each so large that it would take more than a team of oxen to drag it from its place?'

Yes, the donkey knew that heath, and the stones too. He had often passed by them on his journeys to the neighbouring town.

'It is said that under those stones lies hidden an enormous treasure of gold,' said the ox. 'That is the story; it is well known. But none has seen that treasure; jealously the stones guard it. Once in every hundred years, how ever, the stones go down to the river to drink. They are only away for a few minutes; then they come rolling back in mad haste to cover their gold again. But if anyone could be there on the heath for those few minutes, it is a won derful sight that he would see while the stones are away. It is now a hundred years, all but a week, since the stones went down to drink.'

'Then a week from to-night the treasure will be uncovered again?' asked the donkey.

'Yes, exactly a week from now, at midnight.'

'Ah, if only our master knew this,' and the donkey sighed heavily. 'If only we could tell him! Then he might go to the heath and not only see the treasure, but gather a sack full of it for himself.'

'Yes, but even if he did, he would never return with it alive. As I told you, the stones are very jealous of their treasure, and are away for only a few minutes. By the time he had gathered up the gold and was ready to escape, the stones would return and would crush him to powder.'

The beggar, who had become very much excited at the story, felt a cold shiver creep over him at these words.

'No one could ever bring away any of it then?' asked the donkey.

'I did not say that. The stones are enchanted. If anyone could find a five-leaved clover, and carry it with him to the heath, the stones could not harm him, for the five-leaved clover is a magic plant that has power over all enchanted things, and those stones are enchanted.'

'Then all he would need would be to have a five-leaved clover.'

'If he carried that with him, the stones could not harm him. He might escape safely with the treasure, but it would do him little good. With the first rays of the sun the treasure would crumble away unless the life of a human being had been sacrificed to the stones there on the heath before sunrise.'

'And who would sacrifice a human life for a treasure!' cried the donkey. 'Not our master, I am sure.'

The ox made no answer, and now the donkey too was silent. The hour had passed in which they could speak in human voices. For another year they would again be only dumb brutes.

As for the beggar, he lay among the hay, shaking all over with excitement. Visions of untold wealth shone before his eyes. The treasure of Plouvinec! Why, if he could only get it, he would be the richest man in the village. In the village? No, in the country – in the whole world! Only to see it and handle it for a few hours would be something. But before even that were possible and safe it would be necessary to find a five-leaved clover.

With the earliest peep of dawn the beggar rolled from the hay, and, wrapping his rags about him, stole out of the stable and away into the country. There he began looking about for bunches of clover. These were not hard to find; they were everywhere, though the most of them were withered now. He found and examined clump after clump. Here and there he found a stem that bore four leaves, but none had five. Night came on, and the darkness made him give up the search; but the next day he began anew. Again he was unsuccessful. So day after day passed by, and still he had not found the thing he sought so eagerly.

The beggar was in a fever of rage and disappointment. Six days slipped by. By the time the seventh dawned he was so discouraged that he hunted for only a few hours. Then, though it was still daylight, he determined to give up the search. With drooping head he turned back toward the village. As he was passing a heap of rocks he noticed a clump of clover growing in a crevice. Idly, and with no hope of success, he stooped and began to examine it leaf by leaf.

Suddenly he gave a cry of joy. His legs trembled under him so that he was obliged to sink to his knees. The last stem of all bore five leaves. He had found his five-leaved clover!

With the magic plant safely hidden away in his bosom the beggar hurried back toward the village. He would rest in the inn until night. Then he would go to the heath, and if the story the ox had told were true, he would see a sight such as no one living had ever seen before.

His way led him past the heath. Dusk was falling as he approached it. Suddenly the beggar paused and listened. From among the stones sounded a strange tap-tapping. Cautiously he drew nearer, peering about among the stones. Then he saw what seemed to him a curious sight for such a place and such a time. Before the largest stone of all stood Bernet, busily at work with hammer and chisel. He was cutting a cross upon the face of the rock.

The beggar drew near to him so quietly that Bernet did not notice him. He started as a voice suddenly spoke close to his ear.

'That is a strange thing for you to be doing,' said the beggar. 'Why should you waste your time in cutting a cross in such a lonely place as this?'

'The sign of the cross never comes amiss, wherever it may be,' answered Bernet. 'And as for wasting my time, no one seems to have any use for it at present. It is better for me to spend it in this way than to idle it away over nothing.'

Suddenly a strange idea flashed into the beggar's mind – a thought so strange and terrible that it made him turn pale. He drew nearer to the stone-cutter and laid his hand upon his arm.

'Listen, Bernet,' said he; 'you are a clever workman and an honest one as well, and yet all your work scarcely brings you in enough to live on. Suppose I were to tell you that in one night you might become rich – richer than the richest man in the village – so that there would be no desire that you could not satisfy; what would you think of that?'

'I would think nothing of it, for I would know it was not true,' answered Bernet carelessly.

'But it *is* true; it is *true*, I tell you,' cried the beggar. 'Listen, and I will tell you.'

He drew still nearer to Bernet, so that his mouth almost touched the stone-cutter's ear, and in a whisper he repeated to him the story he had heard the ox telling the donkey – the story of the treasure that was buried under the stones of Plouvinec. But it was only a part of the story that he told after all, for he did not tell Bernet that anyone who was rash enough to seek the treasure would be crushed by the stones unless he carried a five-leaved clover; nor did he tell him that if the treasure were carried away from the heath it would turn to ashes unless a human life had been sacrificed to the stones. As Bernet listened to the story he became very grave. His eyes shone through the fading light as he stared at the beggar's face.

'Why do you tell me this?' he asked. 'And why are you willing to share the treasure that might be all your own? If you make me rich, what do you expect me to do for you in return?'

'Do you not see?' answered the beggar. 'You are much stronger than I. I, as you know, am a weak man and slow of movement. While the stones are away we two together could gather more than twice as much as I could gather myself. In return for telling you this secret, all I ask is that if we go there and gather all we can, and bring it away with us, you will make an even division with me – that you will give me half of all we get.'

'That seems only just,' said Bernet slowly. 'It would be strange if this story of the hidden treasure proved to be true. At any rate, I will come with you to the heath to-night. We will bring with us some large bags, and if we manage to secure even a small part of the gold you talk of I shall never cease to be grateful to you.'

The beggar could not answer. His teeth were chattering, half with fear and half with excitement. The honest stone-cutter little guessed that the beggar was planning to sacrifice him to the stones in order that he himself might become a rich man.

It was well on toward midnight when Bernet and the beggar returned to the heath with the bags. The moon shone clear and bright, and by its light they could see the stones towering up above them, solid and motionless. It seemed impossible to believe that they had ever stirred from their places, or ever would again. In the moonlight Bernet could clearly see the cross that he had carved upon the largest stone.

He and the beggar lay hidden behind a clump of bushes. All was still except for the faint sound of the river some short distance away. Suddenly a breath seemed to pass over the heath. Far off, in the village of Plouvinec, sounded the first stroke of twelve.

At that stroke the two men saw a strange and wonderful thing happen. The motionless stones rocked and stirred in their places. With a rending sound they tore themselves from the places where they had stood for so long. Then down the slope toward the river they rolled, bounding faster and faster, while there on the heath an immense treasure glittered in the moonlight.

'Quick! quick!' cried the beggar in a shrill voice. 'They will return! We have not a moment to waste.'

Greedily he threw himself upon the treasure. Gathering it up by handfuls he thrust it hurriedly into a sack. Bernet was not slow to follow his example. They worked with such frenzy that soon the two largest sacks were almost

full. In their haste everything but the gold was forgotten.

Some sound, a rumbling and crashing, made Bernet look up. At once he sprang to his feet with a cry of fear.

'Look! look!' he cried. 'The stones are returning. They are almost on us. We shall be crushed.'

'You, perhaps; but not I,' answered the beggar. 'You should have provided yourself with a five-leaved clover. It is a magic herb, and the stones have no power to touch him who holds it.'

Even as the beggar spoke the stones were almost upon them. Trembling, but secure, he held up the five-leaved clover before them. As he did so the ranks of stones divided, passing around him a rank on either side; then, closing together, they rolled on toward Bernet.

The poor stone-cutter felt that he was lost. He tried to murmur a prayer, but his tongue clove to the roof of his mouth with fear.

Suddenly the largest stone of all, the one upon which he had cut the cross, separated itself from the others. Rolling in front of them, it placed itself before him as a shield. Grey and immovable it towered above him. A moment the others paused as if irresolute, while Bernet cowered close against the protecting stone. Then they rolled by without touching him and settled sullenly into their places.

The beggar was already gathering up the sacks. He believed himself safe, but he wished to leave the heath as quickly as possible. He glanced fearfully over his shoulder. Then he gave a shriek, and, turning, he held up the five-leaved clover. The largest stone was rolling toward him. It was almost upon him.

But the magic herb had no power over a stone marked with a cross. On it rolled, over the miserable man, and into the place where it must rest again for still another hundred years.

It was morning, and the sun was high in the heavens when Bernet staggered into the inn at Plouvinec. A heavy, bulging sack was thrown over one shoulder; a second sack he dragged behind him. They were full of gold – the treasure from under the stones of Plouvinec.

From that time Bernet was the richest man in Plouvinec. Madeleine's father was glad enough to call him son-in-law and to welcome him into his family. He and Madeleine were married, and lived in the greatest comfort and happiness all their days. But for as long as he lived Bernet could never be induced to go near the heath nor to look upon the stones that had so nearly caused his death.

NOTES

Source of tale: Emile Souvestre, *En Bretagne* (1899). Retold in W. Branch Johnson, *Folktales of Brittany*, London: Methuen, 1927.

Stories of treasure-seekers, both successful and unsuccessful, abound in faery tradition. The seekers usually discover the presence of the treasure by accident, and then must either search for it or undergo a series of tests and trials destined to lead, eventually, to it. Often, however, the results are ultimately fatal, as here. Fate takes a hand in this instance, of course, and magic is surely working when the beggar finds the five-leaved clover (traditionally recognized as a sign of good luck). Here, too, there is a sense of the age-old clash between Pagan and Christian – the stone marked with the cross saves Bernet from death.

This story was collected in the early nineteenth century in Brittany, and is very clearly an example of a familiar tale being adapted to a particular locale and given the stamp of place and time. Other tales of stones which move, or are in fact people *turned* to stone, are numerous and found throughout the western folklore tradition. Typically it was pagans dancing on the Sabbath who were so afflicted, or sometimes witches, as in the story of the Rollright Stones in Oxfordshire. Here the stones seem to represent an older power which, though it appears to be sleeping, can be awoken under certain circumstances.

THE SON OF THE KING OF ERIN AND THE QUEEN OF THE MOVING WHEEL

THERE WAS A KING in Erin long ago, and he had three sons. On a day this King went out to walk with the queen and look at the waves and the rocks on the strand. After they had walked for a time they saw a boat sailing in from the old sea (the distant sea). When the boat came to land they saw no one on board but a grey-haired old man, who came ashore and walked up to the King and the Queen.

'It is the wonder of the world to me,' said the old man to the King, 'that you never take thought of going out on the water to have amusement and pleasure for yourself.'

'How could I go on the water when I have neither ship nor boat?' asked the King.

'Walk into my boat with the Queen, and I will hold the cable while you sail and get as much sport as you like.'

The two entered the boat, and they were a good while inside sailing this way and that not far from land. At last the old man drew in the boat.

'Will you come out?' asked he of the King.

The King rose and was coming out.

'It is a wonder to me,' said the old man, 'that you, a King, should be so thoughtless as to come out before the Queen. She might fall between the boat and the rock. You should let her go first, and keep your eye on her.'

The King stepped back and told the Queen to go first. The moment she stepped on the rock the grey-haired old man put his foot to the stem of the boat and gave a shove that sent it out nine leagues to sea.

The boat went tossing about in one direction and another till it came to Lonesome Island. The King left the boat then, anchored, and went his way walking till he came to a splendid castle in the middle of the island. He entered the castle; there was no one inside but a woman, the most beautiful that ever he had seen. That was the Queen of Lonesome Island. She made ready a dinner, and both she and the King of Erin ate and drank at the one table.

84

Next morning she had breakfast ready before him. After breakfast they walked to the strand where the boat had been left, but neither ship nor boat was to be seen on sea or land. The King of Erin remained there with the Queen of Lonesome Island for a day and a year. The Queen at that time had a son three months old.

'King of Erin,' said she, 'you may go home if you choose.'

The King made ready to start.

'Do not go,' said she, 'without marking this child in the way that you will know him surely if you meet him again.'

'What mark am I to put on him?' asked the King.

'If you take off the small toe of his right foot it will do him no harm, and the mark will be certain.'

The King did that. The best ship ever seen was ready for him. He sailed away with fair wind and good wishes till he came to his own harbour with speed and in safety. While the King of Erin was on Lonesome Island word had gone out that he was lost. This word was going slowly from one place to another till it came to the White King.

Said the White King to himself: 'Now is my time to collect a fleet, sail to Erin and take that land for my own use.'

He prepared a great fleet and went to Erin. At this time the son of the Queen of Lonesome Island was seven years old. His mother had been training him in all exercises and arts from one room of the castle to another, and great was his skill.

When the White King came with his fleet he sent a challenge to the King of Erin to fight for his crown or lie under tribute and pay the tribute without trouble.

The King of Erin sent back the answer that he would fight and die rather than lie under tribute to any man.

When his own three sons at home heard of his trouble they hurried away to hide where no man could find them.

'Now,' said the Queen of Lonesome Island to her son, whose name was Wishing Gold. 'It is very pleasant for us to be sitting here to-night, but with your father, the King of Erin, it is different. There is great trouble on him.'

'What trouble is on my father?' asked the boy.

'When I sent him wandering on the sea, so that he might come to this island, word went out of Erin through all lands in the world that he was lost. The White King heard this word at last, and now he has gone with a great fleet to take Erin for himself. Your father, unaided by anyone, will go out to-morrow to give battle to the fleet of the White King, and you must give him a day of assistance.'

'Has he not three sons older than I?' asked Wishing Gold.

'That matters not,' said the Queen. 'It was I that brought him to this trouble, and you must assist him.'

Wishing Gold made ready next morning, and, mounting a steed, hurried off to Erin. When the King of Erin was going out, with his sword under his arm, to face the fleet, he saw a horseman rushing in on the water from the old sea, and he said to himself:

'I have time for delay. I will wait till I see where this horseman is going.

85

There are men enough against me if the horseman is with me, and if it is going against me he is there are too many.'

When the horseman came to the fleet of the White King he closed with it and went through like a hawk through small birds, or a fox through hens, making one pile of men's heads, another of their bodies, and a third of their weapons. He killed all and spared none, till he came to the White King himself. Him he led, took under his arm, and threw down before his father and asked:

'Are we to kill this man or let him lie under tribute forever?'

'I will not take his head without reason,' said the King of Erin. 'If he is willing to lie under tribute I will spare him. Oh, but I had not the luck to have the like of you for a son.' The boy drew the shoe from his right foot, showed that his little toe was missing, and told his story. The King of Erin knew his son then and rejoiced.

The White King was glad to escape, and promised to pay tribute without trouble. Wishing Gold was for turning back on the spot to his mother, but his father would not let him go till he had spent two or three days in Erin.

Next day the King had a great hunt, and when they were starting the Queen would not let Wishing Gold out of her sight.

'I like him so well,' said she, 'that I must have him with me while he stays in Erin.'

It was a delight to the King that the Queen was so fond of Wishing Gold, and he told him to stay with her that day. When the King and his men had gone the Queen went to the old druid and said:

'I will have the head taken off you unless you tell me how to put an end to Wishing Gold.'

'You are the worst woman I have ever seen,' said the druid. 'You wish to kill the boy who saved your husband and your kingdom.'

'I know well that unless I put him to death he will have the kingdom and my own sons will be without it.'

'Very well,' said the druid, 'I will tell you what to do. On the island where this boy was reared there are no banks; the place is flat and level. Take him now to the "Wonderful Banks" beyond this castle, and he will say that in truth they are wonderful. You can say then that they are no wonder to you; that your own sons leap down from them and then spring back to the top again. When he hears this he will try to do it himself, and he will leap to the bottom.'

The Queen did as the druid advised. Wishing Gold leaped down, and when he was springing back and was near the highest point of the bank she was at the brink and pushed him; he lost balance, rolled down and out into the sea. He was dashed from one wave to another till at last he was thrown in on an island. He rose and walked on to the middle of the island; there he found a house, and going in, saw a white trout broiling on a spit before a fire. 'I will eat that trout,' said he to himself. Then he thought, 'It is not mine, and I will not touch it.' He went outside to look about and saw hurrying towards him a terrible giant with five heads and five necks. The giant let such a laugh out of him that a man might have seen through his throat all that was in his body.

'You ugly beast,' said Wishing Gold, 'Why are you laughing like that?'

'I am glad to have your flesh to eat to-day; that's why I'm laughing,' said the giant.

'You haven't me yet,' said Wishing Gold.

The two then faced each other and began. Wishing Gold was better and far better than the giant, so he brought him to the ground, cut off the five heads, and sprang between them and the body.

'If you had not done that,' said one of the heads, 'I should be now on my body, and neither you nor all the world could put me off again.'

'I have done a good work,' said Wishing Gold. Then he went to the house, saying to himself, 'I will eat the trout,' but he thought and said: 'By all that I have been taught, there never is one in a place but there may be more.' So he went out to look, and saw coming a far greater giant, with five heads and five necks.

As soon as the giant came near they closed in combat, but Wishing Gold was stronger and far stronger than the giant, and he brought him to the ground, drew his sword, cut off the five heads, and sprang between the heads and the body.

'Only that you did that,' said a tongue in one of the heads, 'I should be now on my body and all the world could not put me off.'

Wishing Gold went in thinking to eat the trout and he ate it. As soon as he had eaten it he said to himself: 'There may be other giants in the place.' He went out and saw the third giant coming, and soon he was before him. They closed and fought in the way that they made hardness out of softness and softness out of hardness, and if people came from the lower to the upper world it was to look at the wonder of this battle that they came, but at last Wishing Gold was stronger and far stronger than the giant, so he put him to the ground, drew out his sword, cut the five heads off him, and sprang between the heads and the body.

'Only that you did that,' said one of the heads, 'I should be on my body now, and you, with all the world besides, would not put me off.'

'I've done a good deed,' said Wishing Gold. He went in then and sat down and said to himself: 'As these three were in one place their mother must be in it, too.' He rose and went out and soon saw a dreadful old hag coming. He and she fell to fighting and fought for three days and nights. Wishing Gold was doing no harm to the old hag, but the old hag was squeezing the heart out of him, until at last he was thinking: 'It is here my death is.'

That moment his mother's voice spoke behind him. 'Wishing Gold,' said she, 'think not that I am here to help you. If you were to lose your life ten times I would not help you, since you are so simple and keep not in mind what I've told you so often. It is a disgrace for a hero to fight three days and nights with an old woman. Often have I told you that all the world cannot do the old hag any harm while she has the long net on her.'

By hearing his mother's words Wishing Gold grew strong, thrust the point of his sword in between the net and body of the hag and cut the net to the top of her head, when she had no greater strength than another, and he killed her. He went home with the mother then, and she was teaching him exer cises and arts of all kinds.

The report had gone through the seven kingdoms that Wishing Gold was lost. 'It is my time now,' said the White King. 'No need for me to be lying under tribute to the King of Erin. I will give him battle while he has no assistance.'

'I will go, too,' said the Spotted King, 'I will put the King of Erin under tribute to myself and make him release the White King.'

The two Kings made ready a great fleet and set out for Erin. When they reached land the Spotted King sent his message to the King of Erin: 'You are to release the White King and pay tribute to me without trouble, or fight for the kingdom.' The King of Erin sent back this answer: 'I will fight to my death before I will give up my own and go under tribute to any man.'

The battle was to be next day. The King of Erin's three sons hid where no man could find them. Wishing Gold and his mother were sitting at home that evening.

'Very comfortable are we this night,' said the Queen of Lonesome Island, 'but it is not the same with your father in Erin; he has great trouble on him now.'

'What is the trouble that is on my father?' asked Wishing Gold.

'When you were thrown down the Wonderful Banks by the Queen of Erin word went through the seven kingdoms that you were lost, and now the White King and the Spotted King have gone with a great fleet to conquer your father and lay him under tribute, you must give him a day of assistance to-morrow.'

'Sure, my father has three sons older than I.'

'It was I who began all this trouble,' said the Queen, 'when I sent your father wandering through the waters and brought him here, so you must help him.'

'You know how they treated me when I was in Erin before,' said Wishing Gold.

'I do,' said the mother, 'and I will put you in the way now to save yourself from the like again. Here is a belt to tie around your body, and if man or woman wishes to harm you the belt will tighten and warn you.'

Wishing Gold mounted his steed and started for Erin.

Next morning the King of Erin was going out, with his sword under his arm, to face the enemy, when he saw a horseman riding in from the old sea.

'I may delay awhile,' thought the King, 'if it is to help me that horseman is coming I have time enough, and if it is against me he is, I am too soon.'

When the horseman came he attacked the two armies, and went through them as a hawk through small birds or a fox through hens; he made a heap of their heads, a heap of their bodies, and a heap of their weapons, till he gave sore death to them all except the two Kings; these he took to his father, one under each of his arms, and asked, 'Am I to kill these men or put them under tribute?'

'Put double tribute on the White King and single on the Spotted King.'

The two Kings promised to pay without trouble, and glad they were to escape, so they went away, each to his own place. Now Wishing Gold was for going home, but the father would not let him go without spending two or three days with himself.

Next day they had a great hunt, and Wishing Gold went to it, for the Queen dared not ask him to stay with her that turn. After all had gone she went to the old druid and said:

'I will put you to death unless you tell me how to kill Wishing Gold.'

'I will tell you how to do that,' said the druid. 'Kill a cock, take the blood in a bottle to bed with you and say that you'll die very soon, take some blood in your mouth, then spit it out, send a horseman to the mountain with a message to the King saying that he'll not have a sight of you in life unless he comes quickly; and it is not one horseman or two that you will send, but one after another. When the King comes in haste and asks what trouble is on you, this is what you will say, "I cannot live unless you get a cure for me." "What cure must I get?" he will ask. Say to him, "There is nothing in the world to cure me but a bottle of water from the well at the castle of the Queen of the Moving Wheel in the Eastern world, and Wishing Gold can bring it." The King will say then, "That cure is what you'll never get."'

The Queen did as the Druid advised and sent a horseman to the mountain to look for the King, and then a second, and then horseman after horseman. So the King hurried back and asked what was wrong with her.

'I am for death very soon,' said she. 'Is there anything to cure you?' 'Nothing can cure me but a bottle of water from the well of the Queen of the Moving Wheel in the eastern world.'

'How can that be got?' asked the King.

'Wishing Gold could bring it if you would send him.'

'He will never go one step for it at my command,' said the King. 'You have three sons of your own, and I will not spare them if they like to go.'

The three made ready and were for starting. Wishing Gold thought it a shame for him to stop behind, so the four went together. They travelled a very long time, till at length and at last they came to a house, and when they went in a fine woman met them. She caught Wishing Gold by the hand and gave him great welcome. She brought food and drink for the four, and an old man lying on a bed called:

'Daughter, dear, who is this man, and you giving him such a welcome?'

'Wishing Gold, the son of your sister and of the King of Erin. It is he that will give you the tidings, you have not heard the like of them for many a day.'

'Is it not bad, and too bad,' said the old man to Wishing Gold, 'that you are there and I here and I not able to go to you?'

'That is nothing,' said Wishing Gold, 'I will go to you.'

So Wishing Gold drew his chair to the bed, and of all questions that the old man asked the first was: 'Where are you going, and what brought you this way?'

Wishing Gold told all from the first to the last.

'I have seen,' said the old man, 'many a King and King's son passing this house to look for that water, but never a man of them have I seen going home. It is better for you to go back.'

'I will never go back; I will lose my life or get the water.'

When the eldest son of the King of Erin heard of the great danger before him, the soul left him, and he fell dead.

'Well,' said Wishing Gold, 'if we were few enough before this, we are fewer now, but if we get the water we will bring you to life.'

Then they put the body in a box with green leaves to keep it fresh. Next day the three travelled on till near night, when they saw a house in the distance. They hurried on. When they entered the house a fine woman caught Wishing Gold by the hand and gave him a warm welcome. She made ready a supper, and when they had eaten, an old man on a bed called out:

'How is it, daughter dear, that you have such welcome for this man?'

'It is not every one I would welcome in this way,' said she, 'this is the son of your sister and of the King of Erin; he will give news of the brother that you have not seen this long time.'

'It is bad that you are there and I here, and I without power to go to you,' said the old man to Wishing Gold.

'There is nothing wrong, except what is wrong with you, if you cannot come to me I can go to you,' said the King's son. He drew his chair to the bed-side, and they began to talk.

'Where are you going?' asked the old man. 'I suppose it is not to see me that you are here.'

Wishing Gold told him everything.

'I have seen,' said the old man, 'Kings and Kings' sons enough to cover half the world going for that water, but never a man of them returning. If you take my advice you'll not go a step beyond this, but turn home in good season.'

'I will not turn home,' said Wishing Gold. 'I will go till I have the water or lose my life.'

When the second son of the King of Erin heard of the danger and of all who had lost their lives he dropped dead.

'I thought,' said Wishing Gold, 'that we were enough as three, but we are fewer now. If I get the water, however, I will bring him to life.' They found a box, packed the body in it with green leaves, and away they went next morning.

The two travelled all day till near night, when they came to a house, and were met by a beautiful woman, who welcomed Wishing Gold greatly. She brought supper, and then an old man lying in the corner cried out:

'Daughter dear, how is this that you have such welcome for a stranger?'

'Oh, this is the son of your sister and of the King of Erin,' cried the woman.

'Oh, nephew, it is bad enough that you are there, and I without power to go to you.'

'There is nothing wrong but what is wrong with you,' said Wishing Gold. 'I will go to you,' and he drew his chair to the bed. The two began to talk.

'What brought you here?' asked the old man. 'I suppose it was not the wish to see me, though it would be no wonder if it was, and you my sister's son.'

'It was not,' said Wishing Gold. 'I am on my way to the kingdom of the Moving Wheel to get a bottle of water for the Queen of Erin.'

'I have seen many a King and King's son and champion going for that water, but not a man of them has ever come back. That is a terrible place!

Between this and the castle of the Moving Wheel are three bridges on the Queen's land, guarded by three dogs of hers, and their mouths open so widely that you would think they could swallow the world. But as you have come this far, and as you are a son born for luck, you may get the water. The Queen sleeps only once in seven years, and then she sleeps for a day and a year; when ready to sleep she raises her castle to the sky. When she is sleeping everything belonging to her, all her servants and guards are sleeping as well, though you would think they were awake, for all have their eyes open. If you cross the bridges, the greatest wall in the world is between them and the well, a wall with standing spears on top of it. But if you are such a champion as you seem, you may clear the wall. But near the four corners of the wall are four cats, and the sight of these is enough to frighten any man. Each cat has a poison tail on her, and each has poison teeth, and eyes open and staring, as if to spring at you in an instant. If you pass the cats without trouble you will get the water. When you have lifted the water from the well you will see a tree in the middle of the garden, and on the tree three red apples, a large, a middle sized, and a small one; pick the three apples and throw the largest one up to the sky, hit the castle and you will bring it a third of the way toward the earth, throw the middle-sized apple and bring it another third; catch the apple each time before it reaches the ground and put it in your pocket. Throw the small one and the castle will come to the earth. After that, unless you make a leap and catch the wheel at the corner, and keep it steady till the castle is settled, it will never stop moving; then go to the kitchen door where there is a cart load of keys; strive to find the key of the hall door; you may not find the right key for a day and a year, and you may find it in a minute.'

When the third son of the King of Erin heard this he fell dead from terror.

'I see,' said Wishing Gold, 'I am worse off now, for I am alone.'

Next morning he washed his face and hands and started on; he travelled till he came to the first bridge. The terrible dog was there, with bared teeth and eyes staring, as if ready to spring.

'A bird could not fly through the air and escape that dog,' thought Wishing Gold, 'but I will pass or lose my life.'

He went forward warily, crossed the bridge without trouble, for the dog was asleep; he passed the other two bridges in the same way, and cleared the wall at one bound, though it would be enough for a bird to fly over it, and sharp spears standing straight from the top. Wishing Gold was now in the garden; he walked up to the wall, watched the cats carefully, found them asleep, filled the three bottles with water, and set them aside. He went then to the middle of the garden, took the three apples from the tree, threw up the largest and struck the castle in the clouds; the castle came down one-third of the distance. He caught the apple, put it in his pocket, then threw the middle-sized one, and the castle came down the second third; threw the smallest apple and the castle came to the earth. Wishing Gold sprang at the wheel and kept it still till the castle was firm. He went next to the hall door, looked at the great pile of keys, and said to himself: 'I might be here all my life before I could hit on the right key, but I have often heard my mother say that the key of the hall is the biggest of all.'

He picked out the biggest key and tried it, the door opened at the first

91

turn. In the door of every room he found the key in the lock from that out. He opened all the doors in the castle and came to the room where the Queen of the Moving Wheel was asleep. he wrote on a piece of paper that the son of the King of Erin had visited her while she was sleeping and left this paper in her bosom. He came out then, locked all the doors behind him, threw the small apple at the castle, the castle rose in the air one-third of the distance; he threw the middle-sized apple, it rose another third; then the largest apple, and the castle went far into the clouds, where it had been before. He caught each apple as it came down and put them on the tree where he had found them, took the bottles, cleared the wall, crossed the three bridges and came to the third old man, his uncle, who was lying in bed, rubbed him with the water, and left him as young as a boy of fifteen; rubbed the youngest son of the King of Erin, and he came to life.

The two travelled on then till they came to the house of the second old man, rubbed him and he became as if fifteen years old; rubbed some on the second son of the King of Erin and he came to life.

The three travelled on till they came to the third old man, rubbed him with the water, made him young, rubbed the eldest son of the King of Erin; he came to life and the four travelled on.

While they were walking, Wishing Gold in front, the three, who were a little behind, said among themselves: 'Wishing Gold will tell of all that has happened; it would be better to kill him and take the water ourselves.'

The belt of warning began to tighten that moment.

'I know,' said Wishing Gold to the three, 'what you would like, and I will tell you what I will do. I will give you the water; take it home. I will go my own road, to my mother, and never be seen again in Erin. If I give you the water and go it is not because I am in dread of you, for I could kill a hundred like you.'

He gave them the water. They went home, and he went to Lonesome Island. When they reached the castle the King was outside watching.

'Where is Wishing Gold?' asked he.

'It matters not where he is,' said they; 'when he saw what work was before him he fell dead from fright. There was no good in him.'

'That is not true,' said the father. 'Wishing Gold did the whole work and was killed. You stood back until all was over, and that is why you are here.'

They would not confess. When the Queen of Erin heard that Wishing Gold was dead, she had no need of the water. She sprang out of bed, as well as ever.

Wishing Gold and his mother were exercising for a day and a year, and Wishing Gold was so active and skilful that in place of his mother driving him through the rooms he was driving her, and she had as much as she could do to save herself. But one night, as they sat by the fire, she said:

'We are very comfortable here, but there will be need of you in Erin to-morrow early.'

'I will never go to Erin! I have had my fill of that country.'

'No matter, you must go this time. When the Queen of the Moving Wheel woke in her castle she saw before her a child three months old. She sprang out of bed. The line you wrote and left with her fell to the floor. She read it

Wishing Gold prepares to lower the castle by throwing the apples

and is raging with anger. She has come now to your father's castle in Erin to destroy the kingdom or take the head off that son of the King of Erin who entered the castle while she was asleep. She has challenged the King's eldest son to face her at midday to-morrow. She will know that he is not the man; she will destroy him and his two brothers, and then your father and his kingdom, unless you stand before her. I will tell you what to do. She is such a champion that no one in the world is safe from her, but if you can be outside her tent in the morning before she rises, and have the first blow on the pole of combat which is there, and if you defend yourself from her first and second blow, I will save you from the third.'

Wishing Gold took his best weapons, and next morning early was in Erin outside the tent of the Queen of the Moving Wheel and had the first blow on the pole of combat. She made one spring out of bed and shouted:

'Who is this who has dared to strike a blow before my tent?'

'Your master,' said Wishing Gold.

'You will know who is master when I am before you,' replied she.

The Queen took her arms, came out, rose from above him in the air, and came down. He defended himself from the crown of his head to the soles of his feet, and saved himself from her first blow.

'Good champion,' said she, 'this is what no one in the world could do before you. But if you saved yourself from the first you will not the second time.'

She rose above again, and as she came down he defended himself from the crown of his head to the soles of his feet, and saved himself the second time.

'Good champion,' said she, 'this is a thing which I thought no one in the world could do, but I will finish you now.'

'Wishing Gold!' cried the Queen of Lonesome Island, from behind, 'I would not spare the mother of my child, if the mother of my child would not spare me.'

'How can Wishing Gold be the father of my child?' asked the Queen of the Moving Wheel. 'It was prophesied from of old that he was to be my husband, and it was for him that I was guarding myself. It was written on the paper that fell from my bosom that the son of the King of Erin came to my castle.'

'Of course, Wishing Gold is the son of the King of Erin, because I sent the King of Erin wandering so that he might come to my island, where I was waiting for him, for there is no good blood in the world but what is in the King of Erin.'

When the Queen of the Moving Wheel heard all this, she caught Wishing Gold by the hand, kissed him, and had great welcome for him.

All went then to the castle of the King of Erin, and Wishing Gold and the Queen of the Moving Wheel were married. Wishing Gold was giving presents to every one in the castle, and the Queen of Erin, who was anxious, cried:

'Will you leave me without any gift?'

'I have not given your gift to any one yet,' said Wishing Gold.

He drew out a beautiful ring, the loveliest ever seen, and gave it to her.

She was delighted, and put it on her finger. The ring began to tighten.

'Wishing Gold,' said she, 'I fear that your gift is not good.'

'My gift is a true one,' said he.

'Wishing Gold, take the ring from my finger.'

'The whole world could not take off the ring till you tell me the truth,' said Wishing Gold. 'The ring will have the finger off your hand and the head off your body unless you tell me who is the father of your eldest son.'

'Who is his father, but the King of Erin?'

'There is not a drop of the King's blood in his body.'

'Wishing Gold, take off the ring!' cried the Queen.

'The whole world could not take it off till you tell the truth, for 'tis a true gift.'

'Well,' said the Queen, 'the King and I had no children. I was in dread that the crown would be lost. The father of my eldest son is the King's pig stick-er.'

'So I believe,' said Wishing Gold. 'It is little good that is in him.'

'Take the ring off my finger,' cried the Queen.

'Not till you tell me who is the father of your second son.'

'The King's gardener.'

'I believe that, too,' said Wishing Gold. 'He was not much better than the eldest.'

'Take the ring off my finger,' cried the Queen.

'Not till you tell me who is the father of your youngest son.'

'The King's driver.'

'I see,' said Wishing Gold, 'whatever blood was in them was in the last.'

When the King of Erin heard all this he was raging, and said: 'I will have them all burned to ashes.'

'Do not burn them,' said Wishing Gold, 'leave them.'

The King of Erin married the Queen of Lonesome Island then, and went to live in her castle. Wishing Gold and his Queen went to the kingdom of the Moving Wheel and lived there all their lives.

NOTES

Source of tale: Jeremiah Curtin, *Irish Folk Tales*, Dublin: Talbot Press, 1944.

This is another classic story, containing all the essential ingredients of the wonder tale, including the hero who is born from a contrived meeting with a mortal and a faery woman – in this case the Queen of Lonesome Island whom we first met in 'Coldfeet' (see pages 14–23) – the successive battles with giants and then with their haglike mother (it seems that every story has three giants, each more fierce than the one before, who have a hag for a mother), and the final recognition of the hero as the rightful heir to the King of Erin. Here, however, there are some intriguing details which should not go unnoticed. The training which takes place between the hero, Wishing Gold, and his mother reflects not only the training of many heroes by women warriors – the prime example being Cuchulainn's period

95

of warrior-training by the woman-warrior Scathach – but also the general tradition of women being as active in battle as their menfolk. Then there is the curious detail of the net which covers the old woman whom Wishing Gold must fight. Only when this is cut off is he able to kill her. This, I believe, relates to the idea of hair containing the power of an individual. The hag's protection is her hair, woven like a net around her; once Wishing Gold has pierced it, she becomes weak. The hero's name marks him out as a type of solar hero, helped to achieve his apogee by a series of assistants. Once again, these are a number of old men, each one older than the last; but here they are the brothers of the Queen of Lonesome Island, and each one is so weakened by age and infirmity that they cannot get out of bed. I find myself thinking of the wounded Grail King every time Wishing Gold encounters one of them, for he too is unable to rise from his bed, and is eventually cured by a simple youth with a magical vessel (the Grail). This again goes to indicate a fascinating relationship between these folk-tales and the high romantic works of the Arthurian tradition.

The description of the floating castle is also reminiscent both of the revolving castle found in several Grail texts and of the 'four-cornered castle, three times revolving', encountered by Arthur and his warriors in the ninth-century poem *Prieddeu Annwn*, which describes a raid on the otherworld. This sequence, in particular, also bears a remarkable resemblance to the thirteenth-century German romance of Gawain called *Diu Crone* ('The Crown'). Here, like Wishing Gold, the hero enters a revolving castle where he finds a woman seated on a revolving wheel who turns rapidly from dark to light and back again as the wheel turns. Although this does not happen in the story given here, the similarity is sufficient to suggest that these may derive from a common source. In the Gawain romance the figure is representative of both Dame Fortune, who spins the wheel of life, and Lady Sovereignty, who bestows the magical power of the land upon her chosen favourites. Each and every one of the encounters experienced by Wishing Gold – as with so many of these stories – is a stage in an initiatory pattern which results in his being accepted by his natural father and otherworldly mother as the rightful inheritor of their combined power and sovereignty.

THE SHEE AN GANNON AND THE GRUAGACH GAIRE

HE SHEE AN GANNON was born in the morning, named at noon, and went in the evening to ask his daughter of the king of Erin.

'I will give you my daughter in marriage,' said the king of Erin; 'you won't get her, though, unless you go and bring me back the tidings that I want, and tell me what it is that put a stop to the laughing of the Gruagach Gaire, who before this laughed always, and laughed so loud that the whole world heard him. There are twelve iron spikes out here in the garden behind my castle. on eleven of the spikes are the heads of kings' sons who came seeking my daughter in marriage, and all of them went away to get the knowledge I wanted. Not one was able to get it and tell me what stopped the Gruagach Gaire from laughing. I took the heads off them all when they came back without the tidings for which they went, and I'm greatly in dread that your head'll be on the twelfth spike, for I'll do the same to you that I did to the eleven kings' sons unless you tell what put a stop to the laughing of the Gruagach.'

The Shee an Gannon made no answer, but left the king and pushed away to know could he find why the Gruagach was silent.

He took a glen at a step, a hill at a leap, and travelled all day till evening. Then he came to a house. The master of the house asked him what sort was he, and he said: 'A young man looking for hire.'

'Well,' said the master of the house, 'I was going to-morrow to look for a man to mind my cows. If you'll work for me, you'll have a good place, the best food a man could have to eat in this world, and a soft bed to lie on.'

The Shee an Gannon took service, and ate his supper. Then the master of the house said: 'I am the Gruagach Gaire; now that you are my man and have eaten your supper, you'll have a bed of silk to sleep on.'

Next morning after breakfast the Gruagach said to the Shee an Gannon: 'Go out now and loosen my five golden cows and my bull without horns, and drive them to pasture; but when you have them out on the grass, be careful you don't let them go near the land of the giant.'

The new cowboy drove the cattle to pasture, and when near the land of the giant, he saw it was covered with woods and surrounded by a high wall. He went up, put his back against the wall, and threw in a stretch of it; then he went inside and threw out another great stretch of the wall, and put the five golden cows and the bull without horns on the land of the giant.

Then he climbed a tree, ate the sweet apples himself, and threw the sour ones down to the cattle of the Gruagach Gaire.

Soon a great crashing was heard in the woods, – the noise of young trees bending, and old trees breaking. The cowboy looked around, and saw a five-headed giant pushing through the trees; and soon he was before him.

'Poor miserable creature!' said the giant; 'but weren't you impudent to come to my land and trouble me in this way? You're too big for one bite, and too small for two. I don't know what to do but tear you to pieces.'

'You nasty brute,' said the cowboy, coming down to him from the tree, ''tis little I care for you;' and then they went at each other. So great was the noise between them that there was nothing in the world but what was looking on and listening to the combat.

They fought till late in the afternoon, when the giant was getting the upper hand; and then the cowboy thought that if the giant should kill him, his father and mother would never find him or set eyes on him again, and he would never get the daughter of the king of Erin. The heart in his body grew strong at this thought. He sprang on the giant, and with the first squeeze and thrust he put him to his knees in the hard ground, with the second thrust to his waist, and with the third to his shoulders.

'I have you at last; you're done for now!' said the cowboy. Then he took out his knife, cut the five heads off the giant, and when he had them off he cut out the tongues and threw the heads over the wall.

Then he put the tongues in his pocket and drove home the cattle. That evening the Gruagach couldn't find vessels enough in all his place to hold the milk of the five golden cows.

After supper the cowboy would give no talk to his master, but kept his mind to himself, and went to the bed of silk to sleep.

Next morning after breakfast the cowboy drove out his cattle, and going on farther than the day before, stopped at a high wall. He put his back to the wall, threw in a long stretch of it, then went in and threw out another long stretch of it.

After that he put the five golden cows and the bull without horns on the land, and going up on a tree, ate sweet apples himself, and threw down the sour ones to the cattle.

Now the son of the king of Tisean set out from the king of Erin on the same errand, after asking for his daughter; and as soon as the cowboy drove in his cattle on the second day, he came along by the giant's land, found the five heads of the giant thrown out by the cowboy the day before, and picking them up, ran off to the king of Erin and put them down before him.

'Oh, you have done good work!' said the king. 'You have won one third of my daughter.'

Soon after the cowboy had begun to eat sweet apples, and the son of the king of Tisean had run off with the five heads, there came a great noise of

The cowboy prepares to cut the tongues out of the heads of the five-headed giant

young trees bending, and old trees breaking, and presently the cowboy saw a giant larger than the one he had killed the day before.

'You miserable little wretch!' cried the giant; 'what brings you here on my land?'

'You wicked brute!' said the cowboy, 'I don't care for you;' and slipping down from the tree, he fell upon the giant.

The fight was fiercer than his first one; but towards evening, when he was growing faint, the cowboy remembered that if he should fall, neither his father nor mother would see him again, and he would never get the daughter of the king of Erin.

This thought gave him strength; and jumping up, he caught the giant, put him with one thrust to his knees in the hard earth, with a second to his waist, with a third to his shoulders, and then swept the five heads off him and threw them over the wall, after he had cut out the tongues and put them in his pocket.

Leaving the body of the giant, the cowboy drove home the cattle, and the Gruagach had still greater trouble in finding vessels for the milk of the five golden cows.

After supper the cowboy said not a word, but went to sleep.

Next morning he drove the cattle still farther, and came to green woods and a strong wall. Putting his back to the wall, he threw in a great piece of it, and going in, threw out another piece. Then he drove the five golden cows and the bull without horns to the land inside, ate sweet apples himself, and threw down sour ones to the cattle.

The son of the king of Tisean came and carried off the heads as on the day before.

Presently a third giant came crashing through the woods, and a battle followed more terrible than the other two.

Towards evening the giant was gaining the upper hand, and the cowboy, growing weak, would have been killed; but the thought of his parents and the daughter of the king of Erin gave him strength, and he swept the five heads off the giant, and threw them over the wall after he had put the tongues in his pocket.

Then the cowboy drove home his cattle; and the Gruagach didn't know what to do with the milk of the five golden cows, there was so much of it.

But when the cowboy was on the way home with the cattle, the son of the king of Tisean came, took the five heads of the giant, and hurried to the king of Erin.

'You have won my daughter now,' said the king of Erin when he saw the heads; 'but you'll not get her unless you tell me what stops the Gruagach Gaire from laughing.'

On the fourth morning the cowboy rose before his master, and the first words he said to the Gruagach were:

'What keeps you from laughing, you who used to laugh so loud that the whole world heard you?'

'I'm sorry,' said the Gruagach, 'that the daughter of the king of Erin sent you here.'

100 | 'If you don't tell me of your own will, I'll make you tell me,' said the cow-

boy; and he put a face on himself that was terrible to look at, and running through the house like a madman, could find nothing that would give pain enough to the Gruagach but some ropes made of untanned sheepskin hanging on the wall.

He took these down, caught the Gruagach, fastened his two hands behind him, and tied his feet so that his little toes were whispering to his ears. When he was in this state the Gruagach said: 'I'll tell you what stopped my laughing if you set me free.'

So the cowboy unbound him, the two sat down together, and the Gruagach said: -

'I lived in this castle here with my twelve sons. We ate, drank, played cards, and enjoyed ourselves, till one day when my sons and I were playing, a wizard hare came rushing in, jumped on our table, defiled it, and ran away.

'On another day he came again; but if he did, we were ready for him, my twelve sons and myself. As soon as he defiled our table and ran off, we made after him, and followed him till nightfall, when he went into a glen. We saw a light before us. I ran on, and came to a house with a great apartment, where there was a man with twelve daughters, and the hare was tied to the side of the room near the women.

'There was a large pot over the fire in the room, and a great stork boiling in the pot. The man of the house said to me: "There are bundles of rushes at the end of the room, go there and sit down with your men!"

'He went into the next room and brought out two pikes, one of wood, the other of iron, and asked me which of the pikes would I take. I said, "I'll take the iron one;" for I thought in my heart that if an attack should come on me, I could defend myself better with the iron than the wooden pike.

'The man of the house gave me the iron pike, and the first chance of taking what I could out of the pot on the point of the pike. I got but a small piece of the stork, and the man of the house took all the rest on his wooden pike. We had to fast that night; and when the man and his twelve daughters ate the flesh of the stork, they hurled the bare bones in the faces of my sons and myself.

'We had to stop all night that way, beaten on the faces by the bones of the stork.

'Next morning, when we were going away, the man of the house asked me to stay a while; and going into the next room, he brought out twelve loops of iron and one of wood, and said to me: "Put the heads of your twelve sons into the iron loops, or your own head into the wooden one;" and I said: "I'll put the twelve heads of my sons in the iron loops, and keep my own out of the wooden one."

'He put the iron loops on the necks of my twelve sons, and put the wooden one on his own neck. Then he snapped the loops one after another, till he took the heads off my twelve sons and threw the heads and bodies out of the house; but he did nothing to hurt his own neck.

'When he had killed my sons he took hold of me and stripped the skin and flesh from the small of my back down, and when he had done that he took the skin of a black sheep that had been hanging on the wall for seven years and clapped it on my body in place of my own flesh and skin; and the sheepskin grew on me, and every year since then I shear myself, and every bit of wool I use for the stockings that I wear I clip off my own back.'

When he had said this, the Gruagach showed the cowboy his back covered with thick black wool.

After what he had seen and heard, the cowboy said: 'I know now why you don't laugh, and small blame to you. But does that hare come here still to spoil your table?'

'He does indeed,' said the Gruagach.

Both went to the table to play, and they were not long playing cards when the hare ran in; and before they could stop him he was on the table, and had put it in such a state that they could not play on it longer if they had wanted to.

But the cowboy made after the hare, and the Gruagach after the cowboy, and they ran as fast as ever their legs could carry them till nightfall; and when the hare was entering the castle where the twelve sons of the Gruagach were killed, the cowboy caught him by the two hind legs and dashed out his brains against the wall; and the skull of the hare was knocked into the chief room of the castle, and fell at the feet of the master of the place.

'Who has dared to interfere with my fighting pet?' screamed he.

'I,' said the cowboy; 'and if your pet had had manners, he might be alive now.'

The cowboy and the Gruagach stood by the fire. A stork was boiling in the pot, as when the Gruagach came the first time. The master of the house went into the next room and brought out an iron and a wooden pike, and asked the cowboy which would he choose.

'I'll take the wooden one,' said the cowboy; 'and you may keep the iron one for yourself.'

So he took the wooden one; and going to the pot, brought out on the pike all the stork except a small bite, and he and the Gruagach fell to eating, and they were eating the flesh of the stork all night. The cowboy and the Gruagach were at home in the place that time.

In the morning the master of the house went into the next room, took down the twelve iron loops with a wooden one, brought them out, and asked the cowboy which would he take, the twelve iron or the one wooden loop.

'What could I do with the twelve iron ones for myself or my master? I'll take the wooden one.'

He put it on, and taking the twelve iron loops, put them on the necks of the twelve daughters of the house, then snapped the twelve heads off them, and turning to their father, said: 'I'll do the same thing to you unless you bring the twelve sons of my master to life, and make them as well and strong as when you took their heads.'

The master of the house went out and brought the twelve to life again; and when the Gruagach saw all his sons alive and as well as ever, he let a laugh out of himself, and all the Eastern world heard the laugh.

Then the cowboy said to the Gruagach: 'It's a bad thing you have done to me, for the daughter of the king of Erin will be married the day after your laugh is heard.'

'Oh! then we must be there in time,' said the Gruagach; and they all made away from the place as fast as ever they could, the cowboy, the Gruagach, and his twelve sons.

On the road they came to a woman who was crying very hard.

'What is your trouble?' asked the cowboy.

'You need have no care,' said she, 'for I will not tell you.'

'You must tell me,' said he, 'for I'll help you out of it.'

'Well,' said the woman, 'I have three sons, and they used to play hurley with the three sons of the king of the Sasenach, and they were more than a match for the king's sons. And it was the rule that the winning side should give three wallops of their hurleys to the other side; and my sons were winning every game, and gave such a beating to the king's sons that they complained to their father, and the king carried away my sons to London, and he is going to hang them there to-day.'

'I'll bring them here this minute,' said the cowboy.

'You have no time,' said the Gruagach.

'Have you tobacco and a pipe?' asked the cowboy of the Gruagach.

'I have not,' said he.

'Well, I have,' said the cowboy; and putting his hand in his pocket, he took out tobacco and a pipe, gave them to the Gruagach, and said: 'I'll be in London and back before you can put tobacco in this pipe and light it.'

He disappeared, was back from London with the three boys all safe and well, and gave them to their mother before the Gruagach could get a taste of smoke out of the pipe.

'Now come with us,' said the cowboy to the woman and her sons, 'to the wedding of the daughter of the king of Erin.'

They hurried on; and when within three miles of the king's castle there was such a throng of people that no one could go a step ahead. 'We must clear a road through this,' said the cowboy.

'We must indeed,' said the Gruagach; and at it they went, threw the people some on one side and some on the other, and soon they had an opening for themselves to the king's castle.

As they went in, the daughter of the king of Erin and the son of the king of Tisean were on their knees just going to be married. The cowboy drew his hand on the bridegroom, and gave a blow that sent him spinning till he stopped under a table at the other side of the room.

'What scoundrel struck that blow?' asked the king of Erin.

'It was I,' said the cowboy.

'What reason had you to strike the man who won my daughter?'

'It was I who won your daughter, not he; and if you don't believe me, the Gruagach Gaire is here himself. He'll tell you the whole story from beginning to end, and show you the tongues of the giants.'

So the Gruagach came up and told the king the whole story, how the Shee an Gannon had become his cowboy, had guarded the five golden cows and the bull without horns, cut off the heads of the five-headed giants, killed the wizard hare, and brought his own twelve sons to life. 'And then,' said the Gruagach, 'he is the only man in the whole world I have ever told why I stopped laughing, and the only one who has ever seen my fleece of wool.'

When the king of Erin heard what the Gruagach said, and saw the tongues of the giants fitted into the heads, he made the Shee an Gannon kneel down by his daughter, and they were married on the spot.

Then the son of the king of Tisean was thrown into prison, and the next day they put down a great fire, and the deceiver was burned to ashes.

The wedding lasted nine days, and the last day was better than the first.

NOTES

Source of tale: Jeremiah Curtin, *Myths and Folk Lore of Ireland*, Boston: Little, Brown and Co., 1890.

This is an unusual tale in that it actually has an otherworldly being for a hero. The Shee an Gannon (Fairy of the Gannon) is a prodigiously large and powerful character, as witness his summary dealing with the usual three giants, and unlike his human counterparts he needs no magical helpers to accomplish his curious mission – to find out why the Gruagach Gaire (laughing Gruagach) no longer laughs. The reason for his quest, to win the hand of the daughter of the King of Erin, is reminiscent of the quest undertaken by the Welsh hero Culhwch to win the hand of Olwen; but here the similarity ends.

The Gruagach is one of a number of such strange characters who populate the Irish traditional tales. The word literally means 'hairy one', from *gruag*, hair, and probably accounts for the story of how he came by his hairy pelt. Curtin, who collected this story, thought that the Gruagachs were more likely to be solar beings than many of the figures suggested by certain writers. Other commentators have concentrated on the wildman aspect of the Gruagach, his hairiness and tricky nature seeming to tie him in with the image of the wildman so beloved of medieval storytellers. These curious characters were believed to be representative of the natural state, but to be lesser beings than humans. In fact they are probably identifiable with the nature spirits who haunt the woods and waysides of the land.

The magical hare, however, is even more interesting. The hare was a sacred animal among the Celtic peoples, and was associated with prediction. Thus, before her great battles against the Roman armies, the Celtic queen Boudicca used to release a hare from beneath her cloak. Then, according to the way the hare ran, she was able to prognosticate the outcome of the ensuing battle. A wizard hare is thus doubly powerful, and its actions are indicative of both a Druidic and magical connection.

THE LEGEND OF LLYN-Y-FAN-FACH

HEN THE EVENTFUL STRUGGLE made by the Princes of South Wales to preserve the independence of their country was drawing to its close in the twelfth century, there lived at Blaensawdde near Llanddeusant, in Carmarthenshire, a widowed woman, the relict of a farmer who had fallen in those disastrous troubles.

The widow had an only son to bring up, and Providence smiled upon her, and despite her forlorn condition, her livestock had so increased in course of time that she could not well depasture them upon her farm, so she sent a portion of her cattle to graze on the adjoining Black Mountain, and their most favourite place was near the small lake called Llyn-y-Fan-Fach on the north-western side of the Carmarthenshire Fans.

The son grew up to manhood, and was generally sent by his mother to look after the cattle on the mountain. One day, in his peregrinations along the margin of the lake, to his great astonishment, he beheld, sitting on the unruffled surface of the water, a Lady; one of the most beautiful creatures that mortal eyes ever beheld, her hair flowed gracefully in ringlets over her shoulders, the tresses of which she arranged with a comb, whilst the glassy surface of her watery couch served for the purpose of a mirror, reflecting back her own image. Suddenly she beheld the young man standing on the brink of the lake, with his eyes rivetted on her, and unconsciously offering to herself the provision of barley bread and cheese with which he had been provided when he left home.

Bewildered by a feeling of love and admiration for the object before him, he continued to hold out his hand towards the lady, who imperceptibly glided near to him, but gently refused the offer of his provisions, saying:

Cras dy fara;
Nid hawdd fy nala.

Hard baked is thy bread!
'Tis not easy to catch me;

and immediately dived under the water, and disappeared, leaving the love-stricken youth to return home, a prey to disappointment and regret that he had been unable to make further acquaintance with one, in comparison with whom the whole of the fair maidens of Llandeusant and Myddfai, whom he had ever seen were as nothing.

On his return home the young man communicated to his mother the extraordinary vision he had beheld. She advised him to take some unbaked dough or 'toes' the next time in his pocket, as there must have been some spell connected with the hard baked bread, or *Bara cras*, which prevented his catching the lady.

Next morning, before the sun had gilded with its rays the peaks of the Fans, the young man was at the lake, not for the purpose of looking after his mother's cattle, but seeking for the same enchanting vision he had witnessed the day before; but all in vain did he anxiously strain his eyeballs and glance over the surface of the lake, as only the ripples occasioned by a stiff breeze met his view, and a cloud hung heavily on the summit of the Fan, which imparted an additional gloom to his already distracted mind.

Hours passed by, the wind was hushed, and the clouds which had enveloped the mountain had vanished into thin air, before the powerful beams of the sun, when the youth was startled by seeing some of his mother's cattle on the precipitous side of the acclivity, nearly on the opposite side of the lake. His duty impelled him to attempt to rescue them from their perilous position, for which purpose he was hastening away, when, to his inexpressible delight, the object of his search again appeared to him as before, and seemed much more beautiful than when he first beheld her. His hand was again held out to her, full of unbaked bread, which he offered with an urgent proffer of his heart also, and vows of eternal attachment. All of which were refused by her, saying:

Llaith dy fara!
Ti ni fynna.

Unbaked is thy bread!
I will not have thee.

But the smiles that played on her features as the lady vanished beneath the waters raised within the young man a hope that forbade him to despair by her refusal of him, and the recollection of which cheered him on his way home. his aged parent was made acquainted with his ill-success, and she suggested that his bread should next time be but slightly baked, as most likely to please the mysterious being, of whom he had become enamoured.

Impelled by an irresistible feeling, the youth left his mother's house early next morning, and with rapid steps he passed over the mountain. He was soon near the margin of the lake, and with all the impatience of an ardent lover did he wait with a feverish anxiety for the reappearance of the mysterious lady.

The sheep and goats browsed on the precipitous sides of the Fan; the cattle strayed amongst the rocks and large stones, some of which were occasionally loosened from their beds and suddenly rolled down into the lake; rain and sunshine alike came and passed away, but all were unheeded by the youth, so wrapped up was he in looking for the appearance of the lady.

The freshness of the early morning had disappeared before the sultry rays of the noon-day sun, which in its turn was fast verging towards the west as the evening was dying away and making room for the shades of night, and hope had well nigh abated of beholding once more the Lady of the Lake. The young man cast a sad and last farewell look over the waters, and, to his astonishment, beheld several cows walking along its surface. The sight of these animals caused hope to revive that they would be followed by another object far more pleasing; nor was he disappointed, for the maiden re-appeared, and to his enraptured sight, more lovelier than ever. She approached the land, and he rushed to meet her in the water. A smile encouraged him to seize her hand; neither did she refuse the moderately baked bread he offered her; and after some persuasion, she consented to become his bride, on condition that they should only live together until she received from him three blows without a cause,

Tri ergyd diachos.

Three causeless blows.

And if he ever should happen to strike her three such blows, she would leave him for ever. To such conditions he readily consented, and would have consented to any other stipulation, had it been proposed, as he was only intent on then securing such a lovely creature for his wife.

Thus the Lady of the Lake engaged to become the young man's wife, and having loosed her hand for a moment, she darted away and dived into the lake. His chagrin and grief were such that he determined to cast himself headlong into the deepest water, so as to end his life in the element that had contained in its unfathomed depths the only one for whom he cared to live on earth. As he was on the point of committing this rash act, there emerged out of the lake *two* most beautiful ladies, accompanied by a hoary-headed man of noble mien and extraordinary stature, but having otherwise all the force and strength of youth. This man addressed the almost bewildered youth in accents calculated to soothe his troubled mind, saying that as he proposed to marry one of his daughters, he consented to the union, provided the young man could distinguish which of the two ladies before him was the object of his affections. This was no easy task, as the maidens were such perfect counterparts of each other that it seemed quite impossible for him to choose his bride, and if perchance he fixed upon the wrong one, all would be for ever lost.

Whilst the young man narrowly scanned the two ladies, he could not perceive the least difference betwixt the two, and was almost giving up the task in despair, when one of them thrust her foot a slight degree forward. The motion, simple as it was, did not escape the observation of the youth, and he discovered a trifling variation in the mode with which their sandals were tied.

This at once put an end to the dilemma, for he, who had on previous occasions been so taken up with the general appearance of the Lady of the Lake, had also noticed the beauty of her feet and ankles, and on now recognizing the peculiarity of her shoe-tie he boldly took hold of her hand.

'Thou hast chosen rightly,' said her father, 'be to her a kind and faithful husband, and I will give her, as a dowry, as many sheep, cattle, goats, and horses, as she can count of each without heaving or drawing in her breath. But remember, that if you prove unkind to her at any time, and strike her three times without a cause, she shall return to me, and shall bring all her stock back with her.'

Such was the verbal marriage settlement, to which the young man gladly assented, and his bride was desired to count the number of sheep she was to have. She immediately adopted the mode of counting by *fives*, thus: – One, two, three, four, five – One, two, three, four, five; as many times as possible in rapid succession, till her breath was exhausted. The same process of reckoning had to determine the number of goats, cattle, and horses respectively; and in an instant the full number of each came out of the lake when called upon by the Father.

The young couple were then married, by what ceremony was not stated, and afterwards went to reside at a farm called Esgair Llaethdy, somewhat more than a mile from the village of Myddfai, where they lived in prosperity and happiness for several years, and became the parents of three sons, who were beautiful children.

Once upon a time there was a christening to take place in the neighbourhood, to which the parents were specially invited. When the day arrived, the wife appeared very reluctant to attend the christening, alleging that the distance was too great for her to walk. Her husband told her to fetch one of the horses which were grazing in an adjoining field. 'I will,' said she, 'if you will bring me my gloves which I left in the house.' He went to the house and returned with the gloves, and finding that she had not gone for the horse, jocularly slapped her shoulder with one of them, saying, 'go! go!' (*dos, dos*) when she reminded him of the understanding upon which she consented to marry him: – That he was not to strike her without a cause; and warned him to be more cautious for the future.

On another occasion, when they were together at a wedding, in the midst of the mirth and hilarity of the assembled guests, who had gathered together from all the surrounding country, she burst into tears and sobbed most pitifully. Her husband touched her on the shoulder and enquired the cause of her weeping: she said, 'Now people are entering into trouble, and your troubles are likely to commence, as you have the *second* time stricken me without a cause.'

Years passed by, and their children had grown up, and were particularly clever young men. In the midst of so many worldly blessings at home the husband almost forgot that there remained only *one* causeless blow to be given to destroy the whole of his prosperity. Still he was watchful lest any trivial occurrence should take place, which his wife must regard as a breach of their marriage contract. She told him, as her affection for him was unabated, to be careful that he would not, through some inadvertence, give the last and only blow, which, by an unalterable destiny, over which she had no control, would separate them forever.

It, however, so happened that one day they were at a funeral, where, in the midst of the mourning and grief at the house of the deceased, she appeared in the highest and gayest spirits, and indulged in immoderate fits of laughter, which so shocked her husband that he touched her, saying, 'Hush! hush! don't laugh.' She said that she laughed 'because people when they die go out of trouble,' and, rising up, she went out of the house, saying, 'The last blow has been struck, our marriage contract is broken, and at an end! Farewell!' Then she started off towards Esgair Llaethdy, where she called her cattle and other stock together, each by name. The cattle she called thus: –

> *'Mu wilfrech, Moelfrech,*
> *Mu olfrech, Gwynfrech,*
> *Pedair cae tonn-frech,*
> *Yr hen wynebwen.*
> *A'r las Geigen,*
> *Gyda'r Tarw Gwyn*
> *O lys y Brenin;*
> *A'r llo du bach,*
> *Sydd ar y bach,*
> *Dere dithau, yn iach adre!*

> Brindled cow, white speckled,
> Spotted cow, bold freckled,
> The four field sward mottled,
> The old white-faced,
> And the grey Geingen,
> With the white Bull,
> From the court of the King;
> And the little black calf
> Tho' suspended on the hook,
> Come thou also, quite well home!'

They all immediately obeyed the summons of their mistress, the 'little black calf,' although it had been slaughtered, became alive again, and walked off with the rest of the stock at the command of the Lady. This happened in the spring of the year, and there were four oxen ploughing in one of the fields, to these she cried,

> *Pedwar eidion glas*
> *Sydd ar y maes,*
> *Deuwch chwithau*
> *Yn iach adre.*

> The four grey oxen,
> That are on the field,
> Come you also
> Quite well home!

111

Away the whole of the livestock went with the Lady across Myddfai mountain, towards the lake from whence they came, a distance of above six miles, where they disappeared beneath its waters, leaving no trace behind except a well marked furrow, which was made by the plough the oxen drew after them into the lake, and which remains to this day as a testimony of the truth of this story.

What became of the affrighted ploughman – whether he was left on the field when the oxen set off, or whether he followed them to the lake, has not been handed down to tradition; neither has the fate of the disconsolate and half-ruined husband been kept in remembrance. But of the sons it is stated that they often wandered about the lake and its vicinity, hoping that their mother might be permitted to visit the face of the earth once more, as they had been apprised of her mysterious origin, her first appearance to their father, and the untoward circumstances which so unhappily deprived them of her maternal care.

In one of their rambles, at a place near Dôl Howel, at the Mountain Gate, still called 'Llidiad y Meddygon,' The Physician's Gate, the mother appeared suddenly, and accosted her eldest son, whose name was Rhiwallon, and told him that his mission on earth was to be a benefactor to mankind by relieving them from pain and misery, through healing all manner of their diseases; for which purpose she furnished him with a bag full of medical prescriptions and instructions for the preservation of health. That by strict attention thereto, he and his family would become for many generations the most skilful physicians in the country. Then promising to meet him when her counsel was most needed, she vanished. But on several occasions she met her sons near the banks of the lake, and once she even accompanied them on their return home as far as the place still called 'Pant-y-Meddygon,' The Dingle of the Physicians, where she pointed out to them the various plants and herbs which grew in the dingle, and revealed to them their medicinal qualities or virtues; and the knowledge she imparted to them, together with their unrivalled skill, soon caused them to attain such celebrity that none ever possessed before them. And in order that their knowledge should not be lost, they wisely committed the same to writing, for the benefit of mankind throughout all ages.

NOTES

Source of tale: Sir John Rhys, 'A Legend of the Lady of the Lake', Y Cymmrodor, 1881.

This is one of the most famous Welsh folk-tales, largely because it has such an unusual history, dating from the distant past to the late nineteenth century. The great Celtic scholar Sir John Rhys, who included the story in an essay on the legend of the Lady of the Lake in 1861, copied it from the version collected by the author of a book on the Physicians of Myddfai, published by the Welsh MSS society in 1861. The source given there is one John Evans, a tiler of Myddfai, a David Williams, also of the area, who was nearly 90 at the time, and an Elizabeth Morgan, who was herself a native of the same village. This alone places the remembered lineage of the story at least as far back as the 1700s, though it is almost certainly much older. Rhys, in a note accompanying the text, notes that Rhiwallon and his sons became physicians to Rhys Gryg, lord of Llandovery and Dynefor, 'who gave them rank, lands, and privileges at Myddfai for their maintenance in the practice of their art and science, and the healing and benefit of those who should seek their help'. Thus those who could not afford to pay for medical advice were enabled to do so free of charge. Such a truly royal foundation could not fail to attract notice, and in a comparatively short time the physicians of Myddfai were famous. Rhys adds:

> Of the lands bestowed upon the *Meddygon*, there are two farms in Myddfai parish still called *Llwyn Ifan Feddyg*, the Grove of Evan the Physician, and *Llywn Meredydd Feddyg*, the Grove of Meredith the Physician. *Esgair Llaethdy*, mentioned in the legend, was formerly in the possession of the above descendants, and so was *Ty Newydd*, near Myddfai.

The last of the Physicians who practised at Myddfai appear to have been David Jones who died in 1719, and his son John who died in 1739, and who resided for some time at Llandovery.

Rees Williams of Myddfai is recorded as one of the *Meddygon*. His great grandson was the late Rice Williams M.D. of Aberystwyth, who died in 1842 aged 85, and appears to have been the last of the physicians descended from the mysterious Lady of Llyn-y-Fan, except perhaps for Dr C. Rice Williams who also lived at Aberystwyth. However, there may still be surviving members of the family alive today.

Such a detailed line of descent, which can be documented in this way, is rare indeed, but only goes to show that within many of these ancient traditional tales are to be found much that is as true as it is fascinating. The theme of the triple blow which results in a severing of any bond between the couple is extremely ancient and appears in numerous stories across the world.

THE EAGLE OF LOCH TREIG

ONCE UPON A TIME there was a big old Eagle dwelling in the midmost height of Loch Treig, where often her kind was. She was gray with age ever since she could remember, and she therefore imagined she was the oldest creature alive in her generation. But as a precaution, lest her contemporary might be surviving somewhere, she resolved to take a tour round the first opportunity she could get.

One year there came the very coldest Beltane Eve she had ever felt or seen, and she thought that would be a good excuse for her to put her secret intention into action; and in the early morning of that Beltane Day itself, rather than any other day, before the other birds had tasted water, she starts on her journey's quest.

Not a living creature that would meet her, provided only the hue of age were on it, that she would not ask, 'Didst ever see such a cold Beltane Eve as last night?' But none had seen it.

However, the day was but beginning, and she was keeping forward like this, without rest and without repose, till a kindly old Wren met her.

'Hail to the Wren, this yellow day of Beltane,' quoth she. 'Sawest thou ever a Beltane Eve so cold as last night?' But old as were the figure and fashion of the Wren, he was not aware that he had. He had no knowledge of a creature that was older than himself, but he heard that there had been for a long, long time an old Water-ousel at Bunruaidh, and if he were still living it was probable, if the like had come, that he had seen it; and he pointed out the road to her. She gave thanks to the Wren, and off she goes to the smithy at Bunruaidh.

She arrived, but nothing was before her save a cold ruin – common and gentle had departed, except the Water-ousel; and he himself was blind with age long since, and was after making a hole in the anvil a-cleaning his beak. She gave the Beltane greeting to the Ousel, and she told the reason of her journey.

'Sawest thou ever,' said she, 'Beltane Eve so cold as last night?'

The Water-ousel gave a piteous shrug, and said he had never seen it, and
had not heard mention of the like; but that there had been an old Stag
frequenting Choill Innse for ages, there was no knowing since when, and that
his bristles had been grizzled with age ever since he himself could remember
being a little fledgling winging among the bushes.

'It was a frequent practice with him time after time since then,' said he,
'to come over for a ceilidh with me to put past the long winter's night, and to
give me news of the state of the country; but that has ceased. The last journey
he was over here, age was lying so heavily on him that I am afraid he has not
the power to move very far. We spent so long in each other's neighbourhood
that I take delight, as you can understand, in his old belling, hoarse as he is,

The big, old eagle of
Loch Treig

when I hear him in the dawn. He is the oldest creature who survives to-day, so far as my friends and acquaintances go; and if you call upon him when going past, tell him the reason of your journey, and that you have seen me; and if change has not come on him' (that is, if he is not dead), 'he will make you heartily welcome.'

He then recounted to her certain affairs that happened in the generation of the chiefs whom he remembered seeing – about the feats of his forefathers, and the fate of his family. When they were bidding each other good-morning, he prayed and pressed her to call on him the next time she would be going to Choill Innse; and she found the Stag crouched in the shelter of an old alder stump, and icicles on the nostrils of his nose.

She gave him the Beltane greeting, and told him the reason of her journey.

'Didst ever see,' said she, 'Beltane Eve so cold as last night?'

The Stag was so old that he 'let his antler fall on his shoulder-blade;' but he said very, very leisurely that he did not remember that he had ever seen one. She found him hospitable and courteous, and he inquired kindly about the blind Ousel. They then gave a short space to story-telling and genealogy, and the Eagle was about to claim the honour of age; but, when they were separating, the Stag said that there was a One-eyed Trout in the lochan of Coire na Ceanainn, with whom he had become acquainted when he was a young calf at his mother's foot, coming over Làirig-leacach from Béinn-a'-Bhric.

'The dimness of age was on him even then,' said he; 'and if thou hast time, it is worth thy while going to see him – he is fine at a crack.'

Thus it was that she started off again, and that she reached the lochan.

She drank the cup of acquaintance with the One-eyed Trout, and she told the reason of her journey.

'Didst ever see Beltane Eve so cold as last night?'

The Trout said that he had – one other night, and that it was so cold that although he was in the heat of his blood (that is, young and hot-blooded), and in the prime of his strength, he was obliged to begin to cut capers through the water to keep warmth in himself.

'And,' said he, 'one of the leaps that I took, I jump out of the water and strike my forehead against the dark stone yonder; but the bitterness of the frost was so intense, that before I could get myself back my eye stuck to the stone, and that left me blind of an eye to-day.'

When the Eagle heard that, she gave the deference of age to the Trout; and she returned to Aird-mheadhoin to tell her tale to the young brood.

They saw many a fair, sunny day after that; but, so long as she could move a wing, not a Beltane Day, hot or cold, went by that she did not go for a little while for a ceilidh with those excellent old folks – the Water-ousel, the Stag, and the Trout.

The old eagle speaks to the stag

NOTES

Source of tale: Winifred M. Parker, *Gaelic Fairy Tales*, Glasgow: Archibald Sinclair, 1908.

This story is a favourite one among Celtic storytellers, and variations of it can be found in both Ireland and Wales. In the Irish version it is the old blind Salmon of Asseroe who wins the name of oldest, but there he loses his eye, not on a stone but from having it pecked out by the Hawk of Achill. In Wales there is another story, remembered in an old poem, *The Dialogue of Arthur and the Eagle*, where the subject is not the search for the oldest animal, but an account of a human soul given the form of the eagle. This relates very clearly to the practice of shamanic journeying, where the shaman travels out of the body to the otherworld in search of wisdom or knowledge to bring back. Often he will travel in animal form or be assisted by an animal helper who is a spirit in this form. It is very clear from the story given here that this whole tale is an account of such a journey, and it is evident from the original names of the characters – 'antlered one' for the stag and 'the smith' for the ousel (blackbird) – that there is an underlying humanity about these creatures. Very possibly, as in Native American traditional tales, 'Crow' and 'Coyote' are also people who, while in possession of these names, partake of the nature of the creature.

The fact that the eagle sets out on her quest at Beltane Eve (30 April) is not without significance. This was a sacred feast-day among the Celts, a time to celebrate the beginning of the summer and seek the gifts of the otherworld, which was seen as being particularly close at this time. Thus the old eagle travels to find if anyone ever remembers a colder Beltane, and is sent onwards to the successively older creatures, until she finally meets the salmon, who was regarded as a repository of wisdom in Celtic tradition. This may be because of the great age which salmon attain, but a story which speaks of the salmon swimming in the otherworld Well of Segais, and eating the nuts which fall from the nine trees of wisdom which grow around it, may well offer a more likely explanation.

This story is, of course, related very closely to all those in which the hero is helped by a series of people or creatures, each of which is older than the former. See pages 14–23 in particular for examples of this theme.

THE LEECHING OF KAYN'S LEG

HERE WERE FIVE HUNDRED blind men, and five hundred deaf men, and five hundred limping men, and five hundred dumb men, and five hundred cripple men. The five hundred deaf men had five hundred wives, and the five hundred limping men had five hundred wives, and the five hundred dumb men had five hundred wives, and the five hundred cripple men had five hundred wives. Each five hundred of these had five hundred children and five hundred dogs. They were in the habit of going about in one band, and were called the Sturdy Strolling Beggarly Brotherhood. There was a knight in Erin called O'Cronicert, with whom they spent a day and a year; and they ate up all that he had, and made a poor man of him, till he had nothing left but an old tumble-down black house, and an old lame white horse. There was a king in Erin called Brian Boru; and O'Cronicert went to him for help. He cut a cudgel of grey oak on the outskirts of the wood, mounted the old lame white horse, and set off at speed through wood and over moss and rugged ground, till he reached the king's house. When he arrived he went on his knees to the king; and the king said to him, 'What is your news, O'Cronicert?'

'I have but poor news for you, king.'

'What poor news have you?' said the king.

'That I have had the Sturdy Strolling Beggarly Brotherhood for a day and a year, and they have eaten all that I had, and made a poor man of me,' said he.

'Well!' said the king, 'I am sorry for you; what do you want?'

'I want help,' said O'Cronicert; 'anything that you may be willing to give me.'

The king promised him a hundred cows. He went to the queen, and made his complaint to her, and she gave him another hundred. He went to the king's son, Murdoch Mac Brian, and he got another hundred from him. He got food and drink at the king's; and when he was going away he said, 'Now I am very much obliged to you. This will set me very well on my feet. After all that I have got there is another thing that I want.'

'What is it?' said the king.

'It is the lap-dog that is in and out after the queen that I wish for.'

'Ha!' said the king, 'it is your mightiness and pride that has caused the loss of your means; but if you become a good man you shall get this along with the rest.'

O'Cronicert bade the king good-bye, took the lap-dog, leapt on the back of the old lame white horse, and went off at speed through wood, and over moss and rugged ground. After he had gone some distance through the wood a roebuck leapt up and the lap-dog went after it. In a moment the deer started up as a woman behind O'Cronicert, the handsomest that eye had ever seen from the beginning of the universe till the end of eternity. She said to him, 'Call your dog off me.'

'I will do so if you promise to marry me,' said O'Cronicert.

'If you keep three vows that I shall lay upon you I will marry you,' said she.

'What vows are they?' said he.

'The first is that you do not go to ask your worldly king to a feast or a dinner without first letting me know,' said she.

'Hoch!' said O'Cronicert, 'do you think that I cannot keep that vow? I would never go to invite my worldly king without informing you that I was going to do so. It is easy to keep that vow.'

'You are likely to keep it!' said she.

'The second vow is,' said she, 'that you do not cast up to me in any company or meeting in which we shall be together, that you found me in the form of a deer.'

'Hoo!' said O'Cronicert, 'you need not to lay that vow upon me. I would keep it at any rate.'

'You are likely to keep it!' said she.

'The third vow is,' said she, 'that you do not leave me in the company of only one man while you go out.' It was agreed between them that she should marry him.

They reached the old tumble-down black house. Grass they cut in the clefts and ledges of the rocks; a bed they made and laid down. O'Cronicert's wakening from sleep was the lowing of cattle and the bleating of sheep and the neighing of mares, while he himself was in a bed of gold on wheels of silver, going from end to end of the Tower of Castle Town.

'I am sure that you are surprised,' said she.

'I am indeed,' said he.

'You are in your own room,' said she.

'In my own room,' said he. 'I never had such a room.'

'I know well that you never had,' said she; 'but you have it now. So long as you keep me you shall keep the room.'

He then rose, and put on his clothes, and went out. He took a look at the house when he went out; and it was a palace, the like of which he had never seen, and the king himself did not possess. He then took a walk round the farm; and he never saw so many cattle, sheep, and horses as were on it. He returned to the house, and said to his wife that the farm was being ruined by other people's cattle and sheep.

'It is not,' said she: 'your own cattle and sheep are on it.'

'I never had so many cattle and sheep,' said he.

'I know that,' said she; 'but so long as you keep me you shall keep them. There is no good wife whose tocher does not follow her.'

He was now in good circumstances, indeed wealthy. He had gold and silver, as well as cattle and sheep. He went about with his gun and dogs hunting every day, and was a great man. It occurred to him one day that he would go to invite the King of Erin to dinner, but he did not tell his wife that he was going. His first vow was now broken. He sped away to the King of Erin, and invited him and his great court to dinner. The King of Erin said to him, 'Do you intend to take away the cattle that I promised you?'

'Oh! no, King of Erin,' said O'Cronicert; 'I could give you as many today.'

'Ah!' said the king, 'how well you have got on since I saw you last!'

'I have indeed,' said O'Cronicert! 'I have fallen in with a rich wife who has plenty of gold and silver, and of cattle and sheep.'

'I am glad of that,' said the King of Erin.

O'Cronicert said, 'I shall feel much obliged if you will go with me to dinner, yourself and your great court.'

'We will do so willingly,' said the king.

They went with him on that same day. It did not occur to O'Cronicert how a dinner could be prepared for the king without his wife knowing that he was coming. When they were going on, and had reached the place where O'Cronicert had met the deer, he remembered that his vow was broken, and he said to the king, 'Excuse me; I am going on before to the house to tell that you are coming.'

The king said, 'We will send off one of the lads.'

'You will not,' said O'Cronicert; 'no lad will serve the purpose so well as myself.'

He set off to the house; and when he arrived his wife was diligently preparing dinner. He told her what he had done, and asked her pardon. 'I pardon you this time,' said she: 'I know what you have done as well as you do yourself. The first of your vows is broken.'

The king and his great court came to O'Cronicert's house; and the wife had everything ready for them as befitted a king and great people; every kind of drink and food. They spent two or three days and nights at dinner, eating and drinking. They were praising the dinner highly, and O'Cronicert himself was praising it; but his wife was not. O'Cronicert was angry that she was not praising it and he went and struck her in the mouth with his fist and knocked out two of her teeth. 'Why are you not praising the dinner like the others, you contemptible deer?' said he.

'I am not,' said she: 'I have seen my father's big dogs having a better dinner than you are giving to-night to the King of Erin and his court.'

O'Cronicert got into such a rage that he went outside of the door. He was not long standing there when a man came riding on a black horse, who in passing caught O'Cronicert by the collar of his coat, and took him up behind him: and they set off. The rider did not say a word to O'Cronicert. The horse was going so swiftly that O'Cronicert thought the wind would drive his head off. They arrived at a big, big palace, and came off the black horse. A stable-

121

man came out, and caught the horse, and took it in. It was with wine that he was cleaning the horse's feet. The rider of the black horse said to O'Cronicert, 'Taste the wine to see if it is better than the wine that you are giving to Brian Boru and his court to-night.'

O'Cronicert tasted the wine, and said, 'This is better wine.'

The rider of the black horse said, 'How unjust was the fist a little ago! The wind from your fist carried the two teeth to me.'

He then took him into that big, handsome, and noble house, and into a room that was full of gentlemen eating and drinking, and he seated him at the head of the table, and gave him wine to drink, and said to him, 'Taste that wine to see if it is better than the wine that you are giving to the King of Erin and his court to-night.'

'This is better wine,' said O'Cronicert.

'How unjust was the fist a little ago!' said the rider of the black horse.

When all was over the rider of the black horse said, 'Are you willing to return home now?'

'Yes,' said O'Cronicert, 'very willing.'

They then rose, and went to the stable: and the black horse was taken out; and they leaped on its back, and went away. The rider of the black horse said to O'Cronicert, after they had set off, 'Do you know who I am?'

'I do not,' said O'Cronicert.

'I am a brother-in-law of yours,' said the rider of the black horse; and though my sister is married to you there is not a king or knight in Erin who is a match for her. Two of your vows are now broken; and if you break the other vow you shall lose your wife and all that you possess.'

They arrived at O'Cronicert's house; and O'Cronicert said, 'I am ashamed to go in, as they do not know where I have been since night came.'

'Hoo!' said the rider, 'they have not missed you at all. There is so much conviviality among them, that they have not suspected that you have been anywhere. Here are the two teeth that you knocked out of the front of your wife's mouth. put them in their place, and they will be as strong as ever.'

'Come in with me,' said O'Cronicert to the rider of the black horse.

'I will not: I disdain to go in,' said the rider of the black horse.

The rider of the black horse bade O'Cronicert good-bye, and went away.

O'Cronicert went in; and his wife met him as she was busy waiting on the gentlemen. He asked her pardon, and put the two teeth in the front of her mouth, and they were as strong as ever. She said, 'Two of your vows are now broken.' No one took notice of him when he went in, or said 'Where have you been?' They spent the night in eating and drinking, and the whole of the next day.

In the evening the king said, 'I think that it is time for us to be going;' and all said that it was. O'Cronicert said, 'You will not go to-night. I am going to get up a dance. You will go to-morrow.'

'Let them go,' said his wife.

'I will not,' said he.

The dance was set a-going that night. They were playing away at dancing and music till they became warm and hot with perspiration. They were going out one after another to cool themselves at the side of the house. They all went out except O'Cronicert and his wife, and a man called Kayn Mac Loy. O'Cronicert himself went out, and left his wife and Kayn Mac Loy in the house, and when she saw that he had broken his third vow she gave a spring through a room, and became a big filly, and gave Kayn Mac Loy a kick with her foot, and broke his thigh in two. She gave another spring, and smashed the door and went away, and was seen no more. She took with her the Tower of Castle Town as an armful on her shoulder and a light burden on her back, and she left Kayn Mac Loy in the old tumble-down black house in a pool of rain-drip on the floor.

At daybreak next day poor O'Cronicert could only see the old house that he had before. Neither cattle nor sheep, nor any of the fine things that he had was to be seen. One awoke in the morning beside a bush, another beside a dyke, and another beside a ditch. The king only had the honour of having O'Cronicert's little hut over his head. As they were leaving, Murdoch Mac Brian remembered that he had left his own foster-brother Kayn Mac Loy behind, and said there should be no separation in life between them and that he would go back for him. He found Kayn in the old tumble-down black house, in the middle of the floor, in a pool of rain-water, with his leg broken; and he said the earth should make a nest in his sole and the sky a nest in his head if he did not find a man to cure Kayn's leg.

They told him that on the Isle of Innisturk was a herb that would heal him.

So Kayn Mac Loy was then borne away, and sent to the island, and he was supplied with as much food as would keep him for a month, and with two crutches on which he would be going out and in as he might desire. At last the food was spent, and he was destitute, and he had not found the herb. He was in the habit of going down to the shore, and gathering shell-fish, and eating it.

As he was one day on the shore, he saw a big, big man landing on the island, and he could see the earth and the sky between his legs. He set off with the crutches to try if he could get into the hut before the big man would come upon him. Despite his efforts, the big man was between him and the door, and said to him, 'Unless you deceive me, you are Kayn Mac Loy.'

Kayn Mac Loy said, 'I have never deceived a man: I am he.'

The big man said to him: 'Stretch out your leg, Kayn, till I put a salve of herbs and healing to it. Salve and binding herb and the poultice are cooling; the worm is channering. Pressure and haste hard bind me, for I must hear Mass in the great church at Rome, and be in Norway before I sleep.'

Kayn Mac Loy said: 'May it be no foot to Kayn or a foot to any one after one, or I be Kayn son of Loy, if I stretch out my foot for you to put a salve of herbs and healing on it, till you tell me why you have no church of your own in Norway, so as, as now, to be going to the great church of Rome to Rome to-morrow. Unless you deceive me you are Machkan-an-Athar, the son of the King of Lochlann.'

The big man said, 'I have never deceived any man: I am he. I am now going to tell you why we have not a church in Lochlann. Seven masons came to build a church, and they and my father were bargaining about the building of it. The agreement that the masons wanted was that my mother and sister would go to see the interior of the church when it would be finished. My father was glad to get the church built so cheaply. They agreed accord-

123

ingly; and the masons went in the morning to the place where the church was to be built. My father pointed out the spot for the foundation. They began to build in the morning, and the church was finished before the evening. When it was finished they requested my mother and sister to go to see its interior. They had no sooner entered than the doors were shut; and the church went away into the skies in the form of a tuft of mist.

'Stretch out your leg, Kayn, till I put a salve of herbs and healing to it. Salve and binding herb and the poultice are cooling; the worm is chamering. Pressure and haste hard bind me, for I must hear Mass in the great church at Rome, and be in Norway before I sleep.'

Kayn Mac Loy said: 'May it be no foot to Kayn or a foot to any one after one, or I be Kayn son of Loy, if I stretch out my foot for you to put a salve of herbs and healing on it, till you tell me if you heard what befell your mother and sister.'

'Ah!' said the big man, 'the mischief is upon you; that tale is long to tell; but I will tell you a short tale about the matter. On the day on which they were working at the church I was away in the hill hunting game; and when I came home in the evening my brother told me what had happened, namely, that my mother and sister had gone away in the form of a tuft of mist. I became so cross and angry that I resolved to destroy the world till I should find out where my mother and sister were. My brother said to me that I was a fool to think of such a thing. "I'll tell you," said he, "what you'll do. You will first go to try to find out where they are. When you find out where they are you will demand them peaceably, and if you do not get them peaceably you will fight for them."

'I took my brother's advice, and prepared a ship to set off with. I set off alone, and embraced the ocean. I was overtaken by a great mist, and I came upon an island, and there was a large number of ships at anchor near it; I went in amongst them, and went ashore. I saw there a big, big woman reaping rushes; and when she would raise her head she would throw her right breast over her shoulder and when she would bend it would fall down between her legs. I came once behind her, and caught the breast with my mouth, and said to her, "You are yourself witness, woman, that I am the foster-son of your right breast." "I perceive that, great hero," said the old woman, "but my advice to you is to leave this island as fast as you can." "Why?" said I. "There is a big giant in the cave up there," said she, "and every one of the ships that you see he has taken in from the ocean with his breath, and he has killed and eaten the men. He is asleep at present, and when he wakens he will have you in a similar manner. A large iron door and an oak door are on the cave. When the giant draws in his breath the doors open, and when he emits his breath the doors shut; and they are shut as fast as though seven small bars, and seven large bars, and seven locks were on them. So fast are they that seven crowbars could not force them open." I said to the old woman, "Is there any way of destroying him?" "I'll tell you," said she, "how it can be done. He has a weapon above the door that is called the short spear: and if you succeed in taking off his head with the first blow it will be well; but if you do not, the case will be worse than it was at first."

'I set off, and reached the cave, the two doors of which opened. The giant's breath drew me into the cave; and stools, chairs, and pots were by its action dashing against each other, and like to break my legs. The door shut when I went in, and was shut as fast as though seven small bars, and seven large bars, and seven locks were on it; and seven crowbars could not force it open; and I was a prisoner in the cave. The giant drew in his breath again, and the doors opened. I gave a look upwards, and saw the short spear, and laid hold of it. I drew the short spear, and I warrant you that I dealt him such a blow with it as did not require to be repeated; I swept the head off him. I took the head down to the old woman, who was reaping the rushes, and said to her, "There is the giant's head for you." The old woman said, "Brave man! I knew that you were a hero. This island had need of your coming to it to-day. Unless you deceive me, you are Mac Connachar son of the King of Lochlann." "I have never deceived a man. I am he," said I. "I am a soothsayer," said she, "and know the object of your journey. You are going in quest of your mother and sister." "Well," said I, "I am so far on the way if I only knew where to go for them." "I'll tell you where they are," said she; "they are in the kingdom of the Red Shield, and the King of the Red Shield is resolved to marry your mother, and his son is resolved to marry your sister. I'll tell you how the town is situated. A canal of seven times seven paces breadth surrounds it. On the canal there is a drawbridge, which is guarded during the day by two creatures that no weapon can pierce, as they are covered all over with scales, except two spots below the neck in which their death-wounds lie. Their names are Roar and Rustle. When night comes the bridge is raised, and the monsters sleep. A very high and big wall surrounds the king's palace."

'Stretch out your leg, Kayn, till I put a salve of herbs and healing to it. Salve and binding herb and the poultice are cooling; the worm is channering. Pressure and haste hard bind me, for I must hear Mass in the great church at Rome, and be in Norway before I sleep.'

Kayn Mac Loy said: 'May it be no foot to Kayn or a foot to any one after one, or I be Kayn son of Loy, if I stretch out my foot for you to put a salve of herbs and healing on it, till you tell me if you went farther in search of your mother and sister, or if you returned home, or what befell you.'

'Ah!' said the big man, 'the mischief is upon you; that tale is long to tell; but I will tell you another tale. I set off, and reached the big town of the Red Shield; and it was surrounded by a canal, as the old woman told me; and there was a drawbridge on the canal. It was night when I arrived, and the bridge was raised, and the monsters were asleep. I measured two feet before me and a foot behind me of the ground on which I was standing, and I sprang on the end of my spear and on my tiptoes, and reached the place where the monsters were asleep; and I drew the short spear, and I warrant you that I dealt them such a blow below the neck as did not require to be repeated. I took up the heads and hung them on one of the posts of the bridge. I then went on to the wall that surrounded the king's palace. This wall was so high that it was not easy for me to spring over it; and I set to work with the short spear, and dug a hole through it, and got in. I went to the door of the palace and knocked; and the doorkeeper called out, "Who is there?" "It is I," said I. My mother and sister recognised my speech; and my mother called, "Oh! it is my son; let him in." I then got in, and they rose to meet me with great joy.

I was supplied with food, drink, and a good bed. In the morning breakfast was set before us; and after it I said to my mother and sister that they had better make ready, and go with me. The King of the Red Shield said, "It shall not be so. I am resolved to marry your mother, and my son is resolved to marry your sister." "If you wish to marry my mother, and if your son wishes to marry my sister, let both of you accompany me to my home, and you shall get them there." The King of the Red Shield said, "So be it."

'We then set off, and came to where my ship was, went on board of it, and sailed home. When we were passing a place where a great battle was going on, I asked the King of the Red Shield what battle it was, and the cause of it. "Don't you know at all?" said the King of the Red Shield. "I do not," said I. The King of the Red Shield said, "That is the battle for the daughter of the King of the Great Universe, the most beautiful woman in the world; and whoever wins her by his heroism shall get her in marriage. Do you see yonder castle?" "I do," said I. "She is on the top of that castle, and sees from it the hero that wins her," said the King of the Red Shield. I requested to be put on shore, that I might win her by my swiftness and strength. They put me on shore; and I got a sight of her on the top of the castle. Having measured two feet behind me and a foot before me, I sprang on the end of my spear and on my tiptoes, and reached the top of the castle; and I caught the daughter of the King of the Universe in my arms and flung her over the castle. I was with her and intercepted her before she reached the ground, and I took her away on my shoulder, and set off to the shore as fast as I could, and delivered her to the King of the Red Shield to be put on board the ship. "Am I not the best warrior that ever sought you?" said I. "You can jump well," said she, "but I have not seen any of your prowess." I turned back to meet the warriors, and attacked them with the short spear, and did not leave a head on a neck of any of them. I then returned, and called to the King of the Red Shield to come in to the shore for me. Pretending not to hear me, he set the sails in order to return home with the daughter of the King of the Great Universe, and marry her. I measured two feet behind me and a foot before me, and sprang on the end of my spear and on my tiptoes and got on board the ship. I then said to the King of the Red Shield, "What were you going to do? Why did you not wait for me?" "Oh!" said the king, "I was only making the ship ready and setting the sails to her before going on shore for you. Do you know what I am thinking of?" "I do not," said I. "It is," said the King, "that I will return home with the daughter of the King of the Great Universe, and that you shall go home with your mother and sister." "That is not to be the way of it," said I. "She whom I have won by my prowess neither you nor any other shall get."

'The king had a red shield, and if he should get it on, no weapon could make an impression on him. He began to put on the red shield, and I struck him with the short spear in the middle of his body, and cut him in two, and threw him overboard. I then struck the son, and swept his head off, and threw him overboard.

'Stretch out your leg, Kayn, till I put a salve of herbs and healing to it. Salve and binding herb and the poultice are cooling; the worm is channering. Pressure and haste hard bind me, for I must hear Mass in the great church at Rome, and be in Norway before I sleep.'

The head of the
slain giant

127

Kayn Mac Loy said: 'May it be no foot to Kayn or a foot to any one after one, or I be Kayn son of Loy, if I stretch out my foot for you to put a salve of herbs and healing on it, till you tell me whether any search was made for the daughter of the King of the Universe.'

'Ah! the mischief is upon you,' said the big man; 'I will tell you another short tale. I came home with my mother and sister, and the daughter of the King of the Universe, and I married the daughter of the King of the Universe. The first son I had I named Machkan-na-skaya-jayrika (son of the red shield). Not long after this a hostile force came to enforce compensation for the King

of the Red Shield, and a hostile force came from the King of the Universe to enforce compensation for the daughter of the King of the Universe. I took the daughter of the King of the Universe with me on the one shoulder and Machkan-na-skaya-jayrika on the other, and I went on board the ship and set the sails to her, and I placed the ensign of the King of the Great Universe on the one mast, and that of the King of the Red Shield on the other, and I blew a trumpet, and passed through the midst of them, and I said to them that here was the man, and that if they were going to enforce their claims, this was the time. All the ships that were there chased me; and we set out on the expanse of ocean. My ship would be equalled in speed by but few. One day a thick dark mist came on, and they lost sight of me. It happened that I came to an island called The Wet Mantle. I built a hut there; and another son was born to me, and I called him Son of the Wet Mantle.

'I was a long time in that island; but there was enough of fruit, fish, and birds in it. My two sons had grown to be somewhat big. As I was one day out killing birds, I saw a big, big man coming towards the island, and I ran to try if I could get into the house before him. He met me, and caught me, and put me into a bog up to the armpits, and he went into the house, and took out on his shoulder the daughter of the King of the Universe, and passed close to me in order to irritate me the more. The saddest look that I ever gave or ever shall give was that I gave when I saw the daughter of the King of the Universe on the shoulder of another, and could not take her from him. The boys came out where I was; and I bade them bring me the short spear from the house. They dragged the short spear after them, and brought it to me; and I cut the ground around me with it till I got out.

'I was a long time in the Wet Mantle, even till my two sons grew to be big lads. They asked me one day if I had any thought of going to seek their mother. I told them that I was waiting till they were stronger, and that they should then go with me. They said that they were ready to go with me at any time. I said to them that we had better get the ship ready, and go. They said, "Let each of us have a ship to himself." We arranged accordingly; and each went his own way.

'As I happened one day to be passing close to land I saw a great battle going on. Being under vows never to pass a battle without helping the weaker side, I went on shore, and set to work with the weaker side, and I knocked the head off every one with the short spear. Being tired, I lay myself down among the bodies and fell asleep.

'Stretch out your leg, Kayn, till I put a salve of herbs and healing to it. Salve and binding herb and the poultice are cooling; the worm is channering. Pressure and haste hard bind me, for I must hear Mass in the great church at Rome, and be in Norway before I sleep.'

Kayn Mac Loy said: 'May it be no foot to Kayn or a foot to any one after one, or I be Kayn son of Loy, if I stretch out my foot for you to put a salve of herbs and healing on it, till you tell me if you found the daughter of the King of the Universe, or if you went home, or what happened to you.'

'The mischief is upon you,' said the big man; that tale is long to tell, but I will tell another short tale. When I awoke out of sleep I saw a ship making for the place where I was lying, and a big giant with only one eye dragging it

129

after him: and the ocean reached no higher than his knees. He had a big fish-ing-rod with a big strong line hanging from it on which was a very big hook. He was throwing the line ashore, and fixing the hook in a body, and lifting it on board, and he continued this work till the ship was loaded with bodies. He fixed the hook once in my clothes; but I was so heavy that the rod could

*"It is not easy to kill him,
but we will devise an expedient
for killing him," said she.*

not carry me on board. He had to go on shore himself, and carry me on board
in his arms. I was then in a worse plight than I ever was in. The giant set off
with the ship, which he dragged after him, and reached a big, precipitous
rock, in the face of which he had a large cave: and a damsel as beautiful as I
ever saw came out, and stood in the door of the cave. He was handing the
bodies to her, and she was taking hold of them and putting them into the
cave. As she took hold of each body she said, "Are you alive?" At last the
giant took hold of me, and handed me in to her, and said, "Keep him apart;
he is a large body and I will have him to breakfast the first day that I go from
home." My best time was not when I heard the giant's sentence upon me.
When he had eaten enough of the bodies, his dinner and supper, he lay down
to sleep. When he began to snore the damsel came to speak to me; and she
told me that she was a king's daughter the giant had stolen away and that she
had no way of getting away from him. "I am now," she said, "seven years
except two days with him, and there is a drawn sword between us. He dared
not come nearer me than that till the seven years should expire." I said to her,
"Is there no way of killing him?" "It is not easy to kill him, but we will devise
an expedient for killing him," said she. "Look at that pointed bar that he uses
for roasting the bodies. At dead of night gather the embers of the fire together, and put the bar in the fire till it be red. Go, then, and thrust it into his eye
with all your strength, and take care that he does not get hold of you, for if
he does he will mince you as small as midges." I then went and gathered the
embers together, and put the bar in the fire, and made it red, and thrust it into
his eye; and from the cry that he gave I thought that the rock had split. The
giant sprang to his feet and chased me through the cave in order to catch me;
and I picked up a stone that lay on the floor of the cave, and pitched it into
the sea; and it made a plumping noise. The bar was sticking in his eye all the
time. Thinking it was I that had sprung into the sea, he rushed to the mouth
of the cave, and the bar struck against the doorpost of the cave, and knocked
off his brain-cap. The giant fell down cold and dead, and the damsel and I
were seven years and seven days throwing him into the sea in pieces.

'I wedded the damsel, and a boy was born to us. After seven years I started forth again.

'I gave her a gold ring, with my name on it, for the boy, and when he was
old enough he was sent out to seek me.

'I then set off to the place where I fought the battle, and found the short
spear where I left it; and I was very pleased that I found it, and that the ship
was safe. I sailed a day's distance from that place, and entered a pretty bay
that was there, hauled my ship up above the shore, and erected a hut there,
in which I slept at night. When I rose next day I saw a ship making straight
for the place where I was. When it struck the ground, a big, strong champion came out of it, and hauled it up; and if it did not surpass my ship it was
not a whit inferior to it; and I said to him, "What impertinent fellow are you
that has dared to haul up your ship alongside of my ship?" "I am Machkan-
na-skaya-jayrika," said the champion, "going to seek the daughter of the King
of the Universe for Mac Connachar, son of the King of Lochlann." I saluted
and welcomed him, and said to him, "I am your father: it is well that you have
come." We passed the night cheerily in the hut.

'When I arose on the following day I saw another ship making straight for the place where I was; and a big, strong hero came out of it, and hauled it up alongside of our ships; and if it did not surpass them it was not a whit inferior to them. "What impertinent fellow are you that has dared to haul up your ship alongside of our ships?" said I. "I am," said he, "the Son of the Wet Mantle, going to seek the daughter of the King of the Universe for Mac Connachar, son of the King of Lochlann." "I am your father, and this is your brother: it is well that you have come," said I. We passed the night together in the hut, my two sons and I.

'When I rose next day I saw another ship coming, and making straight for the place where I was. A big, strong champion sprang out of it, and hauled it up alongside of our ships; and if it was not higher than they, it was not lower. I went down where he was, and said to him, "What impertinent fellow are you that has dared to haul up your ship alongside of our ships?" "I am the Son of the Wet Mantle," said he, "going to seek the daughter of the King of the Universe for Mac Connachar, son of the King of Lochlann." "Have you any token in proof of that?" said I. "I have," said he: "here is a ring that my mother gave me at my father's request." I took hold of the ring, and saw my name on it: and the matter was beyond doubt. I said to him, "I am your father, and here are two half-brothers of yours. We are now stronger for going in quest of the daughter of the King of the Universe. Four piles are stronger than three piles." We spent that night cheerily and comfortably together in the hut.

'On the morrow we met a soothsayer, and he spoke to us: "You are going in quest of the daughter of the King of the Universe. I will tell you where she is: she is with the Son of the Blackbird."

'Machkan-na-skaya-jayrika then went and called for combat with a hundred fully trained heroes, or the sending out to him of the daughter of the King of the Universe. The hundred went out; and he and they began on each other, and he killed every one of them. The Son of the Wet Mantle called for combat with another hundred, or the sending out of the daughter of the King of the Universe. He killed that hundred with the short spear. The Son of Secret called for combat with another hundred, or the daughter of the King of the Universe. He killed every one of these with the short spear. I then went out to the field, and sounded a challenge on the shield, and made the town tremble. The Son of the Blackbird had not a man to send out: he had to come out himself; and he and I began on each other, and I drew the short spear, and swept his head off. I then went into the castle, and took out the daughter of the King of the Universe. It was thus that it fared with me.

'Stretch out your leg, Kayn, till I put a salve of herbs and healing to it. Salve and binding herb and the poultice are cooling; the worm is channering. Pressure and haste hard bind me, for I must hear Mass in the great church at Rome, and be in Norway before I sleep.'

Kayn Mac Loy stretched his leg; and the big man applied to it leaves of herbs and healing; and it was healed. The big man took him ashore from the island, and allowed him to go home to the king.

Thus did O'Cronicert win and lose a wife, and thus befell the Leeching of the leg of Kayn, son of Loy.

NOTES

Source of tale: Joseph Jacobs, *More Celtic Fairy Tales*, London: David Nutt, 1894.

This is one of the best stories from Joseph Jacobs' second classic collection, *More Celtic Fairy Tales*, and it is really not one but two stories, artfully joined together. The second part, which really concerns Kayn and his wounded leg, in turn includes a whole sequence of stories, broken up by the repetition of the formulaic 'run' (or wordplay) in which the 'big man' offers to heal Kayn and Kayn keeps on asking for another part of the story. There is actually enough material here to fill a dozen books and as such it is a testimony to the immense virility and imaginative richness of the Celtic folk-story tradition.

There are several age-old themes here, beginning of course with the triple promise which O'Cronicert makes to his otherworldly wife, and which he inevitably breaks, just as does the hero in 'The Legend of Llyn-y-Fan-Fach' (see pages 106–14). The second familiar motif is the encounter with the giant woman with the huge breasts. Once the hero has seized one of them – and in this instance actually placed it between his teeth – the woman is regarded as his foster-mother and must serve him accordingly. We saw the same motif in 'The Lad of the Skin Coverings' (see page 35–45).

The oldest-known version of this story dates back to at least the twelfth century, and it can be found in a manuscript from the fifteenth century. In a version collected by Archibald Campbell in 1871, it ran to 142 pages and included 24 episodes, making it one of the longest folk-stories of its kind ever to be recorded. Here we have a shortened version, which nonetheless possesses all the characteristics of the wonder tale. Several other versions exist, including one contained in a manuscript, dated 1762, called *Ceithearnach Caol Riabhach* or *The Slender Grey Kerne*, in which the Ceithearnach assumes a series of different names, one of which is Cian or Cein (Kayn), under which name he heals a man whose foot has been hurt. In this same text the opening concerns the visit of a huge company of 'Importunate Bards' who visit the king of Connaught in order to test his famed hospitality. It is possible that the fantastic account of the Sturdy Strolling Beggarly Brotherhood may be a variant of this, since the story emerged in its present form at a time when the old system of patronage was breaking down, with much animosity on the part of the bards and their former patrons, who on one side were regarded as pariahs and on the other as oppressive overlords.

The notion of the wife who is found in the shape of a deer is repeated in a famous story from the Fionn cycle, where Fionn himself marries a woman named Sabha who occasionally takes the form of a deer even after they are married. This may well be a distant echo of the worship, among the early Celts, of a deer goddess. In one of the variant versions of the present story, collected by Campbell in the 1880s, the wife is a hare – another example of the magical nature of the hare in Celtic tradition (see also notes to 'The Shee an Gannon and the Gruagach Gaire', pages 104–5).

The episode in which the giant is killed by having a heated spike thrust into his eye is, of course, reminiscent of the blinding of the Cyclops Polyphemus in the Greek story of Odysseus and his return from Troy. How it found its way into this tale is not hard to understand, since the Classical stories were popular among the educated people of Ireland at this time. It may well be that some noble patron, having heard a traditional Celtic version from a wandering storyteller, suggested some further details from the Greek story.

THE SPIRIT OF ELD

NCE UPON A TIME there lived at the back of Beinne-nan-Sian a goatherd of the name of Gorla of the Flocks, who had three sons and one daughter. The herding of the kids was entrusted to the little Jewel of the Golden Hair. On a day of days, when she was out on the breast of the hill herding the kids, there came down a tuft of magic mist as white as the snow of one night; and after it had turned the shoulder of the hill, it surrounded the lonely little Jewel, and she was no more seen.

At the end of a day and a year after that, Ardan, the eldest son of the herd, said, –

'A year to-day my sister, the little Jewel of the Golden Hair, went away, and it is a vow and a word to me that I will not take rest nor repose day or night till I trace her out and share her fate.'

'Son,' quoth his father, 'if thou didst vow that, I will not hinder thee; but it would have become thee, before the word went out of thy mouth, to ask thy father's leave. – Rise, wife, and prepare a bannock for thy big son, and he going on a long journey.'

His mother rose, and she prepared a big bannock and a little bannock.

'Now,' quoth she, 'my son, dost thou prefer the big bannock with thy mother's anger, because of thy going without leave, or the little bannock with her blessing?'

'For me,' quoth he, 'the big bannock; and keep the little bannock and thy blessing for those that choose them.' He departed, and in the twinkling of an eye he was out of sight of his father's house.

He sent splashes from every pool, and dust from the top of every hillock. He was keen journeying, without sparing of sole or instep, or muscle or sinew. He would overtake the swift March wind that was before him, but the swift March wind that was behind him would not catch him up. At last hunger struck him. He sits on a gray stone to eat the big bannock. The Black Raven of the Wilderness comes and sits on a snout of rock above his head.

'A morsel, a morsel, son of Gorla of the Flocks,' quoth the Raven.

'Not a morsel shalt thou get,' quoth the son of Gorla. 'Neither bite nor sup shalt thou get from me – hideous, stare-blind, star-blind, swarthy creature; – it is little enough for myself.'

When that was over the brow of his chest he hied forth again at bounding speed. He would overtake the swift wind of March that was before him, but the swift wind of March that was behind him would not catch him up. The mossy places trembled as he drew near them, the dew fell from the bushy purple heather, and the red grouse cock fled to the highest bog. The evening was beginning to grow dusky – the dark, black clouds of night were coming, and the tranquil silken clouds of day journeying away; the little, nestling, twittering, golden-yellow birds taking rest at the foot of the bushes and in the tops of the thickets – in the deer-haunted dells, and each place they chose as best; but though they were, not so the son of Gorla of the Flocks. He saw a little house of light far from him; and though far from him, he was not long in reaching it.

When he went in he saw an old person, seemingly a great gray-haired stalwart man, contentedly taking his ease on a long bench on the other side of the fire, and a comely maiden combing the luxuriant locks of her flowing golden hair on the opposite side.

'Come ben, young fellow,' quoth the Old Man, and he rising; 'thou art welcome. Often has my bright light attracted the traveller of the hills. Come in, and warmth and shelter be thine, and every relief that is in the mountain bothy. Sit down, and, if it be thy will, let thy tale be heard.'

'I am a youth,' said the big son of the herd, 'who is seeking service. Thy bright light attracted me to seek a night's warmth and shelter.'

'If thou wilt stay with me,' said the Old Man, 'to the end of the year, herding my three dun polled cows, thou shalt get thy reward, and there will not be cause for complaining.'

'That were not my advice to him,' quoth the Maid of the Golden Hair and the Silver Comb.

'Advice without asking,' quoth the big son of Gorla, 'never got respect. I will take thine offer, man; in the dawn of the morning I am thy servant.'

Before the belling of the deer in the rocky summits the Maid with the Golden Hair and the Silver Comb milked the three dun polled cows.

'There thou hast them now,' said the Old Man. 'Go behind them, follow them; do not turn them back, do not baulk them – they will seek their own pasture – and let them travel as they like. Wait thou behind them; and let whatever pleases come in thy road, do not part from them. Be thine eye on them, and on them alone; and no matter what thou seest or hearest, do not give an eye to it. This is thy duty: be faithful, trust my word; be painstaking, and thy toil shall not be without reward.'

He went after the cattle, and followed them. He was not long gone when he saw a golden cock and a silver hen running before him on the plain. He gave chase; but though they were now and again as he thought in his grasp, he failed to hold them fast. He returned from the vain pursuit, and reached the place where the three dun polled cows were grazing, and he began again to tend them; but he was not long behind them when he saw a little gold rod

135

and a little silver rod cutting capers on the plain, and he immediately began the pursuit of them.

'It cannot be,' quoth he, 'that these are not easier to catch than the birds that cheated me a short while ago.'

He stretched out after them; but, though he would be pursuing them yet, he would not catch them. He began herding again; but, as he was following the dun polled cows, he saw a grove on which was every fruit that he had ever seen, and twelve fruits he had not seen. He begins to satiate himself with the fruits. The dun polled cows turned their faces homewards, and he followed them. The Maid with the Golden Hair milked them, but instead of good milk they gave only thin milk. The Old Man understood how it was.

'Young man without truth and without faithfulness,' said he, 'thou didst break thy promise.'

He lifted his magic rod – he strikes the youth and makes of him a pillar of stone, that stood three days and three years at the side of the fire in the mountain bothy, as a memorial of the breaking of troth and covenant of hiring.

When another day and year had gone by, Red Ruais, the middle son of Gorla, said, –

'Two days and two years have gone past since my beautiful sister went away, and it is a day and a year since my eldest brother went; it is a vow and a word to me to depart to-day in search of them, and to share their fate.'

Exactly as it happened to the eldest brother in every way, so it happened to the middle son; and he is a pillar of stone at the house end of the mountain bothy, as a reminder of broken troth and covenant of hiring.

A day and a year after this the youngest son, Brown Caomhan of good fortune, said, –

'There are now three days and three years since we lost my beautiful sister. The brothers of my love departed to seek her. Now, father, if it is pleasing to thee, allow me to go after them and to share their fate, and let not my mother hinder me. I entreat your leave – do not refuse me.'

'Thou hast my leave and my blessing, Caomhan, and thy mother shall not hinder thee.'

'Shall I prepare,' said his mother, 'the big bannock without my blessing, or the little bannock with the goodwill of my heart and the longing of my soul?'

'Thy blessing, O mother, give thou to me; and whether big or little come at its heel, I am content. Poor to me would be the inheritance of the great world and thy curse at its foot. On the blessing of a mother it is not I that will pour contempt.'

Brown Caomhan, son of Gorla of the Flocks, 'lifted on himself,' and his heart was full as the house of his father and mother was left behind in the mist. He set off at bounding speed; he reaches the wood of the roedeer; he sits under a tree to eat that bannock which his kind mother baked for him.

'A morsel, a morsel,' quoth the Black Raven of the Wilderness. 'A morsel for me, Caomhan, and I feeble.'

'Thou shalt get a morsel, poor creature,' said Caomhan. 'It is likely that thou art needier than I. It will suffice for both of us; the blessing of a mother is at its foot.'

The first son, turned into a pillar of stone

137

He rose and betook himself on his journey. He took shelter at the Old Man's, and departed to herd the three dun polled cows. He saw the golden cock and the silver hen, but he turned away his eyes – he followed the cattle. He saw the gold rod and the silver rod, but he remembered his promise, and he did not go in chase of them. He reached the grove; he saw the fruit that was beautiful and fair to the sight, but he did not taste it.

The three dun polled cows went past the wood, and they reached a wide moor where there was a 'heather-burning' – the long heather on fire. They went towards it. The fire was spreading on the plain, threatening to burn himself and the dun polled cows; but they went through it – he did not try to stop them, for this was the promise he had given. He followed them through the fire, and not a single hair of his head was burnt. He sees after that a large river, swollen with the mountain floods. Over it went the dun polled cows, and after them undaunted went Caomhan.

A short while after that he sees a beautiful white house of worship on a green plain, back of the wind and face to the sun, from out of which he heard the sound of sweet songs and tuneful hymns. The cattle lay down on the ground, and Brown Caomhan went in to hear the tidings of joy. It was not long he was listening to the message of happiness when a giddy youth came in at the door of the house of worship, with wild eye, and panting, saying that the dun polled cows were in the standing corn, and that he should go and chase them out.

'Begone,' said Caomhan; ''twere easier for thee, thou booby, to put them out thyself, than running thus and "the breath in thy chest" to bring the tale to me. I will listen to the acceptable words.'

A little while after that the same lad came back, frenzy and fury in his eye, and his breath in his chest.

'Out, out, son of Gorla of the Bens,' said he; 'our dogs are chasing thy share of cows. If thou be not out in the twinkling of an eye, thou wilt not see another sight of them.'

'Away with thee, booby,' quoth Brown Caomhan. 'It were easier for thee to restrain thy share of dogs, than coming thus with the breath in thy chest to tell it to me. I will listen to the tidings of joy.'

When worship was over Caomhan went out, and finds the three dun polled cows putting off their weariness, without motion from the place in which he had left them. They rose and moved on the homeward way, and Caomhan followed them. He had not been long behind them when he saw a broad plain, so bare that he could see the thinnest thorn on the bare ground; and he perceived a mare and a fleet mettlesome young foal grazing, and they as plump and fleshy as the seal of the great ocean. 'This is extraordinary,' quoth Brown Caomhan. A short while after that he sees another plain, under a crop of waste pasture, on which were a mare and a foal, in whose backs the awl of the brogues would not stand for leanness.

He sees after that a lochan of water, and many gay, joyous, fresh, bright young people journeying with sweet and joyful noise and in merry companies to the upper end of the lochan, to the land of the sun, under the shade of the fragrant trees. He heard the murmuring of the burns that were in the country of the sun, the warbling of the birds, the tune of a stringed instrument he did not know, and of musical instruments he had never heard before.

He perceived other companies of sad people journeying to the lower end of the lochan to the country of darkness. Fearful was the scream they raised. A cause of horror was the smiting of their palms. Mist and dark clouds were over the gloomy, dark glen to which they were journeying, and Caomhan heard heavy thundering. 'That is indeed strange,' said he.

He followed the three dun polled cows. The night was then purposing to be a wild one, nor had they knowledge of shelter or dwelling in which to put it past; but who should meet Caomhan but the Dog of the Great Mull; and no sooner did the honest helpmate and the good host meet him than he gave him an invitation, and that not churlishly, but hospitably and heartily, to put past three-thirds of his fatigue and the whole night with him.

He was entertained that night right kindly by the Dog of the Great Mull in the dry, water-tight cave, if that would suffice along with sweet flesh of lambs and kids, without lack, without scant, without stint, and at the time of departing in the morning, enough for the day's journey.

'And now,' said the Dog of the Great Mull, 'fare thee well, Caomhan! Success to thee wherever thou goest; good luck in thy journeying and movements. I offered thee hospitality, and thou didst not refuse it; thou didst take heartily and cheerfully what I offered. Thou didst put past the night in the cave of the Dog of the Great Mull; thou didst trust in him, thou didst pledge his friendship, and he will not deceive thee. Now, consider my words. If ever thou art in a hard case or strait in which fleetness of foot and ready action will be of use to thee, think on the Dog of the Great Mull; wish greatly for him, and I will be at thy side.'

The same kindness and hospitality met him the next night from that host-in-himself, the swift-circling, wide-ranging Black Raven of the corrie of the crags, on whom sleep would not lie nor sun rise till he would have what would suffice for himself and for him that would come and go. With short jumps, clapping his wings, he guided him with the points of his wings through the paths of the goat-tracks to the hollow of a secure cleft of the rock, where he asked him to put past three-thirds of his fatigue and the whole night with him.

He was entertained that night well and very well with the Black Raven of the corrie of the crags, if flesh and venison would suffice; and at the time of going in the morning, he said to him, –

'Caomhan, son of Gorla of the Peak, take with thee what will suffice thee for thy journey – the stranger's portion I never missed; – and remember my last words. If it ever befall thee to be in a case or strait in which a strong wing and courage that never failed can be of use to thee, remember me. Warm is thine heart and kind thine eye; thou didst trust thyself to me; thou hast ere this fed the Raven of the Wilderness, and didst share with him thy provisions. I am thy friend; thou didst put past the night in the hollow of the rocks; rely on me.'

On the third night Caomhan met with no less fellowship and hospitality from the brown, sharp-eyed Otter, the expert, nimble searcher, with whom a meal for man or boy would not be lacking so long as it was to be got on sea

or land. Although nothing was to be heard in his den but the squealing and mewing of cat, and badger, and marten and polecat, he led him without dread, without fear, without 'sidestart,' stoutly, bravely, cunningly, warily, sharp-sightedly, with minute knowledge, to the mouth of the cairn, where he asked him to put past with him three-thirds of his weariness and all the night. Thanks to none else if he was not entertained that night by the Brown Otter of the stream, the ever-wandering if fish of every kind that was better than another would suffice, and a dry, snug, fat bed of the flotsam of the high spring storm tides and the cockscomb seaweed of the black shore.

'Put past the night, Caomhan,' said the Otter; 'thou art heartily welcome. Sleep peacefully; the Otter is a keenly-observant watchman.'

When the day came and Caomhan was starting on his journey, the Otter went as escort a while on the way with him.

'Fare thee well, Caomhan,' said he; 'thou hast made a friend of me. If hard adversity or tight necessity come to thee, in which he who swims the stream or dives under the sea can do thee service, remember me, and I will be at thy side.'

He found the three dun polled cows in the little hollow in which he had left them. They got up, and towards the height of the same evening he and they reached safely and easily the mountain bothy.

There was welcome and joy at meeting in the house when Caomhan arrived. He was entertained without scant and without niggardliness. The Old Man inquired 'how it had risen to him' (that is, 'things had gone with him') since he went away, and he began to tell that. The Old Man praised him because he had had nothing to do with any one thing he saw till he reached the house of the melodious hymns, because there was nought in all those other things but vain glamour to deceive him.

'I will open to thee the dark perplexity of the matter later,' said the Old Man; 'and I will discover to thee the interpretation of each sight that put great wonder on thee. Thou wast faithful, Caomhan. Ask thy reward, and thou shalt get it.'

'That will not be heavy to thee, I hope,' quoth Caomhan, 'and it will be plentiful enough for me. Restore to me, alive and well as when they left the house of their father, the sister of my affection and the brothers of my love that thou hast under enchantment, and neither gold piece nor silver shilling will Caomhan want.'

'Youth, thy request is high,' said the Old Man. 'There are difficulties between thee and that thou seekest above what it is in thy power to combat.'

'Name them,' said Caomhan, 'and let me contend with them as best I can.'

'Listen then. In the high mountain up yonder is the swift roe of slenderest foot; her equal does not exist; dappled and curly-haired is her side, and her horns like the antlers of the red deer. On the beautiful loch near to the land of the sun is a duck that surpasses all other ducks – a green duck with a golden neck. In the dark linn of the yellow corrie there is a white-bellied, red-gilled trout, and his tail like the silver of brightest hue. Away, and bring home here the curly-haired, dappled hind of the mountain, the exquisite duck of the golden neck, and the trout that can be known from every trout, and I will tell thee about the sister of thine affection and the two brothers of thy love.'

Caomhan follows the cows through the 'heather-burning'

141

Brown Caomhan departed. The Maiden of the Golden Hair and Silver Comb went after him.

'Caomhan,' saith she, 'take courage; thou hast the blessing of thy mother and the blessing of the poor. Thou didst stand by thy promise; thou gavest reverence to the house of sweet hymns. Go, and remember my parting words: Never yield.'

He took the hill – he sees the roe of the mountain, her like was not in the mountain; but when he was on one ben the roe was on another ben, and he might as well attempt the fleeting clouds of heaven. He was on the point of yielding, when he remembered what the Golden-haired Maiden had said.

'Oh,' said Caomhan, 'that I had the Dog of the Great Mull and the swift feet with me now!'

No sooner did he speak the word than the honest Dog was at his side; and, after he had taken a cast or two round the mountain, he left the curly-haired hind at the sole of his foot.

After that Caomhan betook himself to the lochan, and he sees the green duck of the golden neck flying above his head.

'Oh,' said Caomhan, 'that I had now the Black Raven of the Wilderness, strongest of wing and sharpest of eye!'

No sooner had he said this than he saw the Black Raven of the Wilderness approaching the lochan; and instantly he left the green duck with the golden neck at his side.

After that he arrived at the dark, black linn, and sees the white-bellied, silvery, beautiful fish swimming from bank to bank.

'Oh,' said Caomhan, 'that I had the Brown Otter who swims the stream and dives under the wave!'

In the twinkling of an eye, who was sitting on the bank of the burn but the honest Otter. He looked into Caomhan's face with kindliness; he went quickly out of sight, and out of the dark, black linn of the sea-trout he took the white-bellied trout of brightest hue, and laid it at Caomhan's feet.

He started for home, and leaves the roe, the duck, and the beautiful trout on the threshold of the mountain bothy.

'Success and prosperity to Brown Caomhan!' said the Old Man. '"None ever set his shoulder to it in earnest that did not win through." Come in, Caomhan, and when the Maid of the Golden Hair and Silver Comb milks the three dun polled cows, I will open to thee the riddle of the matter, and we will draw wisdom from the hiring and journey of Caomhan.'

THE RIDDLE OF THE TALE OPENED

'Thou didst not leave the house of thy father and mother without their leave. The blessing of thy father and thy mother was at thy foot, Caomhan. Thou didst not refuse a morsel to the hungry in his distress. The blessing of the poor was at thy foot, Caomhan.

'Thou didst make an engagement; thou didst promise and didst fulfil; and the reward of the righteous is at thy heel, Caomhan.

'Thou didst see the golden cock and the silver hen temptations of evil –

the glamour that gold and silver cast over the eye – thou didst remember thy promise; thou didst walk in the path of thy duty; good fortune was with Caomhan. The tempter tried thee again under the form of a golden rod and a silver rod. These were apparently easier to catch; but thou didst remember thy promise and didst follow the cattle.

'When he did not succeed in tempting thee with gold and silver, he tried to deceive thee with the beautiful fruit of the wood. He put before thee every fruit that ever thou sawest, and twelve fruits that thou hadst not seen; but thou didst turn away.

'When he did not gain what was in his mind with gold and silver, nor with the fruit that was pleasant to the eye, he tried thy courage – the flame and the flood; but thou wentest through them in the path of thy duty, and thou didst understand that they were only illusions. Thou didst hear the voice of the holy songs, the sound of the sweet hymns. Thou didst go in, and didst do well; but the tempter followed thee even there. Thou answeredst him well: "I will listen to the word."

'Thou didst see the bare pasturage, and the high-spirited mare with her playful colt rejoicing on it. It is often thus, Caomhan, in the world: the house of hospitality is often ill supplied, but peace, rejoicing, and prosperity are its prop. Thou didst see the pasture going waste, and every four-footed creature perishing with leanness: thus in the world is the house of the niggardly man; there is plenty in it, but he has not the heart to enjoy it. There is mean saving in the midst of plenty. There is a grub at the root of every stem, and every blossom is withered.

'Thou didst see the beautiful lochan – thou didst hear the joyful shout of the happy companies that journeyed to the land of the sun. There hast thou those who considered my entreaty, and who were wise in their day. Thou didst hear the agonizing lamentations of the other people who journeyed to the land of gloom. Those are the people without understanding, without truth, without faithfulness, who neglected every warning; and now are they keening wretchedly.

'Thou didst not put contempt on the friendliness and hospitality of the poor; thou didst accept in kindness what was generously offered; thou didst not shame the needy – in this way thou didst bind friendship. Thou didst stand to thy promise – thou didst follow the cattle – thou didst win thy reward. I trusted thy courage. Difficulties did not terrify thee; thou didst put thy shoulder to them, and didst succeed. Thou didst learn that neither the Dog of the Great Mull, the Black Raven of the Wilderness, nor the brown fishing Otter were without their use. Thou didst not yield. And now, Caomhan, son of Gorla of the Flocks, listen to me.

'"Restore to me," thou saidst, "my beautiful sister and the brothers of my love that thou hast under enchantment." Under enchantment, Caomhan! What is enchantment? – the cunning device of the crafty, the foolish excuse of the timorous. What is enchantment? – the bugbear of fools, a cause of dread to the faint-hearted – a thing that was not, and that is not, and shall not be. Against the dutiful and the upright there is no magic nor device. Thy sister, the Jewel of the Golden Hair and the Silver Comb, thou shalt take home with thee; but thy brothers, though they are living, laziness and faithlessness made of them wanderers, without home and without friend. Go thou to thy father's house, Caomhan, and store in thy heart what thou hast seen and heard.'

'And who art thou that speakest?' said Caomhan.

'I am,' said the Old Man, 'the Spirit of Eld. Fare thee well, Caomhan. May the blessing of Age be on thy journeying and on thy going!'

NOTES

Sourceof tale: Winifred M. Parker, *Gaelic Fairy Tales*, Glasgow: Archibald Sinclair, 1908.

This extraordinary and powerful tale may seem to owe something to Christianity in its shape and underlying message. In fact, it looks back to an older and simpler time, when the qualities of truth, faithfulness and understanding were common enough. Beneath the surface references to 'hymns' of joy, valleys of gloom and faithless behaviour lies a deeply moving account of a youth's journey of self-discovery. Helped, as so often in these tales, by animals who possess more than a little of human nature and qualities, he travels into the inner worlds, where he meets with the spirit of the past – for so I take Eld to be, rather than the more superficial sense of 'age'. From him Caomhan ('the noble friendly one') learns some salutary lessons – lessons which would have been useful to his brothers Ardan ('pride') and Ruais ('windbag'). Their selfish and boorish behaviour place them under the enchantment of stone – an enchantment which is here explained as of their own doing; an important idea, which goes further towards explaining the true nature of magic than any of the other stories in this book. For the rest, there are all the trappings of the otherworld journey: the strange creatures, the wonderful landscape through which the hero passes, and the magical beings he encounters along the way. The Black Raven is probably a play on the word *biatach*, which has two meanings: a raven and a farmer who held his land rent-free, in return for which he was bound to entertain travellers and the soldiers of his chief on the march. This is a story that repays re-reading, since on each occasion it yields up a deeper level of meaning.

THE BIRD OF THE GOLDEN LAND

 N A TIME which was long ago there lived a King in Erin, and he had three sons. Though the King had land and ruled people, he was not rich. The crown on his head was more precious than all he had in the world besides. The crown was his principal treasure.

There was a bird in the world at that time which used to fly to the castle windows and sing there, sing the most wonderful song ever heard in Erin. Nothing gave the King so much pleasure as the music of that bird, which was called the Bird of the Golden Land.

Now it happened one day above another that the eldest son of the King came to his father in the morning and said:

'Father, I am old enough to marry; will you find me a wife?'

The King made no answer, and the young man went out.

What should happen at noon of the same day but this, that the second son came to the King and the words that he used were: 'Father, I am old enough to marry; will you find me a wife?'

The King said nothing to this son either.

In the evening of the very same day the youngest son came and stood before the King.

'Well, my son,' said the King, 'what is your message this time?'

'I am old enough, father, to marry; will you find me a wife?'

The King made no reply, said nothing to this son any more than to the other two, and the young man went out.

The father sat wondering and thinking, thought long over his sons, and of what he could do for them. 'I have little to give my children,' said he to himself, 'and it is very hard to divide that little between them. If I make two parts of my lands, give one-half to the oldest son, the other to the second, the crown to the third, the other two will be dissatisfied. The crown is worth more than the whole kingdom; my sons will quarrel with one another and fight for the crown.'

The King thought all night and dreamt of his trouble. Next day he sent for his three sons, and this is what he said to them:

'It is hard for me to divide what I have among you. If I give equal parts of the kingdom to two and the crown to the third the division will be unjust, for the crown is worth far more than all my lands, and we cannot divide the crown nor make parts of it. Nothing can be settled in that way, but I will do this with you: The Bird of the Golden Land comes to this castle whenever it pleases her and goes when she likes; she stays here a day or an hour and remains away a short time or long in like manner. Nothing pleases me like that bird. If I had her with me always I could live with delight. Bring me the Bird of the Golden Land; the man who brings her will get the crown.'

'I will go for the Bird of the Golden Land,' said the eldest son.

'I will go for that bird,' said the second.

'I will bring that bird with me,' cried the youngest.

The three brothers made ready, and away they went next day; they travelled together till they came to a crossroad.

'It is time now,' said the eldest, 'for each to go his own way.'

'No,' said the second, 'it is late; let us stop together for this night, and in the morning each may take the road he likes best.'

At nightfall the three brothers came to a house and went in. A woman rose as they entered and gave them a hundred thousand welcomes.

'I wonder,' said the eldest brother, 'how you know us. I did not think there was a person on this road who would know us.'

'I know,' said she, 'who you are, where you are going, and what you are looking for. You are the King's sons, and you are looking for the Bird of the Golden Land.'

'We are looking for that bird,' said the brothers. They spent the night in the house. Next morning, after breakfast, an old man rose from a bed in one corner, and spoke to the young men.

'You have come by the straight road up to this,' said he. 'Now you must take a side path. I will go with you and give you what advice and assistance I can. Let the eldest and strongest take that great sledge lying there, let the second man take the cradle, and the youngest the rope that is coiled at the side of it, and come with me.'

The brothers took the sledge, the cradle, and the rope, and the four men went on together till they came to a broad flat rock.

'Now,' said the old man to the eldest brother, 'give your best blow on that rock.'

The King's son struck a great blow. A large piece fell from the rock. Underneath was an opening of such depth that no man could see the end of it.

'This,' said the old man, 'is the road which you must take to find the Golden Land. There is no other road by which you can go. Whichever one of you wishes may go down in the cradle. If he has luck he will go to the bottom in safety, but he may strike rocks on the way and be killed. The man who reaches the bottom will be on the straight road. He may win the bird or he may lose his life.'

'I will go down,' said the eldest of the three brothers.

They fastened the rope to the cradle and let him down. Soon he began to strike against the rocks on one side and the other, and was greatly terrified in the darkness; he whistled and they drew him up.

'I will go,' said the second brother.

He went in and was let down, but did not go even as far as the eldest when he whistled and was taken up again.

'I will go now,' said the youngest, 'if you have rope enough to carry me to the bottom.'

'I have rope and to spare,' said the old man.

The youngest went into the cradle and stayed inside till it reached the very bottom. He saw a straight road there before him, and going on it was soon in a beautiful country. He walked and walked on for a long time till at length and at last he came to a high, roomy castle. A woman came out to meet him, and said:

'You are a hundred thousand times welcome, son of the King in Erin.'

''Tis the wonder of the world,' said the young man, 'that you know me. I did not think there could be any one down in this land who knew me.'

'I know you,' said the woman, 'and I know what brought you and what is on your mind. I will give you what advice and assistance I can. You have come the straight road up to this time, but there is great hardship and labor before you. It would take seven years to walk the road which you have to travel and seven years to come back, but you can ride there, do your work, and ride back again a day and a year on a horse that I will give you. You need to be back in a day and a year at the opening to the upper land, for the old man and your two brothers will think that long enough and too long to be waiting above in Erin. That stable beyond is full of fine horses. Among them is the swiftest and best one in the world. Go now and take your choice of them.'

The King's son went to the stable, looked at all the horses, looked a second and a third time, and said to himself: 'These horses are too tall by far and too high for me. If I were thrown the fall would kill me.'

Looking around he saw behind the door a poor, shaggy, wretched little mare, and thought, 'If I comb and clean that little mare she may serve me far better than any one of all these tall horses.'

The King's son combed, cleaned, then saddled and bridled the mare and led her out of the stable, and never stopped till he came to the castle with her.

'I see,' said the woman when she saw the mare, 'that you will have luck, for you brought with you the best horse in the stable.'

The King's son left good health with the woman and went forward with all speed on his journey. When they had gone a long and a very long time the mare spoke and said:

'King's son, look around. Tell me what you see.'

'What do I see,' said the King's son, 'but a lovely, a beautiful land?'

'Look between my two ears.'

He looked between her ears and saw a great, mighty sea.

'Ho! ho!' said the King's son. 'I see a broad, swelling sea.'

'Well,' said the mare, 'if you are the right King's son we can cross that sea without trouble.'

147

They came soon to the sea; the mare ran over on the water as though it were land, and they reached the other side without danger.

'Where are you now?' asked the horse.

'I am sitting near your tail, almost falling.'

'I would rather you were in some other place.'

They travelled on and on.

'Look between my ears,' said the mare. 'What do you see?'

'A broader sea by far than the one we crossed.'

'If you are the right King's son we'll cross this sea as well as the other.'

They crossed the second sea, and when on the opposite shore the mare spoke.

'Where are you now?' asked she.

'I'm out your ears at almost falling.'

'I would you were in some other place.'

She went forward now with great swiftness, went far, and then said:

'Look between my ears a third time.'

'Ah, there is a terrible sea before us now.'

'There is a broad and terrible sea before us,' said the mare, 'but if you are the right King's son we may cross this one as well as the others, though not so easily; if you are not the right man there is no escape for us. In the sea are three very small islands. On these I can rest, and in this way pass over.'

The mare rushed ahead till she came to the first little island, and rested. After that she sped on again over the water till she came to the second island and rested, then to the third, and at last reached the shore.

'Where are you sitting now?' asked the mare.

'In the middle of your back on the saddle.'

'That is the place where I wish you to be.'

They went on now for a long time without adventure, till at length and at last they saw in the distance a great shining castle.

'I wonder,' said the King's son, 'who lives in that splendid place.'

'That is the castle of the King of the Golden Land,' said the mare, 'and the thing you are looking for is in that castle. Now I will tell you what to do. Behind the castle are thirteen stables. At the first stable you come to ten stable boys will run out to take from you the mare you are sitting on, to comb her and care for her. Drive them away and tell them that you will take care of your own horse. Go on without stopping or paying attention to the hostlers till you leave twelve stables behind you. Dismount at the thirteenth and lead me in.'

The King's son rode to the first stable. Ten hostlers ran out to take his horse.

'Stand aside,' said the King's son. 'I take care of my own horse.'

At each stable the hostlers ran out and at each the King's son drove them away. At the thirteenth he drove away the hostlers, led in his mare, and tied her in a manger. That moment the King came out raging with anger and cried:

'How dare you take your beast into this stable? Are my hostlers not good enough to care for your horse? Besides, why come to this empty place?'

'Any place will do me,' said the King's son. 'I care for my own horse.

Surely, the King of the Golden Land will not deny me the choice of stables nor deny me the pleasure of caring for the horse that brought me over such a long road?'

'I know,' said the King, 'why you have come. You are in search of the Bird of the Golden Land.'

'I am,' said the King's son.

'If you are,' said the King, 'you must work for her. Come with me now to the castle.'

The King's son went with him.

'To-morrow at sunrise,' said the King, 'I will hide, and if you cannot find me before sunset you will lose your head.'

After a while the King's son went back to his mare and told her all. 'What am I to do?' asked he. 'The King will hide, I cannot find him, and he will take the head off me?'

'Sleep there under the manger before me,' said the mare. Raising her right leg she gave him a tip of her hoof. He was asleep in a moment and did not wake till next morning when the mare gave him a tip of her hoof and roused him.

'Where shall I find the King?' asked the young man.

'Walk into the garden,' said the mare. 'You will find it full of beautiful maidens, each one will praise you, show you beautiful flowers, ask you to look at her, walk with her. Give no heed to the maidens, look not at one of them; go straight to the end of the garden where there is a tree and on it a single red apple. Pluck that apple, make two of it. The King will come out.'

The King's son did all as the mare commanded. Every maiden in the garden was teasing the young man to go with her, was showing him beautiful flowers, but he never lifted his eyes to look at the flowers or the maidens. He hurried forward to the tree and picked the apple, saying: 'This is the nicest, most beautiful apple that I have seen in my life. I will take it with me to Erin.'

'Indeed, then, you will not,' said the King's daughter. 'That is my father's apple, and you must leave it behind you.'

'Very well, for your sake,' said he, 'I will take only half of it with me; I will give you the rest.'

With that he drew his knife and made two halves of the apple, and out jumped the King.

'Oh,' cried the King, 'that is one cut on my head to-day.'

'I am sorry,' said the King's son from Erin: 'but how was I to know that such a great mighty King as you would be inside in an apple?'

They both went to the castle that day. 'Now,' said the King, 'I will hide again in the morning. If you do not find me before sunset you will lose your head.'

The King's son went to the stable in the evening and told the mare all. She put him to sleep as on the evening before under the manger in front of her, and he slept there till sunrise. Then the mare struck him a tip of her hoof and told him to rise.

'Where shall I find the King to-day?' asked the King's son.

'Go straightway from this to the castle kitchen. A great many maidens will be there before you. They will laugh at you, tease you, push, and slap you with towels, but never look at them or mind them. Walk up to the fire. The cook will give you a bowl of warm broth with no spoon in it. You will say,

149

"I must find a spoon." Walk then to the cupboard. There you will see a three-headed pin. Take the pin, cut it open with your knife. You will find the King.'

The King's son from Erin did as the mare had commanded; went to the kitchen, avoided the maidens, took the bowl of broth, and saying, 'I must have a spoon for my soup,' went to the cupboard, found a three-headed pin and took it up.

'This,' said he, 'is the best pin I have seen ever in any place, I will take it home with me to Erin.'

'Indeed, then, you will not,' said the King's daughter; 'that pin belongs to my father, and you are not to take it.'

'For your sake,' said he, 'I will take only half of it. I will give you the other half.'

He drew out his knife then and cut the pin; the King sprang forth.

'Oh,' cried he, 'I have two cuts in my head now, one yesterday, and one to-day.'

'I am sorry,' said the King's son from Erin, 'but how was I to think that such a great mighty King as you could be in a three-headed pin.'

The King took him to the castle that day and said: 'I will hide to-morrow at sunrise. If you find me before sunset you will be safe, if you fail I'll have your head.'

The King's son went to his mare and told all. She put him to sleep as before and roused him in the morning.

'Where am I to find the King to-day?' asked the young man.

'It will be harder work to-day, but you will find him. Take some grains of barley and go to that pond near the garden; you will see a duck swimming around by herself in the water; throw the barley to her on the bank, she'll come toward you; while she is picking the grain catch her, and tell her to lay an egg. She will refuse; say then that you will kill her. She will lay an egg; the King will be in that egg.'

Next morning the King's son went out to the lake, taking barley as the mare had told him. He threw it, caught the duck, and told her to lay an egg.

'How can I lay an egg when I have none?' asked the duck.

'That's one to me, lay the egg or I'll kill you this minute.' The duck laid the egg and the King's son took it, saying: 'This is the finest egg that I have ever seen anywhere. I will keep this egg and eat it myself.'

'Indeed then you will not keep that egg nor eat it,' said the King's daughter. 'That egg belongs to my father.'

'I will be generous,' said the King's son from Erin; 'I will give you one half of it.'

With that he split the egg in two. The King sprang up, let a roar out of him. 'O–h!' cried he, 'there are three cuts on my head to-day.'

'How sorry I am,' said the King's son from Erin, 'but could I think that such a great, noble monarch as you would be hiding in a duck's egg?'

'You have beaten me,' said the King; 'you have found me three times, but I have not finished yet: you must hide in your turn. I will look for you from sunrise till noon, and on the first day of three that I find you I'll have your head. You came to get the Bird of the Golden Land, but if you get that bird you'll work hard for her.'

THE BIRD OF THE
GOLDEN LAND

The King's son went to his mare in the stable. 'Oh, I am in deep trouble this time,' said he.

'How is that?' asked the mare.

'The King of the Golden Land says I must hide, and on the first day of three that he finds me he'll have my head.'

'Sleep there under the manger in front of me,' said the mare, hitting him a tip of her hoof.

He slept till near sunrise, when the mare roused him with a tip of her other foot.

'Where shall I hide from the King?'

The mare made a flea of the King's son, and he was jumping through the stable for himself.

The King came with a brush and curry-comb, combed and brushed the mare, looked everywhere through the stable and outside, but hunt where he would he could not find the King's son. He hunted till noon, and then went back to the castle. The mare called the King's son and made a man of him. 'Go now to the castle,' said she; 'when he sees you the King will ask where you were. Tell him that you did not ask such a question the day he was inside an apple in the garden.'

The King's son went to the castle. 'You beat me to-day,' said the King; 'where were you hidden and in what form were you?'

'I did not ask you such a question the day you were in the apple.'

'We'll make another trial,' said the King.

On the following morning the mare roused the King's son and made a bee of him.

Said the King to himself: 'I must find him to-day,' and he hunted and hunted, looked everywhere, found nothing, and went home at midday.

The mare made a man of the King's son, and he went to the castle in his own shape.

'Oh,' said the King, 'how I looked for you, but where were you, and in what form were you?'

'I did not ask you such a question the day you were in the three-headed pin.'

'We'll make another trial to-morrow. I may find you.'

The King's son from Erin slept till near sunrise next morning, when the mare roused him. She said: 'I'll make you a hair in one of my eyelids to-day; you will be safe there.'

The King came, searched the stable through, searched everywhere, could not find what he wanted. At midday he went home empty-handed, baffled and furious. The mare gave his own form to the King's son from Erin and said:

'Go now to the castle the King will be raging; answer him not a word; please him in every way possible. He only sleeps once in seven years. If you please him he will try a night's rest and all his people will fall asleep with him. You'll find me ready at the castle door. Grasp the cage that is hanging there, mount me, and away with you.'

The King's son from Erin obeyed all these words carefully. The King went to sleep after his trials and efforts. The young man seized the cage, but if he did the bird let a scream out of her that roused every one in the castle. The

King's son sprang into the saddle and away he rode.

'Look behind you,' said the mare, after a time when they were in sight of the sea with three islands, 'and tell me what you see.'

'The largest army I have ever seen is following us.'

'What color is it?'

'White.'

'We can escape that,' said the mare.

She crossed the sea with the three islands.

'Look again,' said she, when in sight of the middle sea.

'A terrible army is after us.'

'What is the color of it?'

'Red.'

'We may escape that army,' and she crossed the middle sea.

'Look behind,' said the mare a third time when in sight of the third and smallest sea.

'I see a still greater army.'

'What is the color of it?'

'Black.'

'We shall escape that army.'

They came to the smallest sea and crossed without difficulty; the army remained on the other side.

At last they reached the castle where the King's son found the mare. The young woman was in front of the castle before him with a hundred thousand welcomes and dancing with delight because he had the bird.

'Do you know who that bird is?' asked she.

'I do not,' said the King's son.

'That bird is a queen with three crowns, the mare that carried you is a queen of two crowns, and I am a queen of one crown. I have a rod here that will give their right forms to the two queens. Once she receives her own form again, the queen of three crowns will have power to make a bird of herself whenever she pleases. The queen of two crowns has not that power, and I have no power to change myself, but another might change us with this rod.'

'Now, do you know what we'll do? We'll give the queen of two crowns to your eldest brother, I will take your second brother, and you will have the queen of three crowns.'

'That is the right thing,' said the King's son, 'if my father is willing.'

'He will be willing,' said the young woman, striking the bird. The bird became the most beautiful woman that ever the sun shone on. Next she struck the mare, and she was the queen of two crowns.

'It is time now for us all to go to Erin. The old man and your brothers will think it too long they are waiting,' said the queen of one crown.

All went to the foot of the opening. The queen of two crowns went into the cradle and the King's son from Erin shook the rope. The three men above drew up the cradle. The eldest brother took the queen of two crowns for himself. The cradle was let down again and the queen of one crown went up. The second brother took her. When the turn came for the queen of three crowns, she said:

'Wait a while; put a stone there in place of me.'

The King's son did so, and when the cradle was drawn almost to the top the men above cut the rope, and the cradle fell then to the bottom.

The two brothers started for home straightway, each thinking of the young queen that he had to marry, but before they reached the house where they took the cradle, the sledge, and the rope, they bethought themselves, remembered their father's promise of the crown, and said to the old man:

'Before we left home we told our father to find wives for us. He did not promise to get us the wives, but he said he would give the crown, which is worth far more than his kingdom, to the man who would bring him the Bird of the Golden Land. We went for that bird, and are going home now without her. What answer are we to give to our father?'

'I will tell you what to do,' said the old man. 'I saw a rod of enchantment with the second woman. I will use it.' With that he went to the queen of one crown, snatched her rod, struck the queen of two crowns, and said: 'Be the Bird of the Golden Land in her cage.' That moment she was a bird in a cage. He gave the rod to the second brother and said:

'Keep that from the woman you are going to marry.'

They went on, came to the old man's house, and spent one night in it. Next morning they started for their father's castle. The old King was glad to see his two sons, but asked in a moment: 'Where is your brother?'

'A rock fell and crushed him on the road,' said the two sons.

'Did you find the bird?'

'I brought her,' said the eldest, and showed a cage to his father. The King had the cage hung near his window. Though he waited and waited there was no song from the cage.

'That is not the Bird of the Golden Land,' said the King.

'I have that bird,' said the younger brother. He went to the queen of one crown, struck her with the rod, made a bird of her, and brought her to his father; but this bird would not sing any more than the other.

When the two brothers left the opening with the two queens and the old man, the queen of three crowns made a bird of herself, the Bird of the Golden Land, flew up through the hole, made a strong woman of herself, let down the rope, and drew up the King's son. The two went on after that, and never stopped till they were in sight of the castle; then the queen of three crowns became the Bird of the Golden Land, flew to a window of the King's chamber, and began to sing. Inside the window was the cage with the queen of one crown in it; in the chamber the King bewailing his youngest son, and sad because he could hear the song of the bird.

'O–h,' cried the King, springing up, 'that is the Bird of the Golden Land, and my youngest son has her.'

The words were scarce out of his mouth when in came the youngest son with the queen of three crowns and she told the whole story. The King in a rage wished to banish his two wicked sons, but forgave them at last.

The second brother took the rod and brought back the other two queens to their own shapes.

The King settled all as he wished and had the Bird of the Golden Land in his castle.

NOTES

Source of tale: Jeremiah Curtin, *Irish Folk Tales*, Dublin: Talbot Press, 1944.

As well as being a perfect example of the wonder tale, this reads like a classic account of a shamanic journey, and I have heard many of its elements repeated in accounts of my own shamanic students. The beginning, in which the hero sets out for the Golden Land by travelling down a deep shaft in the earth, is common to many journey tales of both this and other lands. The helping mare belongs to that vast category of helping animals which we have met so often throughout this collection. She is especially skilled in magic and trickery, and this is fully in keeping with the sacred status of the horse among the Celtic peoples. The wonderful game of hide-and-seek is reminiscent of a form of shamanic 'tag' used in training contemporary students to sharpen their journey skills. To travel in the shape of another creature, and to seek out a partner in another form, is one of the most exciting and challenging aspects of modern shamanic practice. One is reminded, too, of the many poems by the Celtic bard Taliesin, whose work has been shown to contain a largely shamanic content, in which he declares that he has been in the form of a thousand different things: creatures, objects, growing things, stones and so forth. The King's Youngest Son experiences many of these changes in his search for the Bird of the Golden Land, which itself is a probable metaphor for the soul.

In this story, in an interesting variation of the 'Giant Who Had No Heart' theme, discussed in the notes to 'The Bare-Stripping Hangman' (see page 67), the King of the Golden Land hides himself, rather than his soul, in the various objects which the hero must seek out. But he cannot escape the wisdom of the little mare, who knows all and sees all, and instructs the hero where to look on each occasion.

Then, once the King's son had succeeded in capturing the Golden Bird during one of those moments when the King sleeps – once only in seven years – he is pursued not just by one army but by three: significantly they are coloured white, red and black, three colours long believed to be sacred to the Goddess of the Land, as well as to the people of faery. The three wonderful queens, each one with a different magical ability, and each one possessed of one, two, and three crowns, are themselves an image of the triple-aspected goddess who was worshipped at one time throughout most of the world, and by the Celts for longer than most peoples. Even when the three are all together with the three sons, there is a marvellous twist in the tail of this story as the two older brothers try to get the kingdom for themselves; but the magical women cannot be made to be or do what they are not, and in the end all is resolved as it should be.

The queen of one crown is transformed into the Bird of Golden Land

155

In the Kingdom of Seals

THE SEA FAIRIES HAVE GREY skin-coverings and resemble seals. They dwell in cave houses on the borders of Land-under-Waves, where they have a kingdom of their own. They love music and the dance, like the green land fairies, and when harper or piper plays on the beach they come up to listen, their sloe-black eyes sparkling with joy. On moonlight nights they hear the mermaids singing on the rocks when human beings are fast asleep, and they call to them: 'Sing again the old sea croons; sing again!' All night long the sea fairies call thus when mermaids cease to sing, and the mermaids sing again and again to them.

When the wind pipes loud and free, and the sea leaps and whirls and swings and cries aloud with wintry merriment, the sea fairies dance with the dancing waves, tossing white petals of foam over their heads, and twining pearls of spray about their necks. They love to hunt the silvern salmon in the forests of sea-tangle and in ocean's deep blue glens, and far up dark ravines through which flow rivers of sweet mountain waters gemmed with stars.

The sea fairies have a language of their own, and they are also skilled in human speech. When they come ashore they can take the forms of men or women, and turn billows into dark horses with grey manes and long grey tails, and on these they ride over mountain and moor.

There was once a fisherman who visited the palace of the queen of sea fairies, and told on his return all he had seen and all he had heard. He dwelt in a little township nigh to John-o'-Groat's House, and was wont to catch fish and seals. When he found that he could earn much money by hunting seals, whose skins make warm winter clothing, he troubled little about catching salmon or cod, and worked constantly as a seal-hunter. He crept among the rocks searching for his prey, and visited lonely seal-haunted islands across the Pentland Firth, where he often found the strange sea-prowlers lying on smooth flat ledges of rock fast asleep in the warm sunshine.

Two sea fairies from the Land-under-Waves

156

In his house he had great bundles of dried sealskins, and people came
from a distance to purchase them from him. His fame as a seal-hunter went
far and wide.

One evening a dark stranger rode up to his house, mounted on a black,
spirited mare with grey mane and grey tail. He called to the fisherman who
came out, and then said: 'Make haste and ride with me towards the east. My
master desires to do business with you.'

'I have no horse,' the fisherman answered, 'but I shall walk to your
master's house on the morrow.'

Said the stranger: 'Come now. Ride with me. My good mare is fleet-
footed and strong.'

'As you will,' answered the fisherman, who at once mounted the mare
behind the stranger.

The mare turned round and right-about, and galloped eastward faster
than the wind of March. Shingle rose in front of her like rock-strewn sea-
spray, and a sand-cloud gathered and swept out behind like mountain mists
that are scattered before a gale. The fisherman gasped for breath, for
although the wind was blowing against his back when he mounted the mare,
it blew fiercely in his face as he rode on. The mare went fast and far until she
drew nigh to a precipice. Near the edge of it she halted suddenly. The fisherman found then that the wind was still blowing seaward, although he had
thought it had veered round as he rode. Never before had he sat on the back
of so fleet-footed a mare.

Said the stranger: 'We have almost reached my master's dwelling.'

The fisherman looked round about him with surprise, and saw neither
house nor the smoke of one. 'Where is your master?' he asked.

Said the stranger: 'You shall see him presently. Come with me.'

As he spoke he walked towards the edge of the precipice and looked over.
The fisherman did the same, and saw nothing but the grey lonely sea heaving
in a long slow swell, and sea-birds wheeling and sliding down the wind.

'Where is your master?' he asked once again.

With that the stranger suddenly clasped the seal-hunter in his arms, and
crying, 'Come with me,' leapt over the edge of the precipice. The mare leapt
with her master.

Down, down they fell through the air, scattering the startled sea-birds.
Screaming and fluttering, the birds rose in clouds about and above them, and
down ever down the men and the mare continued to fall till they plunged into
the sea, and sank and sank, while the light around them faded into darkness
deeper than night. The fisherman wondered to find himself still alive as he
passed through the sea depths, seeing naught, hearing naught, and still moving swiftly. At length he ceased to sink, and went forward. He suffered no
pain or discomfort, nor was he afraid. His only feeling was of wonder, and in
the thick, cool darkness he wondered greatly what would happen next. At
length he saw a faint green light, and as he went onward the light grew
brighter and brighter, until the glens and bens and forests of the sea kingdom
arose before his eyes. Then he discovered that he was swimming beside the
stranger and that they had both been changed into seals.

Said the stranger: 'Yonder is my master's house.'

The fisherman looked, and saw a township of foam-white houses on the edge of a great sea-forest and fronted by a bank of sea-moss which was green as grass but more beautiful, and very bright. There were crowds of seal-folk in the township. He saw them moving about to and fro, and heard their voices, but he could not understand their speech. Mothers nursed their babes, and young children played games on banks of green sea-moss, and from the brown and golden sea-forest came sounds of music and the shouts of dancers.

Said the stranger: 'Here is my master's house. Let us enter.'

He led the fisherman towards the door of a great foam-white palace with its many bright windows. It was thatched with red tangle, and the door was of green stone. The door opened as smoothly as a summer wave that moves across a river mouth, and the fisherman entered with his guide. He found himself in a dimly-lighted room, and saw an old grey seal stretched on a bed, and heard him moaning with pain. Beside the bed lay a blood-stained knife, and the fisherman knew at a glance that it was his own. Then he remembered that, not many hours before, he had stabbed a seal, and that it had escaped by plunging into the sea, carrying the knife in its back.

The fisherman was startled to realize that the old seal on the bed was the very one he had tried to kill, and his heart was filled with fear. He threw himself down and begged for forgiveness and mercy, for he feared that he would be put to death.

The guide lifted up the knife and asked: 'Have you ever seen this knife before?' He spoke in human language.

'That is my knife, alas!' exclaimed the fisherman.

Said the guide: 'The wounded seal is my father. Our doctors are unable to cure him. They can do naught without your help. That is why I visited your house and urged you to come with me. I ask your pardon for deceiving you, O man! but as I love my father greatly, I had to do as I have done.'

'Do not ask my pardon,' the fisherman said; 'I have need of yours. I am sorry and ashamed for having stabbed your father.'

Said the guide: 'Lay your hand on the wound and wish it to be healed.'

The fisherman laid his hand on the wound, and the pain that the seal suffered passed into his hand, but did not remain long. As if by magic, the wound was healed at once. Then the old grey seal rose up strong and well again.

Said the guide: 'You have served us well this day, O man!'

When the fisherman had entered the house, all the seals that were within were weeping tears of sorrow, but they ceased to weep as soon as he had laid his hand on the wound, and when the old seal rose up they all became merry and bright.

The fisherman wondered what would happen next. For a time the seals seemed to forget his presence, but at length his guide spoke to him and said: 'Now, O man! you can return to your own home where your wife and children await you. I shall lead you through the sea depths, and take you on my mare across the plain which we crossed when coming hither.'

'I give you thanks,' the fisherman exclaimed.

Said the guide: 'Before you leave there is one thing you must do; you must take a vow never again to hunt seals.'

159

The fisherman answered: 'Surely, I promise never again to hunt for seals.'

Said the guide: 'If ever you break your promise you shall die. I counsel you to keep it, and as long as you do so you will prosper. Every time you set lines, or cast a net, you will catch much fish. Our seal-servants will help you, and if you wish to reward them for their services, take with you in your boat a harp or pipe and play sweet music, for music is the delight of all seals.'

The fisherman vowed he would never break his promise, and the guide then led him back to dry land. As soon as he reached the shore he ceased to be a seal and became a man once again. The guide, who had also changed shape, breathed over a great wave and, immediately, it became a dark mare with grey mane and grey tail. He then mounted the mare, and bade the

*Seal-folk listening to
a mermaid's song*

160

fisherman mount behind him. The mare rose in the air as lightly as wind-tossed spray, and passing through the clouds of startled sea-birds reached the top of the precipice. On she raced at once, raising the shingle in front and a cloud of sand behind. The night was falling and the stars began to appear, but it was not quite dark when the fisherman's house was reached.

The fisherman dismounted, and his guide spoke and said: 'Take this from me, and may you live happily.'

He handed the fisherman a small bag, and crying: 'Farewell! Remember your vow,' he wheeled his mare right round and passed swiftly out of sight.

The fisherman entered his house, and found his wife still there. 'You have returned,' she said. 'How did you fare?'

'I know not yet,' he answered. Then he sat down and opened the bag, and to his surprise and delight found it was full of pearls.

His wife uttered a cry of wonder, and said: 'From whom did you receive this treasure?'

The fisherman then related all that had taken place, and his wife wondered to hear him.

'Never again will I hunt seals,' he exclaimed. And he kept his word and prospered, and lived happily until the day of his death.

NOTES

Source of tale: Donald A. Mackenzie, *Wonder Tales from Scottish Myth and Legend*, Glasgow: Blackie and Sons, 1917.

The relationship of mankind and the sea is one that is often explored in Celtic story. The belief that the seashore, a place of the meeting of two worlds, was a doorway into the otherworld infused all stories set there with a particular significance. Thus here we have a detailed description of the Land-under-Waves, and of the relationship which exists between the seals and the undersea folk. Stories of 'selkies', otherworldly beings who can take the shape of seals at will, but put off their skins on land and seem like mortals, abound throughout the islands of Scotland. Human men sometimes marry these seal women, but more often than not their wives soon pine for the land beneath the waves, and return there, leaving families behind who some-times inherit their mother's ability to shapeshift. The MacCodrum family of the Outer Hebrides were reputed to be descended from such a marriage. Here the fisherman had succeeded in stealing the skin of the selkie, and then forced her to marry him; but after she had borne him several children she retrieved her skin and returned to the sea. In Gaelic her descendants are known as 'Clan Codrum of the Seals'.

Interestingly, in this story, there is a distinct difference between the sea faeries and the mermaids, where the latter are seen as making music at the request of the former. It is well known that seals love music, and I well remember seeing my wife wade into the ocean off Widby Island in the Portland Sound in North America, singing to a grey head which bobbed above the surface of the waves for ten minutes before vanishing from sight.

KIL ARTHUR

HERE WAS A TIME long ago, and if we had lived then, we shouldn't be living now.

In that time there was a law in the world that if a young man came to woo a young woman, and her people wouldn't give her to him, the young woman should get her death by the law.

There was a king in Erin at that time who had a daughter, and he had a son too, who was called Kil Arthur, son of the monarch of Erin.

Now, not far from the castle of the king there was a tinker; and one morning he said to his mother: 'Put down my breakfast for me, mother.'

'Where are you going?' asked the mother.

'I'm going for a wife.'

'Where?'

'I am going for the daughter of the king of Erin.'

'Oh! my son, bad luck is upon you. It is death to ask for the king's daughter, and you a tinker.'

'I don't care for that,' said he.

So the tinker went to the king's castle. They were at dinner when he came, and the king trembled as he saw him.

Though they were at table, the tinker went into the room.

The king asked: 'What did you come for at this time?'

'I came to marry your daughter.'

'That life and strength may leave me if ever you get my daughter in marriage! I'd give her to death before I would to a tinker.'

Now Kil Arthur, the king's son, came in, caught the tinker and hanged him, facing the front of the castle. When he was dead, they made seven parts of his body, and flung them into the sea.

Then the king had a box made so close and tight that no water could enter, and inside the box they fixed a coffin; and when they had put a bed with meat and drink into the coffin, they brought the king's daughter, laid her on the bed, closed the box, and pushed it into the open sea. The box went out with the tide and moved on the water for a long time; where it was one day it was not the next, – carried along by the waves day and night, till at last it came to another land.

Now, in the other land was a man who had spent his time in going to sea, till at length he got very poor, and said: 'I'll stay at home now, since God has let me live this long. I heard my father say once that if a man would always rise early and walk along the strand, he would get his fortune from the tide at last.'

One morning early, as this man was going along the strand, he saw the box, and brought it up to the shore, where he opened it and took out the coffin. When the lid was off the coffin, he found a woman inside alive.

'Oh!' said he, 'I'd rather have you there than the full of the box of gold.'

'I think the gold would be better for you,' said the woman.

He took the stranger to his house, and gave her food and drink. Then he made a great cross on the ground, and clasping hands with the woman, jumped over the arms of the cross, going in the same direction as the sun. This was the form of marriage in that land.

They lived together pleasantly. She was a fine woman, worked well for her husband, and brought him great wealth, so that he became richer than any man; and one day, when out walking alone, he said to himself: 'I am able to give a grand dinner now to Ri Fohin, Sladaire Mor (king under the wave, the great robber), who owns men, women, and every kind of beast.'

Then he went home and invited Ri Fohin to dinner. He came with all the men, women, and beasts he had, and they covered the country for six miles.

The beasts were fed outside by themselves, but the people in the house. When dinner was over, he asked Ri Fohin: 'Have you ever seen a house so fine and rich, or a dinner so good, as mine to-night?'

'I have not,' said Ri Fohin.

Then the man went to each person present. Each gave the same answer, and said, 'I have never seen such a house nor such a dinner.'

He asked his wife, and she said: 'My praise is no praise here; but what is this to the house and the feasting of my father, the king of Erin?'

'Why did you say that?' asked the man, and he went a second and a third time to the guests and to his wife. All had the same answers for him. Then he gave his wife a flip of the thumb on her ear, in a friendly way, and said: 'Why don't you give good luck to my house; why do you give it a bad name?'

Then all the guests said: 'It is a shame to strike your wife on the night of a feast.'

Now the man was angry and went out of his house. It was growing dark, but he saw a champion coming on a black steed between earth and air; and the champion, who was no other than Kil Arthur, his brother-in-law, took him up and bore him away to the castle of the king of Erin.

When Kil Arthur arrived they were just sitting down to dinner in the castle, and the man dined with his father-in-law. After dinner the king of Erin had cards brought and asked his son-in-law: 'Do you ever play with these?'

'No, I have never played with the like of them.'

*'What warrior struck
the Pole of Combat?'
he demanded*

'Well, shuffle them now,' said the king. He shuffled; and as they were
enchanted cards and whoever held them could never lose a game he was the
best player in the world, though he had never played a game before in his life.

The king said, 'Put them in your pocket, they may do you good.' Then the
king gave him a fiddle, and asked:

'Have you ever played on the like of this?'

'Indeed I have not,' said the man.

'Well, play on it now,' said the king.

He played, and never in his life had he heard such music.

'Keep it,' said the king; 'as long as you don't let it from you, you're the first musician on earth. Now I'll give you something else. Here is a cup which will always give you every kind of drink you can wish for; and if all the men in the world were to drink out of it they could never empty it. Keep these three things; but never raise hand on your wife again.'

The king of Erin gave him his blessing; then Kil Arthur took him up on the steed, and going between earth and sky he was soon back at his own home.

Now Ri Fohin had carried off the man's wife and all that he had while he was at dinner with the King of Erin. Going out on the road the king's son-in-law began to cry: 'Oh, what shall I do; what shall I do!' and as he cried, who should come but Kil Arthur on his steed, who said, 'Be quiet, I'll go for your wife and goods.'

Kil Arthur went, and killed Ri Fohin and all his people and beasts, – didn't leave one alive. Then he brought back his sister to her husband, and stayed with them for three years.

One day he said to his sister: 'I am going to leave you. I don't know what strength I have; I'll walk the world now till I know is there a man in it as good as myself.'

Next morning he bade good-bye to his sister, and rode away on his black-haired steed, which overtook the wind before and outstripped the wind behind. He travelled swiftly till evening, spent the night in a forest, and the second day hurried on as he had the first.

The second night he spent in a forest; and next morning as he rose from the ground he saw before him a man covered with blood from fighting, and the clothes nearly torn from his body.

'What have you been doing?' asked Kil Arthur.

'I have been playing cards all night. And where are you going?' inquired the stranger of Kil Arthur.

'I am going around the world to know can I find a man as good as myself.'

'Come with me,' said the stranger, 'and I'll show you a man who couldn't find his match till he went to fight the main ocean.'

Kil Arthur went with the ragged stranger till they came to a place from which they saw a giant out on the ocean beating the waves with a club.

Kil Arthur went up to the giant's castle, and struck the pole of combat such a blow that the giant in the ocean heard it above the noise of his club as he pounded the waves.

'What do you want?' asked the giant in the ocean, as he stopped from the pounding.

'I want you to come in here to land,' said Kil Arthur, 'and fight with a better man than yourself.'

The giant came to land, and standing near his castle said to Kil Arthur: 'Which would you rather fight with, – gray stones or sharp weapons?'

'Gray stones,' said Kil Arthur.

They went at each other, and fought the most terrible battle that either of them had ever seen till that day. At last Kil Arthur pushed the giant to his shoulders through solid earth.

'Take me out of this,' cried the giant, 'and I'll give you my sword of light that never missed a blow, my Druidic rod of most powerful enchantment, and my healing draught which cures every sickness and wound.'

165

'Well,' said Kil Arthur, 'I'll go for your sword and try it.'

He went to the giant's castle for the sword, the rod, and the healing draught. When he returned the giant said: 'Try the sword on that tree out there.'

'Oh,' said Kil Arthur, 'there is no tree so good as your own neck,' and with that he swept off the head of the giant; took it, and went on his way till he came to a house. He went in and put the head on a table; but that instant it disappeared, – went away of itself. Food and drink of every kind came on the table. When Kil Arthur had eaten and the table was cleared by some invisible power, the giant's head bounded on to the table, and with it a pack of cards.

'Perhaps this head wants to play with me,' thought Kil Arthur, and he cut his own cards and shuffled them.

The head took up the cards and played with its mouth as well as any man could with his hands. It won all the time, – wasn't playing fairly. Then Kil Arthur thought: 'I'll settle this;' and he took the cards and showed how the head had taken five points in the game that didn't belong to it. Then the head sprang at him, struck and beat him till he seized and hurled it into the fire.

As soon as he had the head in the fire a beautiful woman stood before him, and said: 'You have killed nine of my brothers, and this was the best of the nine. I have eight more brothers who go out to fight with four hundred men each day, and they kill them all; but next morning the four hundred are alive again and my brothers have to do battle anew. Now my mother and these eight brothers will be here soon; and they'll go down on their bended knees and curse you who killed my nine brothers, and I'm afraid your blood will rise within you when you hear the curses, and you'll kill my eight remaining brothers.'

'Oh,' said Kil Arthur, 'I'll be deaf when the curses are spoken; I'll not hear them.' Then he went to a couch and lay down. Presently the mother and eight brothers came, and cursed Kil Arthur with all the curses they knew. He heard them to the end, but gave no word from himself.

Next morning he rose early, girded on his nine-edged sword, went forth to where the eight brothers were going to fight the four hundred, and said to the eight: 'Sit down, and I'll fight in your place.'

Kil Arthur faced the four hundred, and fought with them alone; and exactly at mid-day he had them all dead. 'Now some one,' said he, 'brings these to life again. I'll lie down among them and see who it is.'

Soon he saw an old hag coming with a brush in her hand, and an open vessel hanging from her neck by a string. When she came to the four hundred she dipped the brush into the vessel and sprinkled the liquid which was in it over the bodies of the men. They rose up behind her as she passed along.

'Bad luck to you,' said Kil Arthur, 'you are the one that keeps them alive;' then he seized her. Putting one of his feet on her two ankles, and grasping her by the head and shoulders, he twisted her body till he put the life out of her.

When dying she said: 'I put you under a curse, to keep on this road till you come to the "ram of the five rocks," and tell him you have killed the hag of the heights and all her care.'

166 He went to the place where the ram of the five rocks lived and struck the

pole of combat before his castle. Out came the ram, and they fought till Kil Arthur seized his enemy and dashed the brains out of him against the rocks.

Then he went to the castle of the beautiful woman whose nine brothers he had killed, and for whose eight brothers he had slain the four hundred. When he appeared the mother rejoiced; the eight brothers blessed him and gave him their sister in marriage; and Kil Arthur took the beautiful woman to his father's castle in Erin, where they both lived happily and well.

NOTES

Source of tale: Jeremiah Curtin, *Myths and Folk Tales of Ireland*, Boston: Little, Brown and Co., 1890.

Few stories in this collection gather together such a broad spectrum of themes and incidents from Celtic tradition. Here are strange laws (such as that if someone asks for the hand of the daughter of the king of Erin and does not win her, she rather than her potential suitor must suffer); and even stranger encounters with giants and hags. The theme of the bride who is found floating on the sea in a coffin brings to mind not only the 'Sleeping Beauty' story, with all its complex antecedents, but also the Taliesin story, where the reborn child Gwion is cast adrift in a leather bag, from which he is eventually recovered and brings good fortune to his rescuer just as the king's daughter does at first for the fisherman. The blow that he strikes her, with all that follows thereafter, is probably the last vestige of a longer incident, omitted from this telling in which he struck her three times and thus forfeited both the right to be her husband and any luck she had brought him (see also 'The Legend of Llyn-Y-Fan-Fach', page 106–13). Instead this is used as a jumping-off point for the real hero of the piece, Kil Arthur, to set out on a series of adventures. There is some confusion in the story between the various packs of cards, and the number of giants killed. Though Kil Arthur apparently only slays one of them, he is accused of slaying nine – another indication that is either a corrupt or a badly remembered story, though it may also be a confusion over the giant's magical sword, which is described as 'nine-edged'. The striking of the pole of combat, which initiates the battle, is often referred to in the epic literature of Ireland. It appears that at one time a pole was set up outside the house or village of a hero and that to strike it summoned him to defend his title.

The hag who recalls to life the 400 men is reminiscent of several Celtic figures who possess wonder-working cauldrons. Thus in Welsh myth Ceridwen is the mistress of the Cauldron of Inspiration, from which poets imbibe the *Awen*; while in 'Branwen, Daughter of Llyr' from *The Mabinogion* (Dent, 1937), there is a quest for a cauldron which, like the vessel owned by the hag of the heights in this story, restores the dead to life – though still speechless, since it would not be right to tell what had been seen in the Land of the Dead.

In all this is a rich and complex story which well repays study and re-reading.

THE BATTLE OF THE BIRDS

 WILL TELL YOU A STORY about the wren. There was once a farmer who was seeking a servant, and the wren met him and said: 'What are you seeking?' 'I am seeking a servant,' said the farmer to the wren.

'Will you take me?' said the wren.

'You, you poor creature, what good would you do?'

'Try me,' said the wren.

So he engaged him, and the first work he set him to do was threshing in the barn. The wren threshed (what did he thresh with? Why a flail to be sure), and he knocked off one grain. A mouse came out and she eats that.

'I'll trouble you not to do that again,' said the wren.

He struck again, and he struck off two grains. Out came the mouse and she eats them. So they arranged a contest to see who was strongest, and the wren brings his twelve birds, and the mouse her tribe.

'You have your tribe with you,' said the wren.

'As well as yourself,' said the mouse, and she struck out her leg proudly. But the wren broke it with his flail, and there was a pitched battle on a set day.

When every creature and bird was gathering to battle, the son of the king of Tethertown said that he would go to see the battle, and that he would bring sure word home to his father the king, who would be king of the creatures this year. The battle was over before he arrived all but one fight, between a great black raven and a snake. The snake was twined about the raven's neck, and the raven held the snake's throat in his beak, and it seemed as if the snake would get the victory over the raven. When the king's son saw this he helped the raven, and with one blow takes the head off the snake. When the raven had taken breath, and saw that the snake was dead, he said, 'For thy kindness to me this day, I will give thee a sight. Come up now on the root of my two wings.' The king's son put his hands about the raven before his wings, and before he stopped, he took him over nine Bens, and nine Glens, and nine Mountain Moors.

'Now,' said the raven, 'see you that house yonder? Go now to it. It is a sister of mine that makes her dwelling in it; and I will go bail that you are welcome. And if she asks you, Were you at the battle of the birds? say you were. And if she asks, "Did you see any one like me," say you did, but be sure that you meet me to-morrow morning here, in this place.' The king's son got good and right good treatment that night. Meat of each meat, drink of each drink, warm water to his feet, and a soft bed for his limbs.

On the next day the raven gave him the same sight over six Bens, and six Glens, and six Mountain Moors. They saw a bothy far off, but, though far off, they were soon there. He got good treatment this night, as before – plenty of meat and drink, and warm water to his feet, and a soft bed to his limbs – and on the next day it was the same thing, over three Bens and three Glens, and three Mountain Moors.

On the third morning, instead of seeing the raven as at the other times, who should meet him but the handsomest lad he ever saw, with gold rings in his hair, with a bundle in his hand. The king's son asked this lad if he had seen a big black raven.

Said the lad to him, 'You will never see the raven again, for I am that raven. I was put under spells by a bad druid; it was meeting you that loosed me, and for that you shall get this bundle. Now,' said the lad, 'you must turn back on the self-same steps, and lie a night in each house as before; but you must not loose the bundle which I gave ye, till in the place where you would most wish to dwell.'

The king's son turned his back to the lad, and his face to his father's house; and he got lodging from the raven's sisters, just as he got it when going forward. When he was nearing his father's house he was going through a close wood. It seemed to him that the bundle was growing heavy, and he thought he would look what was in it.

When he loosed the bundle he was astonished. In a twinkling he sees the very grandest place he ever saw. A great castle, and an orchard about the castle, in which was every kind of fruit and herb. He stood full of wonder and regret for having loosed the bundle – for it was not in his power to put it back again – and he would have wished this pretty place to be in the pretty little green hollow that was opposite his father's house; but he looked up and saw a great giant coming towards him.

'Bad's the place where you have built the house, king's son,' says the giant.

'Yes, but it is not here I would wish it to be, though it happens to be here by mishap,' says the king's son.

'What's the reward for putting it back in the bundle as it was before?'

'What's the reward you would ask?' says the king's son.

'That you will give me the first son you have when he is seven years of age,' says the giant.

'If I have a son you shall have him,' said the king's son.

In a twinkling the giant put each garden, and orchard, and castle in the bundle as they were before.

'Now,' says the giant, 'take your own road, and I will take mine; but mind your promise, and if you forget I will remember.'

The king's son took to the road, and at the end of a few days he reached

the place he was fondest of. He loosed the bundle, and the castle was just as it was before. And when he opened the castle door he sees the handsomest maiden he ever cast eye upon.

'Advance, king's son,' said the pretty maid; 'everything is in order for you, if you will marry me this very day.'

'It's I that am willing,' said the king's son. And on the same day they married.

But at the end of a day and seven years, who should be seen coming to the castle but the giant. The king's son was reminded of his promise to the giant, and till now he had not told his promise to the queen.

'Leave the matter between me and the giant,' says the queen.

'Turn out your son,' says the giant; 'mind your promise.'

'You shall have him,' says the king, 'when his mother puts him in order for his journey.'

The queen dressed up the cook's son, and she gave him to the giant by the hand. The giant went away with him; but he had not gone far when he put a rod in the hand of the little laddie. The giant asked him –

'If thy father had that rod what would he do with it?'

'If my father had that rod he would beat the dogs and the cats, so that they shouldn't be going near the king's meat,' said the little laddie.

'Thou'rt the cook's son,' said the giant. He catches him by the two small ankles and knocks him against the stone that was beside him. The giant turned back to the castle in rage and madness, and he said that if they did not send out the king's son to him, the highest stone of the castle would be the lowest.

Said the queen to the king, 'We'll try it yet; the butler's son is of the same age as our son.'

She dressed up the butler's son, and she gives him to the giant by the hand. The giant had not gone far when he put the rod in his hand.

'If thy father had that rod,' says the giant, 'what would he do with it?'

'He would beat the dogs and the cats when they would be coming near the king's bottles and glasses.'

'Thou art the son of the butler,' says the giant and dashed his brains out too. The giant returned in a very great rage and anger. The earth shook under the sole of his feet, and the castle shook and all that was in it.

'OUT HERE WITH THY SON' says the giant, 'or in a twinkling the stone that is highest in the dwelling will be the lowest.' So they had to give the king's son to the giant.

When they were gone a little bit from the earth, the giant showed him the rod that was in his hand and said: 'What would thy father do with this rod if he had it?'

The king's son said: 'My father has a braver rod than that.'

And the giant asked him, 'Where is thy father when he has that brave rod?'

And the king's son said: 'He will be sitting in his kingly chair.'

Then the giant understood that he had the right one.

The giant took him to his own house, and he reared him as his own son. On a day of days when the giant was from home, the lad heard the sweetest

*The trans-
formed raven
offers the
magic bundle*

171

music he ever heard in a room at the top of the giant's house. At a glance he saw the finest face he had ever seen. She beckoned to him to come a bit nearer to her, and she said her name was Auburn Mary but she told him to go this time, but to be sure to be at the same place about that dead midnight.

And as he promised he did. The giant's daughter was at his side in a twinkling, and she said, 'To-morrow you will get the choice of my two sisters to marry; but say that you will not take either, but me. My father wants me to marry the son of the king of the Green City, but I don't like him.' On the morrow the giant took out his three daughters, and he said:

'Now, son of the king of Tethertown, thou hast not lost by living with me so long. Thou wilt get to wife one of the two eldest of my daughters, and with her leave to go home with her the day after the wedding.'

'If you will give me this pretty little one,' says the king's son, 'I will take you at your word.'

The giant's wrath kindled, and he said: 'Before thou gett'st her thou must do the three things that I ask thee to do.'

'Say on,' says the king's son.

The giant took him to the byre.

'Now,' says the giant, 'a hundred cattle are stabled here, and it has not been cleansed for seven years. I am going from home to-day, and if this byre is not cleaned before night comes, so clean that a golden apple will run from end to end of it, not only thou shalt not get my daughter, but 'tis only a drink of thy fresh, goodly, beautiful blood that will quench my thirst this night.'

He begins cleaning the byre, but he might just as well to keep baling the great ocean. After midday when sweat was blinding him, the giant's youngest daughter came where he was, and she said to him:

'You are being punished, king's son.'

'I am that,' says the king's son.

'Come over,' says Auburn Mary, 'and lay down your weariness.'

'I will do that,' says he, 'there is but death awaiting me, at any rate.' He sat down near her. He was so tired that he fell asleep beside her. When he awoke, the giant's daughter was not to be seen, but the byre was so well cleaned that a golden apple would run from end to end of it and raise no stain. In comes the giant, and he said:

'Hast thou cleaned the byre, king's son?'

'I have cleaned it,' says he.

'Somebody cleaned it,' says the giant.

'You did not clean it, at all events,' said the king's son.

'Well, well!' says the giant, 'since thou wert so active to-day, thou wilt get to this time to-morrow to thatch this byre with birds' down, from birds with no two feathers of one colour.'

The king's son was on foot before the sun; he caught up his bow and his quiver of arrows to kill the birds. He took to the moors, but if he did, the birds were not so easy to take. He was running after them till the sweat was blinding him. About mid-day who should come but Auburn Mary.

'You are exhausting yourself, king's son,' says she.

'I am,' said he.

'There fell but these two blackbirds, and both of one colour.'

'Come over and lay down your weariness on this pretty hillock,' says the giant's daughter.

'It's I am willing,' said he.

He thought she would aid him this time, too, and he sat down near her, and he was not long there till he fell asleep.

When he awoke, Auburn Mary was gone. He thought he would go back to the house, and he sees the byre thatched with feathers. When the giant came home, he said:

'Hast thou thatched the byre, king's son?'

'I thatched it,' says he.

'Somebody thatched it,' says the giant.

'You did not thatch it,' says the king's son.

'Yes, yes!' says the giant. 'Now,' says the giant, 'there is a fir tree beside that loch down there, and there is a magpie's nest in its top. The eggs thou wilt find in the nest. I must have them for my first meal. Not one must be burst or broken, and there are five in the nest.'

Early in the morning the king's son went where the tree was, and that tree was not hard to hit upon. Its match was not in the whole wood. From the foot to the first branch was five hundred feet. The king's son was going all round the tree. She came who was always bringing help to him.

'You are losing the skin of your hands and feet.'

'Ach! I am,' says he. 'I am no sooner up than down.'

'This is no time for stopping,' says the giant's daughter. 'Now you must kill me, strip the flesh from my bones, take all those bones apart, and use them as steps for climbing the tree. When you are climbing the tree, they will stick to the glass as if they had grown out of it; but when you are coming down, and have put your foot on each one, they will drop into your hand when you touch them. Be sure and stand on each bone, leave none untouched; if you do, it will stay behind. Put all my flesh into this clean cloth by the side of the spring at the roots of the tree. When you come to the earth, arrange my bones together, put the flesh over them, sprinkle it with water from the spring, and I shall be alive before you. But don't forget a bone of me on the tree.'

'How could I kill you,' asked the king's son, 'after what you have done for me?'

'If you won't obey, you and I are done for,' said Auburn Mary. 'You must climb the tree, or we are lost; and to climb the tree you must do as I say.'

The king's son obeyed. He killed Auburn Mary, cut the flesh from her body, and unjointed the bones, as she had told him.

As he went up, the king's son put the bones of Auburn Mary's body against the side of the tree, using them as steps, till he came under the nest and stood on the last bone.

Then he took the eggs, and coming down, put his foot on every bone, then took it with him, till he came to the last bone, which was so near the ground that he failed to touch it with his foot.

He now placed all the bones of Auburn Mary in order again at the side of the spring, put the flesh on them, sprinkled it with water from the spring. She rose up before him, and said: 'Didn't I tell you not to leave a bone of my body without stepping on it? Now I am lame for life! You left my little finger on the tree without touching it, and I have but nine fingers.'

'Now,' says she, 'go home with the eggs quickly, and you will get me to marry to-night if you can know me. I and my two sisters will be arrayed in the same garments, and made like each other, but look at me when my father says, "Go to thy wife, king's son;" and you will see a hand without a little finger.'

He gave the eggs to the giant.

'Yes, yes!' says the giant, 'be making ready for your marriage.'

Then, indeed, there was a wedding, and it was a wedding! Giants and gentlemen, and the son of the king of the Green City was in the midst of them. They were married, and the dancing began, that was a dance! The giant's house was shaking from top to bottom.

But bed time came, and the giant said, 'It is time for thee to go to rest, son of the king of Tethertown; choose thy bride to take with thee from amidst those.'

She put out the hand off which the little finger was, and he caught her by the hand.

'Thou hast aimed well this time too; but there is no knowing but we may meet thee another way,' said the giant.

But to rest they went. 'Now,' says she, 'sleep not, or else you are a dead man. We must fly quick, quick, or for certain my father will kill you.'

Out they went, and on the blue grey filly in the stable they mounted. 'Stop a while,' says she, 'and I will play a trick to the old hero.' She jumped in, and cut an apple into nine shares, and she put two shares at the head of the bed, and two shares at the foot of the bed, and two shares at the door of the kitchen, and two shares at the big door, and one outside the house.

The giant awoke and called, 'Are you asleep?'

'Not yet,' said the apple that was at the head of the bed.

At the end of a while he called again.

'Not yet,' said the apple that was at the foot of the bed.

A while after this he called again: 'Are you asleep?'

'Not yet,' said the apple at the kitchen door.

The giant called again.

The apple that was at the big door answered.

'You are now going far from me,' says the giant.

'Not yet,' says the apple that was outside the house.

'You are flying,' says the giant. The giant jumped on his feet, and to the bed he went, but it was cold – empty.

'My own daughter's tricks are trying me,' said the giant. 'Here's after them,' says he.

At the mouth of day, the giant's daughter said that her father's breath was burning her back.

'Put your hand, quick,' said she, 'in the ear of the grey filly, and whatever you find in it, throw it behind us.'

'There is a twig of sloe tree,' said he.

'Throw it behind us,' said she.

No sooner did he that, than there were twenty miles of blackthorn wood, so thick that scarce a weasel could go through it.

The giant came headlong, and there he is fleecing his head and neck in the thorns.

'My own daughter's tricks are here as before,' said the giant; 'but if I had my own big axe and wood knife here, I would not be long making a way through this.'

He went home for the big axe and the wood knife, and sure he was not long on his journey, and he was the boy behind the big axe. He was not long making a way through the blackthorn.

'I will leave the axe and the wood knife here till I return,' says he.

'If you leave 'em, leave 'em,' said a hoodie that was in a tree, 'we'll steal 'em, steal 'em.'

'If you will do that,' says the giant, 'I must take them home.' He returned home and left them at the house.

At the heat of day the giant's daughter felt her father's breath burning her back.

'Put your finger in the filly's ear, and throw behind whatever you find in it.'

He got a splinter of grey stone, and in a twinkling there were twenty miles, by breadth and height, of great grey rock behind them.

The giant came full pelt, but past the rock he could not go.

'The tricks of my own daughter are the hardest things that ever met me,' says the giant; 'but if I had my lever and my mighty mattock, I would not be long in making my way through this rock also.'

There was no help for it, but to turn the chase for them; and he was the boy to split the stones. He was not long in making a road through the rock.

'I will leave the tools here, and I will return no more.'

'If you leave 'em, leave 'em,' says the hoodie, 'we will steal 'em, steal 'em.'

'Do that if you will; there is no time to go back.'

At the time of breaking the watch, the giant's daughter said that she felt her father's breath burning her back.

'Look in the filly's ear, king's son, or else we are lost.'

He did so, and it was a bladder of water that was in her ear this time. He threw it behind him and there was a fresh-water loch, twenty miles in length and breadth, behind them.

The giant came on, but with the speed he had on him, he was in the middle of the loch, and he went under, and he rose no more.

On the next day the young companions were come in sight of his father's house. 'Now,' says she, 'my father is drowned, and he won't trouble us any more; but before we go further,' says she, 'go you to your father's house, and tell that you have the likes of me; but let neither man nor creature kiss you, for if you do, you will not remember that you have ever seen me.'

Every one he met gave him welcome and luck, and he charged his father and mother not to kiss him; but as mishap was to be, an old greyhound was indoors, and she knew him, and jumped up to his mouth, and after that he did not remember the giant's daughter.

She was sitting at the well's side as he left her, but the king's son was not coming. In the mouth of night she climbed up into a tree of oak that was beside the well, and she lay in the fork of that tree all night. A shoemaker had a house near the well, and about mid-day on the morrow, the shoemaker asked his wife to go for a drink for him out of the well. When the shoemaker's wife reached the well, and when she saw the shadow of her that was in the tree, thinking it was her own shadow – and she never thought till now that she was so handsome – she gave a cast to the dish that was in her hand, and it was broken on the ground, and she took herself to the house without vessel or water.

'Where is the water, wife?' said the shoemaker.

'You shambling, contemptible old carle, without grace, I have stayed too long your water and wood thrall.'

'I think, wife, that you have turned crazy. Go you, daughter, quickly, and fetch a drink for your father.'

His daughter went, and in the same way so it happened to her. She never thought till now that she was so lovable, and she took herself home.

'Up with the drink,' said her father.

'You home-spun shoe carle, do you think I am fit to be your thrall?'

The poor shoemaker thought that they had taken a turn in their understandings, and he went himself to the well. He saw the shadow of the maiden in the well, and he looked up to the tree, and he sees the finest woman he ever saw.

'Your seat is wavering, but your face is fair,' said the shoemaker. 'Come down, for there is need of you for a short while at my house.'

The shoemaker understood that this was the shadow that had driven his people mad. The shoemaker took her to his house, and he said that he had but a poor bothy, but that she should get a share of all that was in it.

One day, the shoemaker had shoes ready, for on that very day the king's son was to be married. The shoemaker was going to the castle with the shoes of the young people, and the girl said to the shoemaker, 'I would like to get a sight of the king's son before he marries.'

'Come with me,' says the shoemaker, 'I am well acquainted with the servants at the castle, and you shall get a sight of the king's son and all the company.'

And when the gentles saw the pretty woman that was here they took her to the wedding-room, and they filled for her a glass of wine. When she was going to drink what is in it, a flame went up out of the glass, and a golden pigeon and a silver pigeon sprang out of it. They were flying about when three grains of barley fell on the floor. The silver pigeon sprung, and ate that up.

Said the golden pigeon to him, 'If you remembered when I cleared the byre, you would not eat that without giving me a share.'

Again there fell three other grains of barley, and the silver pigeon sprung, and ate that up as before.

'If you remembered when I thatched the byre, you would not eat that without giving me my share,' says the golden pigeon.

Three other grains fall, and the silver pigeon sprung, and ate that up.

'If you remembered when I harried the magpie's nest, you would not eat that without giving me my share,' says the golden pigeon; 'I lost my little finger bringing it down, and I want it still.'

The king's son minded, and he knew who it was that was before him.

'Well,' said the king's son to the guests at the feast, 'when I was a little younger than I am now, I lost the key of a casket that I had. I had a new key made, but after it was brought to me I found the old one. Now, I'll leave it to any one here to tell me what I am to do. Which of the keys should I keep?'

'My advice to you,' said one of the guests, 'is to keep the old key, for it fits the lock better and you're more used to it.'

Then the king's son stood up and said: 'I thank you for a wise advice and an honest word. This is my bride the daughter of the giant who saved my life at the risk of her own. I'll have her and no other woman.'

So the king's son married Auburn Mary and the wedding lasted long and all were happy. But all I got was butter on a live coal, porridge in a basket, and paper shoes for my feet, and they sent me for water to the stream, and the paper shoes came to an end.

The Giant's Daughter

BIDS the BIRDS thatch her FATHER'S BYRE.

NOTES

Source of tale: J.F. Campbell, *Popular Tales of the West Highlands*. Edinburgh: Edmonston & Douglas, 1860. Reprinted by Wildwood House, London, 1983–85.

This is a justly famous story, which extends the genre of the wonder tale to its limits. There are several versions extant, including one from Islay called 'The Widow's Son' which has some interesting variations on the way in which the giant's daughter achieves the tasks set by her father. When it comes to cleaning the byre she says, 'Gather, oh shovel, and put out, oh rake', and the tools work by themselves. In order to thatch the byre with feathers, the giant's daughter throws three grains of barley onto the roof and the birds come and thatch it themselves. Next day the hero has to capture a steed that has 'never seen a blink of earth or air', and she gives him a rusty old bridle which summons the steed which comes and puts its head into it. In the episode of the apples which call out to the giant, these are replaced by cakes which the giant's daughter bakes. Then, when he is pursuing them, instead of the three objects taken from the horse's ears the giant's daughter gives the hero a golden apple and tells him to throw it at a mole on her father's body. When the hero is concerned to miss such a small target, the girl herself does the deed and her father falls dead.

The version which appears here is from the telling of one John Dewar, collected in 1859 by the great John Francis Campbell and included in his monumental collection *Popular Tales of the West Highlands* (1822–85) (Wildwood House, 1983–85). Campbell believed this to be the oldest version, for which reason I have included it here. The opening, with its curious tale of the battle between the birds, is probably the oldest part of the tale, predating the main story considerably. It may indeed belong to the lost cycle of tales relating to animal and bird 'totems' of which 'The Eagle of Loch Treig' (see pages 114–18) is another. There are many parallels between this story and the great classic compendium of Welsh mythic stories bound together under the title 'Culhwch and Olwen' from *The Mabinogion* (Dent, 1937). Here the hero is assisted by the warriors of Arthur (the pre-Arthurian figure) and by the daughter of the giant Ysbaddadden, who helps Culhwch in much the same way as the giant's daughter here. There is also a whole sequence of 'helping animals', which may well derive from the same cycle of tales which is partially present here.

There are echoes, too, of both Norse and Germanic tales. The ladder of bones, though not exactly as given here, appears in Grimm's *Tales*, and the story as a whole has a version which is well known in Norway. Campbell himself suggests that there might be a shadowy memory of early encounters between the tall, fair-haired Gaels and the little, dark-haired aboriginal race of these islands. In the stories, the former gradually became transformed into a race of giants and the little dark people into the heroes of many of these tales. There is also at least a possibility that the tale of the labours of Hercules (who may have had a closer connection with these islands than is generally acknowledged) may also have influenced this tale, in the matter of the cleaning of the stables if nothing more. It is perfectly possible that these old Classical tales were in circulation at the time when the Celtic stories first took shape.

THE QUEST OF EVERLASTING LIFE

OW THE SONS OF THE AGED chief, who traced his ancestry down from Mananan, and, in the manner of that age, spoke of the Son of the Sea as his grandfather (though many centuries intervened), were called Nissyen, and Evnissyen.

The elder of them was fair, the son of his father; the younger of them was dark, the son of his mother. The younger was envious of his brother because he was brave and strong, and was much spoken of by the women of his father's house. He went about in silence and anger, and would lend no hand in the search for the Pearl of Never Die. Rather would he take counsel in secret with weird enchanters that he might despoil his brother's courage, beauty, and strength.

At the corner of a crooked lane, Evnissyen met a little, wizen, old man with three-cornered eyes, from which he looked east, and west, and south, but never straight north.

'What is the matter?' said the little man.

'I hate my brother. He is everything; and I am nothing.'

'Is that all?' said the weird-looking old fellow; and the pupils of his eyes went from one corner to the other, and back again. 'Here, take this, and put it under his bed by day, and at night he will turn black; then the women will look down their noses at him, and the men will spit on him.'

The man gave him a basket containing a snake, and then went his way – down the crooked lane whence he had come.

Nissyen, the elder brother, went to bed early, for he was a famous hunter, and had been abroad that day from early morning. When he arose the next day, and went down to the sea to bathe, he screamed aloud, for the change in his skin terrified him. And when he returned, every one of his father's house regarded him as an intruder, or worse – a spy, and cast him out, for no one would believe him when he said, 'I am Nissyen, the chief's eldest son.'

Then Nissyen sought the chief, and cried, 'Father! father!' But the chief turned his back on him. He went to his mother, and cried, 'Mother! mother!' But his mother drove him from her, as she would a scheming usurper.

And with the steps of the laggard and the weariness of the heavy-hearted, he went his way.

At a place where a river winds by the foot of the mountain, he sat himself down on a great stone, and put his head on his hands.

When he looked up, he saw a little old woman coming along the river-bank, gathering sticks. Every time she gathered a handful of sticks she dropped the heavy bundle from her back and put the handful into it. The bundle was cumbrous, and so heavy that it was bending the old woman's face to the earth.

'How far hast thou to carry the bundle, Grandmother?' said the man.

'Half-way up the mountain,' the cailleach answered.

'I will carry it for thee,' said Nissyen; and he took it from the old woman's back and slung it over his own. But as he went he sighed in heaviness of heart.

'What ails thee, son?'

Nissyen told his story. By the time it was all told they had reached a little house, with its face to the sun and its back to the hill.

'Enter, and be comforted,' said the old woman, 'I will tell thee what thou must do.'

And when they had entered,

'Sit down and rest,' she said.

'But I am young still,' said Nissyen. 'If thou wilt rest thyself, I will kindle thy fire.'

The old woman was pleased by the young man's address. So she sat herself down, and, taking a sparkling crystal, gazed long and intently into it. Meanwhile Nissyen lit the fire, and put on a kettle of fish, savouring it with fragrant herbs. Soon it was cooked.

'Ay,' said the woman, looking up with deliberation from the crystal, 'that is right. Eat and be strong, for I see thee in a vision of happy days. Rest here until the morrow, and I will tell thee how thou may'st win a greater prize than ye do yet think of.'

After supper, Nissyen lay in a corner by the ingle-nook, but only slept by winks. Every time he awoke, to put a few more sticks on the slackening fire, he could hear the old woman in earnest conversation with 'somebodies' he could not see. In the morning she said:

'Rest until the day begins to wane. Then walk where the crooked lane meets the river-bank. There thou wilt meet a man with three-cornered eyes, eyes which look east, and west, and south, but never straight north. He will say, "Why and wherefore, my son? I am the friend to all in trouble, the guide to all who seek joy." Then ye must say so and so. But whatever he may prompt thee to do, thou must refrain, or do the exact opposite.'

At sundown, Nissyen went by the way of the crooked lane and walked in sadness. The man was there, watching for wayfarers by the river-bank, his eyes moving from right to left, and left to right.

'Why and wherefore, my son?' he said. 'I am the friend to all in trouble, the guide to all who seek joy.'

180   Then said Nissyen, Such, and such, is my story.

'And sad withal,' he said. 'But wait here till I go home for my velvet gloves. If, while I am gone, thou should'st see the Queen of the Little People coming by, hide thyself. Do not stop her, or speak.'

The moon comes up over the hill. Then a black cloud covers the face of the moon; darkness is over all.

But no! there is a bright white light far, far away! What is it? A little star is approaching. It is coming along the river-bank. Nearer and nearer it comes. Now a company of Little People appear, and in the centre of the group is a lady, taller than the others. She is dressed in a green cloak, and bears a basket on her left arm, from which there is shining this great light; so pure and white is it, like unto a fallen or imprisoned star.

She approaches the gorse bushes in which Nissyen has hidden himself, but he, holding himself in secret no longer, comes forth, and bowing low, says:

'Hail, Queen! Tell me what I am to do, for such, and such, is my sad plight. I will be thy slave for ever if thou wilt enable me to redeem my father's promise to the great King, and tell me where I may seek, and find, the Pearl of Never Die.'

The bright-robed Queen of the Little People presumed to be amazed at the man's sudden appearance from the midst of the gorse bushes, and, of much earnestness, revolted at the colour of his skin.

'It is the venom of the snake,' she said to her followers, and then, addressing Nissyen, added, 'Rise, and follow me, and I will tell thee whither thou must go, and what thou must do.'

They journeyed along, and soon were on the western coast of our isle, near to the edge of the sea. A vision unfolded itself before their eyes. Ships, bearing all sorts of strange devices on hull and sails, were lying at anchor in the bay; boats were quietly making for the shore.

'Hist!' said the Queen, in a whisper, 'these are the people of the King's house. In the first boat is the King's only daughter, the most beautiful princess beneath the skies. Be strong, and fear not. The blood of yet a greater king courses in thy veins, and this fair lady will be thy mate, of a surety, if thou wilt fulfil thy father's promise, and win back the Pearl of Never Die. But thou must secure and hold fast the Flaming Sword. By it thou may'st overcome many enemies. By thy own firm will thou may'st not be lured from thy quest by any subtle device that may assail a man. Ye must do this, and that.'

And she told him how to go through with it all. Then, with a puff from her lips, the light in the basket went out. In the same instant she disappeared herself, leaving only her sister to bear him company over the beginning of his way.

Nissyen, led by the Queen's little sister, above whose brow a diamond shone like a radiant star, went by the long and rugged path; the road along dangerous cliffs by the edge of the sea, and there, she, too, suddenly left him.

Nissyen descended the cliff, and immediately found himself faced by tall iron bars. He wrestled with the obstruction, bending one bar to the right, and another to the left, making in the end an opening large enough to force himself through.

Soon he found himself in a spacious cave, steeped in the music of running water. Men were gambling with dice, and drinking from horns which they dipped into a great bowl over which there hung the Flaming Sword with its haft of gold.

'This,' he said, 'must be the sword of Mananan, gleaming like sunlight, that shall put every man to flight. Yet it looks too high to reach.'

Following the commands of the Queen of the Little People, he entered the chamber, and walked up boldly.

'Play and drink! Drink and play!' cried the men, offering him their horns full of liquor.

'A'nel, a'nel,' he exclaimed, 'I do not drink to-day, I come for the sword.'

The men burst into laughter.

'So brave a man as thou,' they said, 'hast no enemies. Besides, the Flaming Sword which thou dost seek is beyond thy reach. And, if it were not so, seek peace, gather gladness, drink to the hour that is with us now. Let that content thee. To-day we live, to-morrow we die.'

But he would not, and waited his chance. The men drank themselves into good humour; from good humour they drank themselves into noisy merriment; from noisy merriment they drank themselves into stupor, and finally, into silence.

Nissyen now brought tables and chairs to his aid. And these he buttressed with the men fallen into drunken stupor. With a supreme effort he succeeded, from the topmost ledge, in reaching the sword and cutting it down.

Suddenly a raven cawed, and cawed.

The drunken revellers were on their feet; but none dared approach a man wielding so trusty a weapon. With many a bitter curse he was allowed to pass thence.

Further along he found, as he had been told, a great hall beneath the level of the ground on which he trod. The chamber had no windows, the lightning being solely from the roof. Neither was there any entrance or exit, save by this same opening, and the men who sat below, feasting themselves, were all so fat and indolent, they could not possibly climb the rope which swung unheeded above their heads.

Wines, in casks and leathern bottles, filled one side of the hall, while in a corner of much squalor, among the discarded bones of many feasts, lay, as something of no account, the Pearl of Never Die. Only by risking all might a champion secure it. He did not hesitate. He let himself down by the rope.

The men hailed him as a good fellow, and offered him a seat of the highest honour.

'A'nel, a'nel,' he exclaimed, 'I do not eat to-night.'

No other offence did he offer. Thus he waited his chance. As the men did eat of meats and drink of wine to their repletion, they gave him less, and still less, heed.

Nissyen picked up the discarded Pearl, and put it, for safety, near his heart. Then he seized the rope and began to climb. As he did so, a raven cawed, and cawed.

Instantly the men awoke from their dazed stupor, and in their alarm rushed upon each other, rather than upon Nissyen, whom they could not pursue from fatness.

So he got his way.

Again, on his path, he came to a palace all blazing with light. His way led in at one door, and out by another. No sooner had he passed the entrance than he was greeted by shouts of joy from a company of women.

'Come, come,' they said, 'tarry awhile, and make glad.'

'A'nel, a'nel,' he exclaimed, 'I am under a vow.'

Then they pleaded for the gift of the Pearl. Trusting not his strength of will, against enemies so alluring, he hastened away.

Finally, when hope was dying in his heart, and his limbs were no longer able to support him, he came to a lady of surpassing loveliness, all clothed in white.

'Who art thou, brave man,' she asked, 'that thou hast overcome all thy enemies, and, with thy honour untarnished, hath secured the Flaming Sword?'

'I am Nissyen, my lady,' he made reply, 'the son of the Elder of the Land, grandson of our revered Lord and King Mananan.'

'And thy mission in this Other-World?'

'I came at the bidding of my father, to whom was given the command of Orry, the King, to seek the Pearl of Never Die, and that I have won, above, perchance, all other winnings of my proud day.'

'Is it so precious that thou would'st never yield it up to another?'

'He who holds is ever willing to give. That is the virtue of a gem above all counting of gold. The King did for this cause come hither. And yet it was a vain quest. "*He who finds must of a surety have won; she who receives may only hold with her love, and give with her heart.*" This is the motto of a great treasure. Mananan made gift to his Queen, that she might share his Everlasting Day. And the Queen made gift to her son, the ancestor of my father's house. Then was it lost, for its virtues were gone. But who, my lady, art thou, in this realm of pleasantness, that could envy a prize which, making thee no richer, would leave me, in my father's eye, poor indeed?'

'I am Hilda, the King's daughter,' the lady made reply. 'Not the gem for the treasure's sake, but for the love of a man such as thou did I so boldly make bid. But rest thee, and in the refreshment of thy fatigued body thou wilt awake to find thyself white again, white as the white rose with ruddy bloom.'

Nissyen cast himself down, and with the gem firmly lashed to his body, he was, in the instant, asleep.

When the sun dawned the day, and Nissyen awoke again, behold! he was white again. Beside him stood the little old woman with whom he began his adventure. Her silent gaze was the gaze of mingled sympathy and joy.

'Grandmother,' said Nissyen, in freshened gladness, 'let me make relation of my tale. I have regained the Flaming Sword of Mananan, and found, too, the Pearl of Never Die. But more wonderful than all else, I have met a fair and beautiful lady, one whose loveliness surpasses every word of the Bright Robed Queen.'

'Peace, peace, my son,' said the cailleach impatiently, having no ears for love's thrice-a-thousand-times-told tale.

'Go thou now before the King, bearing on thy back this burden,' she said, showing him a full sack. 'Cast the contents at Orry's feet, saying, "Long live my lord, the King."'

Now, Nissyen had prospered so exceedingly at the advice of the old woman, that, with a willing heart, he picked up the sack of pebbles, and went boldly forth with the heavy load on his back.

In the court of the King, Nissyen threw down his burden, emptying the sack at Orry's feet, as he had been bidden. Lo! every pebble was a diamond as big as a bird's egg! Cut, and cut again, at many angles, the light radiated in every facet of every gem, dazzling the eyes of all onlookers.

Nissyen himself marvelled at the immensity of the riches he had unsuspectingly borne. But, know ye, the little old woman who had thus befriended her son, was a fairy. She had lived ten thousand years, and had kept the Treasury of The Hundred Kings of the Little People. A sack of cut diamonds was but a trifle from the vastness of their store.

Seeing the pleased countenance of the King, and, more than all else, the sweet lady of his journeyings come hence and take her place at Orry's feet, Nissyen brought forth also the Pearl, saying, 'O King, my quest is ended. Here, too, is the Pearl of Never Die.'

A murmur of admiration and delight passed over the whole company.

'Thrice happy youth,' exclaimed the King. 'For this treasure came I hither. Yet have I gathered wisdom rather than riches. From the lips of thy father, of revered memory, I have learned the virtues of this gem. *He who holds must of a surety have found. And he who has found, must of a surety have sought. And he who has sought, must have ploughed the lonely furrow, and braved the angry sea, serving in all courage, honesty, and love.* As a charm, it may only reveal its potency to one of another sex, for that is the foundation of that love which is life and eternal. Thus said the Druids of old time, thus say the old women and physicians of our day, learned in ancient law and custom. But it would as ill become a King to bemean so supreme a gift as to make labour in adding colour to the rose, or to fashion order out of the beauty of the orderless-order of the starry night – all vain and foolish mockery. Say now, what doth thy heart crave, my son, and if it is in thy Lord's giving, it shall be thine.'

'Thy daughter, sire,' said Nissyen, fearlessly, adding not so much as a single word in extenuation of his crime.

The King's countenance clouded at so bold and unexpected a request. But had he not pledged his word? He turned a grave and inquiring look upon his daughter. Hilda's answer was in eyes full of joyful expectancy.

'Then she is thine, and this day shalt thou be made my heir, as truly as my son.'

Hilda flew into her lover's arms, and Nissyen tenderly kissed her, and held her in his fond embrace.

'But stay!' said Orry, in a voice of seeming reproach of himself – as a gentle smile o'erspread his countenance, 'I cannot sell my daughter as the pagans do. And a King cannot be outstripped in the giving. If thou hast taken my daughter, I shall not fail in kingly gifts for her nuptials. Take back the Pearl of Never Die, for while my child shall have joy of thee, and thee of her, my heart can know no sorrow, nor my proud day suffer eclipse or death.'

The mating of Nissyen and Hilda, with the gift to her of the precious Pearl of Never Die, now set amid a spray of flowering myrtle, as so truly honoured

and beloved of the Viking's bride, was immediately celebrated and proclaimed, and the King, the Elders, and all the people of the land of our precious Magic Isle, gave themselves to music and feasting for many days.

Thus was the royal line of Mananan, that began with Partholan, the son of Sera, who came out of heaven, preserved at the coming of Orry the King to the Island of the Lord, the Isle of the Man, to this hour.

NOTES

Source of tale: W. Ralf Hall Caine, *Annals of the Magic Isle*, London: Cecil Palmer, 1926.

The final story in this collection comes from the Isle of Man, a Celtic land rich in lore and tradition. This particular tale, from the pen of W. Ralf Hall Caine, is part of a tradition in the making. Caine drew not only upon the legends and folklore of the Manx, but also upon more general Celtic traditions, weaving them into a cycle of tales which told a coherent story, the quest for the Pearl of Never Die. Thus the brothers, Nissyen and Evnissyen (Efnissien), borrow their names and character from Welsh mythology, in particular from 'Branwen Daughter of Llyr', one of the Four Branches of *The Mabinogion* (Dent, 1937), in which they also appear as mortally opposed to each other. For the rest, the story follows Manx traditions, skilfully woven into something neither old nor new, but the product of the endless re-weaving of the threads of folk-story and lore.

Mannanán mac Lir has long been recognized as the tutelary deity of the Isle of Man, and as such he appears here as the founder of a great dynasty. The story also reflects the coming of the Vikings to the island, and the mingling of blood and traditions between the two peoples is further reflected in this telling. In the story, 'cailleach' means a nun or lonely old woman.

Further Reading

TEXTS

There follows a brief selection from the many hundreds of volumes of Celtic fairy-tales and folk-tales which can be located either from retail outlets or libraries. All are worth seeking out if you love the folklore of these islands.

Caine, W. Ralf Hall, *Annals of the Magic Isle*, London: Cecil Palmer, 1926.

Campbell, John Francis, *Popular Tales of the West Highlands*, 4 vols., London: Wildwood House, 1983–85.

Curtin, Jeremiah, *Hero Tales of Ireland*, London: Macmillan, 1894.
    Irish Folk Tales, Dublin: Talbot Press, 1944.
    Myths and Folk Tales of Ireland, New York: Dover Books, 1975.
    Tales of the Fairies and of the Ghost World, Dublin: Talbot Press, 1895.

Guest, C., *The Mabinogion*, London: J.M. Dent, 1937.

Jacobs, Joseph, *Celtic Fairy Tales*, London: David Nutt, 1892.
    More Celtic Fairy Tales, London: David Nutt, 1894.

Johnson, W. Branch, *Folktales of Brittany*, London: Methuen, 1927.

Lover, S. and Croker, T.C., *Legends and Tales of Ireland*, London: Simpkin, Marshall, Hamilton, Kent & Co., 1889.

MacDougal, J., *Folk and Hero Tales of Argyllshire*, London: David Nutt, 1891.

MacInnes, D., *Folk and Hero Tales of Argyllshire*, London: Folklore Society, No. XXV, 1890.

Mackenzie, Donald A., *Wonder Tales from Scottish Myth and Legend*, Glasgow: Blackie and Sons, 1917.

Matthews, J. (ed.), *From The Isles of Dream*, Edinburgh: Floris Books, 1993.
    Within the Hollow Hills, Edinburgh: Floris Books, 1994.

Parker, Winifred M. (ed.), *Gaelic Fairy Tales*, Glasgow: Archibald Sinclair, 1908.

Williamson, R., *The Craneskin Bag*, Edinburgh: Canongate, 1993.

Yeats, W.B., *Fairy and Folk Tales of the Irish Peasantry*, London: Macmillan, 1888.
    Irish Fairy Tales, London: Macmillan, 1892.

Young, E., *Celtic Wonder Tales*, Edinburgh: Floris Books, 1990.
　　The Tangle-Coated Horse, Edinburgh: Floris Books, 1991.
　　The Wonder-Smith and His Son, Edinburgh: Floris Books, 1992.

COMMENTARIES

There are almost as many good books on the subject of faery traditions as there are collections. Here are just a few of the best ones, together with some basic guides to the Celtic traditions.

Bettelheim, B., *The Uses of Enchantment*, London: Thames and Hudson, 1976.
Bly, R., *Iron John*, Shaftesbury: Element Books, 1992.
Branston, B., *The Lost Gods of England*, London: Thames and Hudson, 1957.
Briggs, K., *The Anatomy of Puck*, London: Routledge & Kegan Paul, 1959.
　　A Dictionary of British Folk-Tales in the English Language, 2 vols., London: Routledge & Kegan Paul, 1970.
　　A Dictionary of Fairies, London: Allen Lane, 1976.
　　The Vanishing People, London: Batsford, 1978.
Briggs, K. and Tongue, R.L., *Folktales of England*, London: Routledge & Kegan Paul, 1965.
Carmichael, A., *Carmina Gadelica*, Edinburgh: Floris Books, 1992.
Clodd, E., *Tom Tit Tot: An Essay on the Savage Philosophy in Folk-Tale*, London: Duckworth, 1898.
Cook, E., *The Ordinary and the Fabulous*, Cambridge: Cambridge University Press, 1969.
Cooper, J.C., *Fairy Tales: Allegories of the Inner Life*, London: Aquarian Press, 1983.
Duffy, M., *The Erotic World of Faery*, London: Hodder & Stoughton, 1972.
Dunsany, Lord, *The King of Elfland's Daughter*, London and New York: Ballantine Books, 1974.
Gaster, M., 'The Modern Origins of Fairy Tales', *Folk-Lore Journal*, V, 1887, 339–51.
Hartland, S., *The Science of Fairy Tales*, London: Methuen, 1925.
Hazlitt, W.C., *Fairy Tales, Legends and Romances Illustrating Shakespeare and other Early English Writers*, London: Frank & William Kerslake, 1875.
Hole, C., *A Dictionary of British Folk-Customs*, London: Hutchinson, 1976.
Jackson, A., 'The Science of Fairy Tales?' *Folklore*, *84*, 1973, 120–41.
Keightley, T., *The Fairy Mythology*, London: Wildwood House, 1981.
Krappe, A.H., *The Science of Folk-Lore*, London: Methuen, 1930.
Logan, P., *The Old Gods: The Facts About Irish Fairies*, Belfast: Appletree Press, 1981.
Macleod, F., *The Laughter of Peterkin*, London: Heinemann, 1927.

McCulloch, J.A., *The Childhood of Fiction*, London: John Murray, 1905.

Mackenzie, D.A., *Scottish Folk-Lore and Folk Life*, Glasgow: Blackie, 1935.

MacNeil, J.N., *Tales Until Dawn: The World of the Cape Breton Storyteller*, Edinburgh: Edinburgh University Press, 1987.

Matthews, C., *Arthur and the Sovereignty of Britain*, London: Penguin Arkana, 1989.

    The Celtic Tradition, Shaftesbury: Element Books, 1995.

    Mabon and the Mysteries of Britain, London: Penguin Arkana, 1987.

Matthews, C. and Matthews, J., *A Fairy Tale Reader*, London: Thorsons, 1993.

    Ladies of the Lake, London: Aquarian Press, 1992.

Matthews, J., *An Arthurian Reader*, London: Thorsons, 1989.

    A Celtic Reader, London: Thorsons, 1990.

    Robin Hood: Green Lord of the Wildwood, Glastonbury: Gothic Image Publications, 1995.

    Taliesin: Shamanism and the Bardic Mysteries in Britain and Ireland, London: Aquarian Press, 1991.

Matthews, J. and Stewart, R.J., *Legendary Britain*, London: Blandford Press, 1989.

Naddair, K., *Keltic Folk and Faerie Tales: Their Hidden Meaning Explored*, London: Century, 1987.

O'Hogain, D., *Myth, Legend and Romance: An Encyclopaedia of the Irish Folk Tradition*, London: Ryan Publishing Co., 1990.

Rees, A. and Rees, B., *Celtic Heritage*, London: Thames and Hudson, 1961.

Rhys, J., *Celtic Folk-Lore, Welsh and Manx*, 2 vols., London: Wildwood House, 1980.

Spence, L., *British Fairy Origins*, London: Aquarian Press, 1989.

    The Fairy Tradition in Britain, London: Rider & Co., 1948.

    The Minor Traditions of British Mythology, London: Rider & Co., 1948.

Stewart, R.J., *Earth Light*, Shaftesbury: Element Books, 1991.

    The Living World of Faery, Glastonbury: Gothic Image Publications, 1995.

    Magical Tales, London: Thorsons, 1990.

    Power Within the Land, Shaftesbury: Element Books, 1992.

    Robert Kirk: Walker Between Worlds, Shaftesbury: Element Books, 1990.

Tolkien, J.R.R., 'On Fairy-Stories', *Tree and Leaf*, London: George Allen and Unwin, 1964.

Trevelyan, M., *Folklore and Folk Stories of Wales*, London: Eliot Stock, 1909.

Warner, M., *From the Beast to the Blonde*, London: Chatto & Windus, 1994.

Wentz, W.Y. Evans, *The Fairy Faith in Celtic Countries*, Oxford: Oxford University Press, 1911.

Yearsley, M., *The Folklore of Fairy-Tale*, London: Watts & Co., 1924.

Index